THEY LAY AT LAST ON
THE VERY EDGE
OF THE INVADERS' BASE

The Commando-Colonel's breath froze in her breast as she stared in silent horror. The clearing was indeed large, and most of it was filled with a deep-space vessel of immense proportions, a battleship, four thousand–class, one of the true space-permanent warships that were the pride of both Navies. Never before had she seen or heard of anything approaching this size on a planet's surface, and of a certainty, her master would never have set her down voluntarily.

More amazing even than her size was her design. She was circular and was crowned by a large command spike rising from her center. This last could be withdrawn into the ship's body during battle.

The Federation unit was fortunate—if the presence of this monster did not render that term laughable—in that there would be no problem in recognizing their targets when the time came for attack. The exhaust ducts and various firing positions were clearly visible on the hull and made excellent points of reference. Her unusual form did not alter that.

There was no shine left to the starship. She had been too long planet-bound for that, but the hull looked sound. Whatever damage she had taken in the crash had since been repaired . . . and those injuries had been considerable.

Ace Books by P.M. Griffin

STAR COMMANDOS

MIND SLAVER

P.M. GRIFFIN

ACE BOOKS, NEW YORK

This book is an Ace original edition,
and has never been previously published.

STAR COMMANDOS:
MIND SLAVER

An Ace Book / published by arrangement with
the author

PRINTING HISTORY
Ace edition / March 1990

ISBN: 0-441-78045-8

Ace Books are published by The Berkley Publishing Group,
200 Madison Avenue, New York, New York 10016.
The name "ACE" and the "A" logo are trademarks
belonging to Charter Communications, Inc.

PRINTED IN THE UNITED STATES OF AMERICA

10 9 8 7 6 5 4 3 2 1

To my aunt, Mollie Griffin Monahan,
whose courage, spirit, and imagination
inspire both the author and the books.

ONE

VARN TARL SOGAN switched off both the tape reader and graphics viewer and sat back in his chair. He closed his eyes. They were burning, and he knew he had spent far too many hours in front of those screens.

Even at that, his efforts seemed useless, foredoomed. There was so much to be learned, and for an instant, he felt overwhelmed by the enormity of the task he had set himself. He had not known nearly so much about the planets of the Arcturian Empire, not even those of the star systems he himself had ruled, planets geophysically stable, populated only by his own race, warrior caste, and the menials who existed to serve them, and by the very few other creatures his kind had permitted to continue sharing those worlds with them.

The worlds constituting the Federation ultrasystem or allied with it were totally different, well-nigh infinitely varied both in themselves and in the life forms they supported, in the races occupying them. No one could hope to learn a fraction of what there was to know about them all.

Recognizing that fact was small comfort to the former Admiral. He had to acquire a great deal of knowledge and acquire it quickly, particularly about the planets in these rim Sectors, if he was to effectively stand their defense as he was sworn to do as part of Ram Sithe's elite troubleshooting unit.

There were only four of them in the company: Commando-Colonel Islaen Connor, their field CO; Commando-Captain Jake Karmikel; Navy Sergeant Bethe Danlo, their demolitions expert and Jake's copilot on the *Jovian Moon;* and himself, now a Captain in the Federation Navy. Sogan had accepted that he could not as yet match either of the two guerrillas in the surplanetary work for which they had been trained, but it behooved him, as second-in-command to Islaen, to at least not prove an impediment to them.

He got to his feet. He was tired, and with no emergency driving him, he saw no reason to push himself, mentally or physically, to the point of exhaustion. He was supposed to be on furlough, after all.

Varn's expression tightened but relaxed again almost in the same moment, partly because he willed it to do so.

Both he and Islaen did need this rest after the almost constant action they had seen since their fateful meeting on Visnu. He had insisted that they take it on Thorne of Brandine because of the many friendships the Colonel formed here while commanding the surplanetary Resistance during the last years of the War.

The usual harsh cast of his features softened. That had been a good move despite the sometimes intense discomfort he felt when he was forced to deal with the local populace, particularly in number. His consort's delight, her pleasure in the beautiful planet herself and in the society of her friends and former comrades, was open for the reading. That was satisfaction enough for him.

It had to be, he thought with an inner sigh. He could expect nothing better. He might compel himself to come here or to other worlds within the great ultrasystem, but he could never expect to find ease or real peace on any of them. Even without the fear of exposure, he doubted he would ever feel really at home, ever see himself as more than an alien, on any Federation world, or anywhere at all now that the Empire was irrevocably closed to him.

The man put that regret out of his mind as he always did when the longing for his own place came over him. He himself had chosen this. He had been aware of the consequences of his decision when he made it. They could not be altered, and the code of a war prince demanded that he accept the decrees of fate and the fruit of his own work without shaming himself with useless protest or whining over that which could not be undone.

Because he could not quite banish the gloom which had settled on his spirit, he left the chamber where he had been working, passing through white lattice doors onto the broad terrace outside.

Part of its fine garden swept around the house and lay below him. Just beyond, within easy sight, tossed Thorne's vast, incredibly wild ocean, eternally beating against the high cliff on which the building stood.

His dark eyes went to it, stayed with it. He loved water, fresh or salt, perhaps as much as he did the starlanes themselves, and this great sea most of all. Its beauty and mystery, its restless grace, touched deep chords within him, and so, too, did its power and the threat that was ever part of it. That mighty force out there could be a comrade to one who knew and respected it, but, like space, it would tolerate neither ignorance nor stupidity for long. Contempt, it would not endure at all.

Varn, Bandit's cold!

Sogan started as a small, brown-feathered creature fluttered to the railing on which his hands were resting.

The gurry's head raised so that her bright, black eyes looked up at him from out of the dark streak that circled her head like a robber's mask. She whistled sharply to emphasize her words, which had issued, not from the supple yellow bill, but directly into his mind.

He cupped his hands around her, cuddling and warming her. "Sorry, small one. I should have shut the door behind me. Thorne is a cool world for you."

Yes.

He brought her inside and discovered he was glad to be out of the breeze himself. Normally, he found the chill more bracing than uncomfortable, but a spacer's tunic alone was not sufficient covering to withstand its bite this close to the water.

The Arcturian opened the top drawer of his desk and removed a small, amber-colored cube from a shallow box partly filled with more of its like. He offered it to the gurry. "Here. This should make up for my freezing you."

The little mammal's delighted purr and the speed with which she moved to accept the prize brought a smile to his lips. Bandit had a liking for anything sweet, and honey crystals ranked high among her favorites.

His attention lifted from her as another's thought brushed against his. *Islaen, welcome!* he responded in the form of speech they shared with no other human.

The Commando-Colonel entered the room, smiling as she caught sight of him. *We're about ready to go,* she told him. *How do I look?*

She did not really have to pose that question. Varn Tarl Sogan

had made no effort to conceal either his admiration or the
pleasure he always took in seeing her in Thornen costume.

Most fair, my Islaen. There will be no other to equal you.

She hesitated. *You're sure you won't come?*

Varn shook his head, smiling. *I should be in the way, Colonel.
You have not yet seen some of those who will be present. They
are all old comrades of yours, and I know full well that you will
want to relive the battles you fought together. My presence
would inhibit any such exchange.*

The woman was forced to agree with that. Thorne's people
were a courteous race, too courteous to discuss their long war
with the invaders who had held their planet for six hard years,
the war she had led as head of the Federation penetration team
sent in to aid their efforts, in front of the commander of those
invaders. Varn Tarl Sogan had been a hated if respected enemy
once, but that hatred changed fast when he cast away all he had
valued in life and very nearly life itself to save Thorne of
Brandine and every living thing upon her from the burn-off
ordered by his deranged commander at the time of the Empire's
surrender.

Even as that passed through her mind, another thought rose up
to trouble her. *Such affairs are easily arranged. Would you
rather that I didn't go to this one? We might try a sail . . .*

Varn looked at her with mock severity. *I am not without
resources, Colonel Connor. I think I can manage to amuse
myself while you are gone.*

She laughed. *Sorry, Varn.—I have been away from you a lot,
though.*

Your pleasure is mine. Besides, he added, nodding at the tape
reader, *I have been putting the time to good use.*

Islaen's brown eyes shadowed. *Too much, maybe. I don't
want you killing yourself, Admiral. You needed this break as
badly as I did.*

I shall do no more for a while, he promised. *Go now, or you
shall be late. It would be a poor payment for all the Doge's
hospitality if you were to keep him waiting.*

Sogan frowned as the gurry flew from the desk to the
Commando's shoulder. *Leave Bandit*, he said quickly, then
hesitated, *unless she would miss too many handouts by staying.*

The woman's eyes sparkled. *No fear of that! I've seen how
you keep that desk stocked.*

He colored slightly but merely raised his hand in farewell.

They both catered to the Jadite creature, but, then, she had more than earned their consideration since she had adopted them on her homeworld and elected to accompany them into space.

He gently stroked the little hen, running the tip of his finger over the sensitive area between her bill and eyes until he had her purring in ecstasy. "Thank you, small one," Sogan said softly. He knew that the gurry heartily enjoyed the attention she received at any gathering and realized that she had remained behind only for his sake.

Varn did not deny that he derived a certain measure of security from her presence and made as great as possible use of her special talents whenever they found themselves on-world. Everyone liked gurries, and all but the most warped or those gripped by powerful, violent emotion quickly fell under the spell of the enormous volume of goodwill the tiny Jadite mammals had the power to transmit, softening those around them not only in their favor but toward their companions as well.

That was a tightly guarded secret known only to the members of his team and to the settlers of Jade of Kuan Yin, as was the fact that gurries could communicate mind-to-mind with those humans they adopted for their own. To the universe at large, they were merely extraordinarily engaging little animals, rarities whose export from Jade was absolutely forbidden save in this one case, an exception made because of the colonists' gratitude to their saviors and Bandit's attachment to the pair.

His finger dropped suddenly to tickle her with somewhat greater force. Varn smiled at her surprised, pleased squawk and parried the return thrust of her beak, hardly realizing what he was doing. He played with her readily now when they were alone like this, although he still would not do so even before Islaen.

A chill touched him, and his eyes quickly ran along the intricately carved walls of the room. Were they, in fact, alone? This was a Thornen house, and unseen watchers might well be present.

Only after his meeting with Islaen Connor had he learned that nigh unto every Thornen structure was riddled with concealed passages and chambers and that his headquarters, his private quarters, were under constant surveillance during most of the occupation. That knowledge had set a heavy load of guilt on him for the damage his own words must have wrought upon his troops. He struggled with it now and with a helpless fear and frustration.

The Arcturian chuckled suddenly, and his mood lightened. He was being a proper fool and insufferably vain besides. There was no reason in all space why any of these people should want to spy on him at this stage in his life. He was no longer of any importance to anyone but his own immediate comrades, and if the hate generated in the War still burned strongly enough to demand his death—well, that could be accomplished readily enough without resorting to an elaborate program of espionage.

"Come, small one," he said to the gurry. "I shall order some food to be brought to us and then get back to work. I do far better by keeping my mind occupied with some concrete problem."

Yes!

Varn laughed aloud, not caring if anyone was watching him. He could not decide whether Bandit had merely been agreeing with his ever-welcome suggestion that they eat or commenting upon his final statement, and he did not press her for clarification. His ego might well be the happier for letting matters rest as they were.

Several hours passed quickly, then a knock roused the war prince from his studies. The disturbance surprised him, but he gave his visitor permission to enter.

A very young man clad in the Doge's blue livery came into the room and advanced until he stood before the desk at which Varn was working. He was obviously ill at ease, for his orders, like those given to the rest of the staff assigned to the house, were explicit in that he was not to intrude at all upon this guest.

Sogan realized what troubled him. He had never enjoyed overawing others, even the menials serving in his palaces, and he spoke quickly to help dispel the Thornen's sense of trespass. "Aye, lad?" he asked. "Mikron, is it not?"

"It is, Lord," the boy replied, pleased to be recognized by this distant, widely famed man. "I am sorry to disturb you, but . . ."

"Go on. I know you would not have come to me without good cause."

"An Admiral Sithe has planeted and has asked to meet with you and Colonel Connor. He is being held in the port area. If you would prefer not to see him, he can be ordered to lift immediately."

"Of course I shall see him! Prepare a flier . . ."

"He will be brought here," the other replied stiffly. "You are the Doge's guests."

"Very well, then, but do not delay him any longer."

"Whatever you wish, Lord."

Sogan gave him a half smile, but his eyes were troubled. "It is rarely good policy to keep any Admiral waiting, lad, and Ram Sithe is a man who has earned his rank. He would not have journeyed all the way from Horus without cause."

"Your instructions will be obeyed at once, Lord," the Thornen assured him, his own voice mirroring concern.

"Recall Islaen as well. Send a fast flier for her."

"Aye, Lord."

Mikron started to turn but suddenly faced the Arcturian again. "You have been named a lord of our people," he said, speaking hastily but with determination. "That is not an honor we give lightly, and no off-worlder's rank counts for anything among us when laid against it."

He bowed low and hurriedly took his leave before the man could recover enough from his astonishment to make him an answer.

TWO

Varn rose to his feet when Navy Admiral Ram Sithe was shown into the room.

The newcomer was a relatively small man with the slim body and fine features typical of his southern Terran subrace. Strength and the aura of command rested on him, and his black eyes were steady. They could be either highly expressive or utterly inscrutable as the situation demanded.

He returned the Arcturian's salute but nodded almost immediately to the chair from which his host had risen and took the one set before the desk himself. "Sit, Captain. We might as well be comfortable."

Sogan obeyed. "I am sorry about the delay at the port, sir."

"No problem. I presumed I wouldn't be admitted quickly. Thornens don't really like having off-worlders wandering around their planet." His eyes sparkled. "They put the time to good use by making sure I understood our relative status, or, rather, to stress that I have none where you and Colonel Connor are concerned."

His hands raised to silence the other's apology. "Relax, Captain. My ego's not that tender. I'm glad you two have found so comfortable a retreat."

Ram Sithe studied Sogan without making his scrutiny obvious. It was not often that he got the chance to do so. His dealings with this pair were almost exclusively conducted through Islaen, and he rarely saw the Arcturian at all.

Varn Tarl Sogan was a moderately tall man, slender of body with a soldier's carriage and a spacer's grace of movement. He had the strong, hard features of his race's warrior caste, and his hair and eyes were the same dark brown, a trait rarely found even in the Empire's highest ruling families, who alone displayed it. There was an authority on him that seemed his by right of birth and a reserve that set him apart from most of his species.

That, too, was part of Sogan's caste and the place he had held within it, but the Terran imagined it had grown into a far more powerful force in the years since his exile. The Spirit of Space only knew, he had cause enough to distrust the greater part of humanity and those other races like it. He had not merited the brutality with which his own had used him, and the features he bore were enough to bring him a hard if fast death in a great many places throughout the Federation.

Despite the darkness of his history and the continuing care required of him, he had retained not only his courage but also the compassion which moved him when he chose to spare Thorne of Brandine, a fact graphically illustrated since he surfaced on Visnu. Those coming to know him even slightly responded to that and to other, less readily definable qualities, and many evinced a sometimes fierce loyalty to him—witness these Thornens' efforts to screen him from disturbance even by a ranking Federation officer.

Ram Sithe himself felt some guilt about troubling him. Both Sogan and his Colonel had surely earned a measure of peace. More than that, they needed it. He had contemplated calling in one of the other Commando units and might still do so, but his instinct demanded that he choose this team, and he had learned long since never to disregard its promptings.

He had intended to see Islaen Connor, though, and it was unfortunate that her absence forced this interview. The Federation Admiral sighed in his heart, though he took care to conceal his thoughts. The war prince had to be uncomfortable behind that frigidly formal mask. Space knew, he was himself. Had there been any justice at all in this grim universe, Varn Tarl Sogan should be facing him as an equal, more than an equal, not as a subordinate, although they should then be representatives of two hostile powers. Sithe often wondered how he would have responded had fate treated him as monstrously. He found it easy to sympathize, to empathize, with the man, now and in a larger sense, and wished there was some way by which he might ease this meeting for both of them, especially since he preferred to hold off discussing the purpose of his visit until the Commando-Colonel was also present.

The Terran started as a feathered ball hurtled itself onto the desk in front of him. "What in space . . ."

The strange creature looked up at him, whistling insistently.

He realized then what it was and ran the tips of his fingers down her back. "Your gurry! She's the talk of every maintenance crew on Horus, but Colonel Connor never brought her to any of her meetings with me."

"That would hardly have been appropriate, sir."

"More's the pity," he replied gruffly. "She's a nice little thing."

Varn's eyes danced for a moment, although his expression did not otherwise change. It seemed that even the famed Admiral Sithe was not immune to Bandit's magic.

Despite his amusement at the immediate response she provoked, his mind sharply repeated his answer to Sithe.

The hen ignored him. By that time, she had assumed as a right her role of acting as a buffer between this human of hers and others of his kind when he chanced to encounter them. Besides, the newcomer was already friendly to them, and his long, sensitive fingers seemed to have been trained in the art of bringing pleasure to a gurry.

She returned to her former perch across the room a few seconds later when the Terran raised his eyes from her to face Varn once more. She knew Sogan did not want her to remain too close, but she was satisfied with her performance. The feeling between the humans was better now.

The war prince was relieved that Bandit had not fluttered to his shoulder as she often did during an interview. Ordinarily, he welcomed her presence or at least was not troubled by it, but this case was different. His disgrace shamed him enough before this one with whom he had so often matched wits and the strength of their fleets. He did not need to further reduce himself in the Terran's eyes.

Sogan felt annoyed with himself. These considerations were inconsequential now. Ram Sithe had not come to Thorne of Brandine without a good reason. What mattered was that his team would probably be in action again well before they had anticipated. "How may we help you, sir?" he asked quietly.

"I periodically check my Commando bases and am currently on such a tour. Perhaps my visit is no more than that."

It was impossible to read the black eyes. Varn did not try. "Thorne is not a base," he responded a little wearily.

"She has become one as far as your team is concerned." He smiled. "You don't appear to believe me, Captain."

Despite himself, the Arcturian answered with a fleeting smile of his own. "I am afraid not, sir."

"Nor do I," a soft voice interjected from the doorway.

Both men looked up. They had not heard or, in Varn's case, felt the Commando-Colonel enter the room.

Varn Tarl Sogan's head raised in pride when he saw the way in which the other man straightened. Those who knew Islaen Connor were accustomed to seeing her either in uniform or, more commonly, in the casual spacer's garb normally adopted by the guerrillas. That plus her rank and her competence tended to blind her associates to her startling beauty, and it pleased him to have that aspect of her receive its just homage as well.

The woman saluted smartly. She was well aware of how ludicrous the gesture must appear in one clad in exotic Thornen costume, and Varn felt her amusement even as she completed it.

Islaen maintained contact with him. She could read her consort's relief at her arrival and sensed that there was more behind it than his dislike of this interview, although his mind shields were so set as to deny her entry into his deeper thoughts.

Another mission? she asked.

I believe so. He has not said yet.

Sogan brought another chair over to the desk so that the Commando might sit beside him. *Are we alone?* his mind demanded sharply.

The Commando was surprised. She knew Varn sometimes brooded over the possibility of their attendants spying on them, but he recognized that as a weakness, a scar, of his and had never before mentioned it to her.

She caught herself. It was not an unreasonable fear now. This conference could be expected to arouse the interest and concern of their hosts. *Aye,* she assured him. *Thorne's people wouldn't violate our privacy without better motive than satisfying their curiosity.*

Once she had settled herself, she turned to their guest. "Well, Admiral, to what do we really owe the honor of this visit? You have a job in mind for us, I presume."

Ram Sithe nodded. "I do if you believe you're fit to take it on. I know the kind of pressure your team, and you two particularly, have had to bear since Visnu, and I don't want to risk burning you out, not for this."

Islaen was quiet for a few seconds. She glanced at Varn and received his almost imperceptible nod in answer to her unvoiced question. "We've had time enough, though a little more would have been better."

"You can take it after this," he promised.

"The problem?" she asked.

"The site is in Quandon Sector."

The Colonel started. "Quandon Sector! That's halfway around the ultrasystem, and . . ."

Sithe nodded. "And is normally serviced out of Deneva, not Horus. I know. I also have Commandos stationed there whom I could've ordered to take it on.

"As you know," he continued, chiefly for Sogan's benefit, since the former Admiral might well not share his companion's knowledge of the region, "it always was a fairly quiet Sector. It still is compared to some of the others, including this one. Quandon's planet-rich, but the War stopped development, and most of those now settled are in the first-ship stage or, at best, first or second generation from it. Most of the worlds have never been formally explored at all, and it's believed that there are probably as many more again yet to be discovered.

"Because of its undeveloped state, Navy and Patrol service has been light and irregular, and there's a chronic, low-grade pirate infestation, but the general paucity of good targets, surplanetary or merchant traffic, has served to hold them in check. They've never become the major threat they represent in some areas. Chiefly, they use the Sector as a rest base, a relatively safe region in which to overhaul their ships, though on a couple of occasions, they've staged major raids involving several packs out of there."

"Things are changing for the worse now that the War's over and development's progressing again?" Islaen asked shrewdly.

"Aye, or that seems to be what's happening."

The Terran leaned forward over his side of the desk, his eyes narrowing as a frown formed and deepened between them. "I'm not so sure it's that simple, and neither are the people on Deneva.

"Ships have been disappearing, right enough, all the ones that concern us from one general area. Vessels of every type have vanished, including a few that should have been of no interest to any wolf pack, and when I use the word 'vanished,' I mean precisely that. No sign of wreckage and no sign of their cargos have surfaced.

"It's hard to spook freighters servicing a rim Sector, but this Quandon situation's getting to the captains operating there. They're threatening to boycott the affected region entirely if something is not done fast. If they do, three fine new colonies are likely to wither."

His eyes went from one to the other of them. "They aren't the only ones who've demanded help, either."

"Who else?" the Commando asked, frowning. He was transmitting strong concern, almost fear. Where was all this leading?

"The pirates themselves."

Both she and her consort straightened. "What?"

Sithe nodded grimly. "Aye. They haven't approached us openly, of course, but some have sent requests for aid under the guise of being merchantmen. It seems their ships have been disappearing as steadily as legitimate craft and without any more trace, including a task force of their own that they sent in to investigate. After that failure, they decided they had enough and came to us, too."

"You wish us to take up that investigation?" Sogan inquired quietly.

"I do."

"You say one area appears to be involved. What does that mean in terms of distance, and do we have any clues, any planet which might be the focus of the trouble? I doubt it originates in the starlanes unless it is some natural phenomenon."

"That is a possibility. Unfortunately, the region's a poorly studied one. We must act under the assumption that the source of the mystery is a more conscious agency, however, and our computers have selected nine planets from four star systems. Any one of them could hold the answers we want. I've pulled together everything we have on them and on the Sector itself. You can study the material while en route there."

"Good enough. We may be able to pick up something from it."

"Direct assault has proven a failure, so I've resolved to be a bit more subtle in our approach. You will be taken as close as is prudent to your target planets on a Patrol cruiser apparently on a routine sweep and will planet in your flier, or in a lifecraft if the distance is too great for the former."

Islaen felt Varn stiffen, although he gave no visible reaction.

He had no will to play the role of passenger on any other's ship.

She was not pleased by that prospect herself, particularly if the Terran meant what he had said just now. "You mention a Patrol cruiser, sir," she said, successfully keeping the sharpness which threatened to invade it out of her voice.

"Aye. A Navy craft would probably attract too much of the attention we wish to avoid. You'll fly to Deneva and pick up the *Free Comet* there. She's a one hundred-class with a record to match anything of her size in the Navy. Patrol-Commander Marta Florr holds the bridge. She's something of a legend herself, as you'll find out from those tapes. —Can you have the *Maid* off-world by tomorrow night, Captain?"

"I keep her space-ready," Sogan replied stiffly. "We could lift within the hour."

"All the better," the Admiral said. "Wait until morning, though. No use in making your departure too hurried even here. As long as you catch the *Free Comet* before her next scheduled lift-off, you're all right."

"Are we to work alone, sir?" the woman asked him.

"No. Captain Karmikel and Sergeant Danlo are already en route to Deneva. They should planet well before you do."

Both were relieved to hear that, but Sogan in particular. The unit was a team in fact, and it was well to know that he would have comrades upon whom he knew he could depend when they entered into potentially hostile territory, be it on the planets of Quandon Sector or on the Stellar Patrol's *Free Comet*.

They discussed the upcoming mission in greater detail, then, after some more general conversation, Ram Sithe took his leave of the pair.

Varn said nothing for some moments after the Admiral had gone. He stood with his back to his companion, apparently staring at the door leading out to the terrace but not actually seeing it.

He felt the Colonel's question touch his mind and turned apologetically. *Sorry. I was thinking.*

Obviously, she responded, frowning. *What's wrong?*

Nothing. He stopped. *No, I lie there.—I have a very ill feeling about all this, Islaen Connor.*

Over and above your dislike of shipping out on this Free Comet? she asked him bluntly.

The man flashed her an angry look but nodded. *Aye.* He shook his head, as if trying to banish the thoughts filling his mind. *It is stupidity, I suppose. Spacer's superstition and nothing more.*

Maybe.

Islaen could put no conviction into her reply. Sogan had experienced misgivings about assignments in the past, and they had proven all too well founded. That coupled with Ram Sithe's strong instinctive belief that their unit must be the one to take this on did not speak well for their upcoming mission.

With a great effort, the war prince threw off the gloom pressing down on him. *Are you very tired?* he asked suddenly.

No, Islaen replied in surprise. *Why?*

I thought we might go for that sail you mentioned this morning. It appears we shall not have another chance for a while.

The Commando stared at him for a moment, then the answer came to her. Varn Tarl Sogan was sorry to be leaving Thorne, a regret sharpened by his ugly premonition regarding the work ahead of them. He wanted, and wanted fairly strongly, to have what might be his final interaction both with her and with the ocean he had come to love.

She nodded her agreement, smiling and screening her own thoughts so that he should not realize she had guessed what lay behind those tight shields of his. *Order the boat, Admiral! I'll be with you as soon as I get into something a bit more appropriate.*

THREE

THE FRENZIED YET ordered activity that preceded lift-off was in full progress around the Patrol cruiser *Free Comet*. To the untrained eye, the scene would have seemed one of utter disorder, but the former Admiral, watching it all from the high observation walk, could only admire the precision and apparent ease with which the hands carried out their complicated tasks. A highly professional crew, he thought with grudging admiration, probably the match of most in the Arcturian Navy.

They had to be. The history of their ship was proof of that. The War had hit the Stellar Patrol hard. Many of its personnel had volunteered or were mustered into the great Federation Navy, and replacements had been nearly impossible to find. Supplies had been equally scarce, to the degree that commanders had been forced to scavenge to meet even their most urgent requirements.

It was a bad time for such general weakness, for never had there been greater need for a strong Patrol fleet. With the best of every Federation planet on the front, the scum that remained behind in wartime in an ultrasystem so governed found an almost clear field for their activities. Pirates flourished, some wolf packs becoming so large as to constitute small fleets, miniature navies in their own right.

The rim planets, with most of their own defensive forces gone and unable to depend on the weakened Patrol for aid, had been hard-pressed to resist the vermin preying upon them and on the few freighters daring enough to continue servicing them.

For year after weary year, the desperately undermanned ships of the Stellar Patrol had fought a seemingly hopeless battle to stem the growing power of these outlaw fleets, which in places became great enough to threaten to destroy from within what countless Federation soldiers were dying to preserve.

The *Free Comet* was one of these. From the time she was commissioned, she had proven a fighter, penetrating endangered star systems and succeeding in her missions with startling regularity.

As her reputation grew, she was given the difficult, then the nearly impossible assignments that arose out of a universe in turmoil, and still she triumphed.

The cruiser's amazing record was directly due to her mistress, Marta Florr of Terra, and to the crew she had forged from the seemingly poor raw material left her by the heavy musters. A daring, resourceful company with a penchant for discovering unorthodox solutions to the challenges confronting them, they had made their starship the terror of every dark-souled spacer operating in Quandon Sector and in those adjoining it. By rights, she seemed a logical choice to aid in the solving of this mystery.

The man glanced at his companion. *We had best be going down, I suppose.*

Aye.

They lifted their packs and stepped onto the descent platform. A few minutes later, they were standing at the base of the cruiser.

Varn ran his eyes up her sleek side. She was a fair ship, showing the care and pride of her crew. She was also a large vessel compared to the *Fairest Maid* and the others of her class with which he now chiefly dealt.

In actuality, though, he knew her to be relatively small. The Patrol had ships four and five times her size, and she would not have served as a lifecraft for one of the giant battleships of the Federation Navy, vessels so immense that they never set down on any planet but were moored like satellites in space.

All this passed through his mind as they approached the boarding ramp. They paused there while Islaen presented their orders to the sentry, a Sirenian if the red tint of her skin spoke true.

The woman spent a long time checking their credentials against her own orders.

Sogan smiled. Her obvious youth plus a certain stiffness in her manner betrayed her as one who faced her first voyage in deep space.

Satisfied at last, the Yeoman returned their papers and gave
the pair formal permission to board. Perhaps because she was so
unfamiliar with her surroundings herself, she volunteered directions both to the Commander's office and to the crew's cabin
before they were forced to ask for them.

They passed through the open hatch but halted once inside. *I
had best see Commander Florr at once,* the Colonel told him.
*Go on and wait for me in the crew's cabin. I'll join you there
when I'm done.*

He frowned slightly. *I might do better to check out our
quarters first.*

*Agreed, but in both services, the first thing a newcomer does
on any ship is head for the crew's cabin for a quick look at his
crewmates, even before he drops off his pack. For us to do
otherwise would mark us as decidedly odd.*

And I am odd enough as it is?

I didn't say that!

The woman saw the rather welcome sparkle in his eyes and
stopped herself. *You wouldn't have been too pleased if I'd
agreed with you,* she told him tartly.

Probably not.—You will keep Bandit with you? he asked
doubtfully as the gurry poked a sleepy head from beneath
Islaen's service jacket.

*Aye. I think it's best to introduce her to the Commander right
away. This isn't a ship noted for pets, apparently, and I don't
want to chance having any problems about keeping her with us.*

They separated then, and Islaen Connor turned into the hall to
her right, following the Sirenian's instructions.

It was fortunate she had them, she realized. There were few
enough around whom she might have asked. This section of the
Free Comet was all but deserted, the greater part of her crew still
being occupied outside and below with the tasks of loading and
fueling.

That was work of no small importance, and she was pleased
with the attention the Patrol agents seemed to devote to it. They
had learned the ways of the starlanes through hard experience,
and they accorded these portside duties the respect they merited,
knowing there would be little opportunity to acquire forgotten
supplies on the rim many weeks hence or to repair the effects of
a careless error now.

It was eerie walking through the empty hall. The life systems had already been activated, and she found herself wondering for whom—or for what.

The feeling was queerly familiar. The Commando placed it suddenly. It was like this when she preceded the salvage crew aboard that projectile-blasted brig in her first year of active service.

Islaen Connor shook off the strangely unsettling sensation. There was reason for it then, she reminded herself. Horror had its place in war. Here all was normal, as it should be.

The guerrilla located the cabin she wanted without difficulty. The door was plain, with nothing to distinguish it from any of the others lining the passageway but its number and the neatly stenciled name of the Commander.

Islaen received an immediate reply to her brisk knock. She entered the cabin and came to attention before the *Free Comet*'s mistress.

She studied the Terran woman closely with eyes and mind and liked what she found, including the intensity and nature of the scrutiny she found turned on herself.

There was an air of ease as well as the expected competence and custom of command about Marta Florr. The neck clasps of her tunic were unfastened, giving even the binding Patrol uniform a relaxed appearance. Her desk was cluttered without giving the impression of a rodent's nest.

She was a classic Terran, though of a type different from those who had given rise to Noreen's offspring. Her body was stocky and strong without real bulk. The features were heavy but were not unattractive for that reason.

Her age was difficult to determine. The lines marring her face and the gray shooting through the otherwise dark hair were born of the care she had known these past years rather than of the effects of time. There was certainly no sign of its blight in her eyes. They were steady, confident, and their particular green color gave them a strangely piercing look. Her hair was worn short rather than in the tightly coiled braids adopted by Islaen and most other female spacers.

Marta returned her passenger's salute and then waved her into a chair. "Welcome, Colonel Connor. I've been eager to meet you after the account Admiral Sithe gave me of your unit's history."

"I hope you won't find us a disappointment, Commander."

"I won't," she declared flatly. "I just hope we won't be going into anything as dramatic as some of your previous missions."

"That's a wish we all share," the guerrilla agreed a trifle grimly.

A sharp chirp drew the older woman's attention to the Colonel's shoulder. "This must be your gurry."

"Aye. Her name's Bandit."

The hen looked directly into Marta Florr's face, her bright, black eyes meeting the human's green ones. She whistled for more attention and purred in apparent delight at receiving even so much notice.

The Terran restrained herself from actually petting the small creature, but a soft, amused smile gentled her expression. "Ordinarily, I don't encourage the presence of animals aboard the *Comet,* but this little thing doesn't look like she'll be much trouble."

"She won't," Islaen Connor assured her. "Besides, Bandit is part of my unit, not merely a mascot."

Marta's smile broadened. "So your papers indicate, but after seeing her, I must confess to a certain difficulty in envisioning an attack gurry in action."

Islaen laughed. "It'd be an unlikely role, all right! Her kind loves just about anyone who fusses over them."

She grew serious once more. "In truth, though, she did go for one of the locals on Hades when he assaulted my second-in-command."

"With what result?" the Patrolwoman asked in some surprise.

"We'd already disarmed him, but she succeeded in defusing a very nasty situation."

"I imagine the idea of doing battle with a gurry would be likely to produce that effect," she agreed. The green eyes narrowed. "Why was your comrade attacked in the first place? It can't have been by the pirates if the trouble was aborted so readily."

"Hades of Persephone suffered heavily during the War. Her people hate anything reminding them of an Arcturian."

"Your teammate did?"

Islaen's head lifted. "Aye, and so would a good third of your crew, to judge by what I've seen of them!"

She quickly turned back to the hen. "Bandit was the real heroine of that mission."

She went on to describe the role the gurry had played in Jake's rescue from the crawlway in which he had been trapped far below Hades' surface.

Marta Florr did stroke the little creature when the Commando finished speaking. "It's hard to believe she could manage so complex a task. We tend not to see intelligence of that level in an animal of this size."

"Jade's gurries are quite bright, and Varnt was directing her during the whole of it. She works very well with him."

Islaen Connor seemed to use the name that Sogan adopted for his alias at the beginning of his life in exile casually, but in fact she had done so intentionally, as she had purposely mentioned the trouble they had experienced on Hades. This one was sharp, maybe too sharp, and she had felt from the beginning of their interview that it would be a better move to draw down Varn's apparent resemblance to their former enemies at once, as if without thought, than hope it would pass unnoticed and have the truth about his race be guessed or suspected during the voyage. That discovery could bring trouble on them all, and the real possibility of such a situation's arising was the cause of most of her reluctance to ship out in a Patrol vessel. Varn's recent history would not be as well known or appreciated in this service as in her own. A similar Navy crew, at least one basing out of Horus, would be well aware of it, and whether they knew his full story or not, they would be friendly toward him, toward them all.

"That's quite a tale, Colonel," Marta told her. "You don't have to fear for Bandit's reception here. So brave a little soldier will always be welcome aboard the *Free Comet*."

"Thank you, Commander."

Their conversation turned to graver matters after that, their mission and what knowledge the *Comet*'s mistress had regarding it, which was chiefly a more detailed repetition of Ram Sithe's earlier account.

At last, the Patrol-Commander rose to her feet. "I hope you'll be comfortable, Colonel." Her eyes narrowed slightly as they fixed curiously on her passenger for a moment, but she did not voice her question. "Your Admiral requested that we give your team as much privacy as possible, and I've turned our Exploratory Force's quarters over for your use. You'll have them to yourselves."

Islaen arose as well. "I'm sorry for that trouble."

"Don't be. It won't hurt my Rangers at all to mingle with the Regulars for a while. They're part of the crew even if they do most of their work on-world. —Your gear has been brought on board. You should check it out as soon as you can. We'll be lifting shortly, but there's still time to secure anything we may have forgotten."

"My other comrades, Captain Karmikel and Sergeant Danlo?" she asked.

"Both have been on board since yesterday morning. They oversaw the equipping of your unit."

"Excellent! You seem to have thought of everything, Commander." She smiled. "You've gone to a considerable amount of trouble for us. We do appreciate it."

Marta Florr touched one of the files on her desk. "According to this, you've more than earned a little consideration, Colonel. The *Free Comet* is glad to supply it."

FOUR

VARN TARL SOGAN stood a moment in the entrance of the starship's crew's cabin.

It was a big room, proportionally very large for the size of the vessel, but the *Free Comet*'s hands spent the bulk of their leisure waking hours here, and it had to be able to accommodate at least the basic interests and moods of a hundred men and women over sometimes very long voyages.

The cabin was designed and outfitted to accomplish that. Its furnishings consisted chiefly of varying numbers of benches and chairs set around a variety of tables, some constructed to support games of chance or skill. All were firmly secured, of course, in deference to the sudden emergencies and turbulence common to life in the starlanes. Sporting machines and both tape readers and graphics viewers were in good supply, and a broad door gave access to the serving area of the galley.

As a whole, the room was brightly lighted, in keeping with its cheerful color scheme, but a line of booths along the starboard wall were darker and looked to be screened to eliminate much of what could at times be a considerable din.

Sogan made his way toward one of the latter, crossing the chamber as swiftly as he could without projecting urgency or haste. He had his choice of place. Ordinarily, the crew's cabin would be crowded at this time, but most of the *Comet*'s hands were busy with lift-off preparations, and there were only a few present, three small groups. All the same, he saw no need to choose a spot that would leave him completely open to their study when more comfortable options were open to him. As it was, he felt as if eyes were boring into him.

The war prince reached the booth. He slid his pack in along the padded seat and sat down himself. He gave a sigh of relief. It was indeed pleasantly shadowed. He would feel far more at ease waiting here than at one of the brightly illuminated tables beyond, but he still hoped Islaen would be quick about finishing up her business with the Patrol-Commander and not keep him sitting in this place too long.

He tensed. He had known full well that most of the attention he imagined he was receiving existed only in his mind, but one group was looking at him. Even as he watched, the four left their table and started toward him.

All were Yeomen, male and fairly young. Three were typical Terran colonials, and each could be the product of any one of several dozen planets, some whose names he did not even know. The fourth was something different. He could not identify his race, either, and Varn felt a crawling sensation pass through his flesh at the sight of him: a mutant, and more than usually repulsive with a skeletal body and a death's head of a face crowned by a comb of stiff orange hair. Not many years before, he would not even have considered the man human, and he had to fight himself now to accord him that dignity in his mind.

His own lack of tolerance was of little importance at the moment. They were definitely heading for his booth.

The shipmen approached rapidly, not stopping until they stood directly above him.

"This seat taken?" one, apparently their leader, inquired.

"Aye, or it soon will be."

The other arched his brows at the coldness of his reply. "You know, friend, not only do you look like one of our former foemen, but you have their delightful manner as well."

Sogan's expression did not alter, but he carefully released the safety catch on the blaster he had already drawn and now held at ready beneath the table. He slipped the control to stun and set it at broad beam to take out all four quickly if he was forced to open up on them. He did not even think to burn them down. There was no true hostility in any of the group. He did not need Islaen Connor's ability to read the emotions of those around her to recognize that.

They did not have to threaten him themselves for their sport to become deadly reality, he thought grimly. There could not be a single man or woman aboard this cruiser who had not lost someone in the recent War. If the others picked up on this baiting in earnest . . .

A second of the Yeomen draped his arm across the mutant's shoulder. "Impossible, Graff! An Arcturian would throw his guts out at the mere thought of having to share a table with Aste, here."

"Perhaps he might later," a voice snapped behind them, "but an Arcturian would give no sign of distress at all while he was forced to endure it."

They whirled to face a small, fair-haired woman. A man was with her, even more openly angry and ready to back her should she be challenged.

She looked from one to the other of them contemptuously, the slate of her eyes dark and stormy with controlled but not concealed fury. "Now that you little boys have amused yourselves, how about blasting off and giving the Captain some peace?"

"Captain!" the mutant hissed. He glanced at Sogan in alarm.

"You don't imagine Commandos or their associates march into battle flaunting insignia, do you, or uniformed at all, for that matter?" she continued smoothly. "For example, I happen to be a Navy Sergeant, and this is Commando-Captain Jake Karmikel here with me."

"We didn't realize . . ."

"Obviously," the former Admiral replied with a frigid control that sent the hearts of his erstwhile tormentors plummeting.

"We—we didn't think, sir," he answered miserably.

"That, too, is obvious." Sogan turned away from him.

"Clear!" The Sergeant's lips formed the word. They obeyed at once, retreating to the table across the big cabin to which she had pointed.

Bethe Danlo slipped into the seat opposite Varn. "You might as well holster that blaster," she told him. "Unless you already have."

"It is secure." He had returned it to its place as soon as he was sure his comrades had the situation under control. "That was a timely arrival," he added. "I was afraid I might have to use it."

"I doubt it would've come to that. You're too good at talking your way out of such spots."

Jake returned from the galley with two steaming mugs. He set them on the table in front of the others. "Jakek," he said. "It's hot, though I won't vouch for the quality.—Relax while I have a talk with our friends over there. They're starting to eye the exit, and I don't want them to bolt before I have a chance to straighten them out."

"They won't bolt," Bethe assured him. "It'd be too easy to identify them. If they're to have any chance at all of keeping off the charges list, they know they'll have to stay put."

She waited until the redhead had gone before turning to Varn. His face was a mask, of course, but his temper was still high, to judge by the stiffness of his body.

"You should've kept Bandit with you," she said conversationally.

"It was more important for Islaen to make a favorable impression on Commander Florr."

The demolitions expert smiled. "Come on, Varn. They had no idea you were brass. Don't tell me your lads never pulled anything on newcomers before a voyage."

"Not on any vessel of mine! It is poor disciplinary procedure, and my captains responded accordingly."

"Aye, and I'll bet it went on all the same.—They meant no real harm."

"No, but if they had managed to sow the idea that I am an Arcturian, I might have had the choice of either fighting the whole crew or burying myself in our quarters for the duration."

Bethe laughed outright. "You'd probably welcome the excuse for the last."

Sogan scowled at her but then smiled himself. She was right. He was overreacting to the incident, more because his pride had been stung than for any really concrete cause.

He watched Karmikel lower himself into a chair at the crewmen's table. "Will he be able to accomplish anything?"

"Jake? Oh sure. He's very persuasive when he wants to be."

She glanced at the exit. "We've just put the flier on board. We might as well go back to our quarters. You can have a look around and then start checking it out. Tell Islaen to meet us there when she's done."

He nodded. Bethe and Jake Karmikel shared the knowledge of their ability to communicate thought-to-thought, the only others to do so. He concentrated, sending out his mind until he found and joined with his consort's.

After a few moments, he severed the contact and came to his feet.

"Let us go, Sergeant."

* * *

The Commando-Captain sat back and looked at the unhappy faces of the four Patrol agents.

"You're safe enough. He's not the kind to put you on charges," he assured them with some mental reservation. Varn Tarl Sogan had been a fairly strict disciplinarian in such matters when he had his own fleet under him.

"That's a relief," Graff muttered. "Our old lady'd have us scrubbing tubes for the rest of the voyage if she found out."

"Look, I know you Regulars must be put out about our coming aboard and being given the VIP treatment, especially about our bumping your Rangers out of their quarters, but we didn't exactly ask for it, either. Both Sogan and I have our own ships, and we'd be a whole lot happier using one or both of those."

He paused and then went on. "Guerrillas don't wear their decorations any more than rank insignia. If we did, you'd see that man doesn't have to prove anything to anybody."

"Decorations?" the Patrolman asked a little curiously, wondering what award or awards the dark-eyed officer had managed to pick up and under what circumstances. The Navy was not exactly generous in distributing them.

"Citations, friend. First-class. Three individual and one shared."

The Yeoman straightened. "That isn't possible!"

Jake smiled. "Visnu. Astarte. Jade. Mirelle."

Aste whistled. No one in either service could fail to recognize those four worlds or be ignorant of the events which had catapulted them into interstellar fame. "By the Spirit ruling all space! You've got to be that special team of Ram Sithe's!"

The Yeoman sitting across from him frowned. "Just what are you doing here?"

"Same as you. Following orders." Once more, his eyes swept the four. "Sogan may strike you as a cold bastard, but you came down on a real sore point with him. He knows what he looks like, and it's gotten him jumped and almost killed on more than one occasion. He's not anxious for a repetition out here."

"We'll pass the word, sir. No one'll bother any of you again."

Jake got to his feet. "Thanks. We'll have enough to do fighting pirates if it comes to that without having to battle each other as well."

* * *

Bethe was just heading into the hangar when Karmikel reached the exploration wing. She smiled and raised her hand in greeting. "How'd you make out?"

"Fine. None of us should have any more trouble from the *Comet*'s crew, except that they'll probably be expecting a few odd miracles from us now."

She groaned. "Terrific! I had more of a boring, restful cruise in mind myself."

The Commando chuckled. "Sorry. That's the penalty on being a genuine hero. You have a reputation to maintain.—Where's the Admiral?"

"Unpacking. I gave him a quick tour of our domain and then left him to settle in before he attacks the flier. He wants to give it a really good overhaul before we lift."

"Wise enough," he agreed. "He's cooled down, I take it?"

"Aye, just about. He had a bit of a scare, but he was mostly annoyed at being run over the jets like a yeoman, and a tyro at that. He got over it fast." She smiled. "Varn's pretty good at laughing at himself, very good really, considering who he is, even if he does have to remind himself to do it occasionally."

"You wasted no time in charging to the rescue," the man remarked.

His companion started to frown, but memory returned to her, and her eyes were dancing devilishly when she turned them on him. "What was that growl I heard on my right when we saw what was going on?" she inquired innocently.

"Force of habit," Jake muttered. "A Commando's always going to stick up for his own." He ignored her laugh. "Any sign of Islaen?"

Bethe nodded. "She just told Varn she's on her way here. Her meeting took some time."

The blond spacer's face softened, and a wistful note crept into her voice. "I wish we could do that," she said, "join our minds the way they do." She put that regret from her. "Come on, let's start getting the tools out. She and Varn won't have that much time for working before we're ordered to strap down."

FIVE

AFTER LEAVING THE Commander's office, the Commando-Colonel stood still a moment to orient herself.

On most Patrol vessels, she knew, the exploration wing was located at the very aft, as much separated as possible from the daily workings of the ship. It should be the same on the *Free Comet*.

She could confirm her deductions easily enough by asking one of the crew, but Islaen made no attempt to do so at this point. She strode purposefully along the hall. If her guess proved wrong, she would seek directions. Otherwise, she would indulge her Noreenan stubbornness and not reveal that she had ever felt the need of them.

There was certainly no lack of possible guides. The corridor had become crowded in the time the interview had taken, and she believed most of the hands were now on board.

This was one of the chief arteries of the vessel, but although many people hurried along it in the performance of their duties, there was very little noise. The Colonel nodded with satisfaction. It was a good crew, right enough. Each member knew his or her task and performed it with a minimum of confusion and verbal command. She had seen some less professional manning of a few of the Navy warships on which she journeyed in the past.

The mix of the races comprising it pleased her as well. The crew was composed of offspring of many diverse systems and included a fair number of mutants. That was much to their advantage, although she thought Sogan might have a little difficulty adapting to their presence. The *Free Comet* could call upon a broad spectrum of the adaptations and the skills acquired

29

by the various branches of the human species in the centuries
since the colonization of the stars began.

It was not too long before the guerrilla officer came to a halt
before a seemingly solid barrier, whose expanse was relieved by
the cunningly set sign of the Far-Roving Star, the insignia of the
Exploratory Force. This both signaled the approach to Ranger
quarters, temporarily her unit's base, and concealed the eye that
would react with the device pinned to her shoulder to admit her.
Even as she approached it, a panel silently slid back.

The exploration wing was laid out on the customary plan. The
Ranger's private quarters were located on either side of a short
corridor. At the end were the equipment storage room and the
hangar, which formed the nerve center for the team during flight.
The latter would be equipped with an air lock to permit the rapid
entrance and exit of the planet rover that was a basic part of
every Ranger company's gear.

Islaen went to what was to be her own cabin first, that on the
farthest end of the hall on the right. She wanted to drop off her
pack and maybe settle in a bit before heading for the hangar. It
would take no more than a few minutes to stow her things. She
had brought little of a personal nature with her. A guerrilla soon
learned the value of traveling light, satisfying most of her needs
from her surroundings.

The woman glanced about her. The cabin was small but
looked comfortable enough. A quick check told her that everything was in order.

She did not bother to examine the chamber in detail. She was
growing increasingly more impatient to check out the hangar and
its contents. She had her own ideas of what they would need,
and she wanted time to correct any omissions before lift-off.

As if in response to her impatience, she felt her consort's mind
touch hers. A moment later, his knock sounded at the door. *I'm
ready, Varn. How does everything check out?*

*Perfectly thus far. Between the Patrol-Commander and our
own comrades, we do not seem to lack for anything.*

He strode inside and lifted Bandit from her shoulder. He held
her at eye level. "I could have used your help earlier, small one.
I hope you did a good job with Commander Florr to make up for
your absence."

Bandit always does well! she responded hotly.

"So you do."

Islaen took the hen out of his hand. *She worked her customary magic.* Concern rose up in her. *What happened, Varn? You just said you'd had some problem.*

It hardly merits such a designation. He described the incident while they were walking toward the hangar.

Once there, both fell silent as they and their comrades finished their inspection of the equipment on which their lives might and probably would soon depend.

The former Admiral had just finished closing the drive compartment of the flier when three sharp blasts of the *Free Comet's* signal siren informed them that very soon now, they would be spaceborne. Already, they could feel the throb of the heavy engines.

The Navy unit secured their tools and retired to their cabins to strap down. There was nothing they could do to aid in the lift-off. The handling of the vessel was strictly the province of the Regulars.

Varn Tarl Sogan lay back on his bunk and slipped the safety netting into place. There could be considerable turbulence before they cleared Deneva's gravity, and the nets were mandatory for crew members and passengers alike.

The whine of the engines became louder. The trembling increased as they were switched into active drive.

Noise and vibration grew, peaked, held at that peak. The vessel rose, slowly at first, almost suspended in the dark Denevan sky, then she broke the invisible chain that kept her planet-bound, and the *Free Comet* raced out into deep space.

The Arcturian sighed as the effects of double gravity were lifted from him. He smiled. Size aside, his *Maid* was considerably the more advanced vessel. No noise, tremor, or change in pressure accompanied her maneuvers.

All sensation of motion disappeared. Varn felt strangely relieved. They should be in deep space soon, well away from the crowded lanes around Deneva.

He, for one, was glad of that. She, like Horus, was a major Sector governmental planet, but both the Naval and Patrol bases were larger here, larger and strange and more dangerous for him. He wanted no part of them or the busy world supporting them, and ordinarily, he would take a keen pleasure in quitting them all.

His dark eyes closed. There was none of that in him now. He

had been forced to leave the *Fairest Maid* behind him, and he
lay here, as helpless as so much inert cargo, on another's vessel,
unable to aid either himself or any of his comrades should some
emergency arise to threaten them.

By all the gods, he thought savagely, those young Yeomen
had been right to taunt him! They, at least, served a useful
purpose on the *Comet*. He was no more than a parasite . . .

Sogan forcibly quelled that line of thought. It was both false
and ridiculous.

Knowing that did not make it rankle any the less. He cast off
his nets, although the release had not been given, and hurriedly
made his way to their flier.

He slipped into the front seat and stared moodily at the
controls. If only there was a near-space viewer!

To many, the vast void of the universe was forbidding, a bleak
and lonely emptiness, but he had always found a beauty and
splendor out there that satisfied a deep hunger inside him.

Its blackness was rich, awesome. The stars were not the cold,
almost monochromatic, lifeless spheres of poet and scientist
alike, but glinting sparks of almost sentient power glowing with
every conceivable color, never any two showing precisely the
same shade or the same spirit. They willed, beckoned in their
infinity, those distant suns, personifying his species' ancient
longing for the ever-far, the ever-unknown.

Why must he be cut off from the sight of them?

Varn's head lowered. It was not that which was tearing at him.
He wanted to be on the *Free Comet*'s bridge. He belonged there.
Centuries, millennia, of breeding and training demanded that he
be there, with full responsibility for the starship and crew resting
on him.

Memory swept over him, unbidden and powerful. The first
command he had ever held was over a cruiser of this class. He
recalled his pride when he first walked onto her bridge, his pride
as success followed success, honor followed honor. He was
happy then despite his ever-growing responsibilities, happy in
his victories and in the service he was able to render to his
comrades and to the Empire he loved well beyond his own life.

Why had death been denied him during those years? he
wondered wearily. Had he fallen in one of those battles from
which his commands, single vessel or fleet, had always emerged
victorious, he would have been honored as one worthy of

respect, one whom his kin could rightly mourn and whose loss they could regret.

Fate had reserved no such kindness for him. He had witnessed the shattering of his ultrasystem, had seen it dragged down in shame in the first major defeat in his people's long history, and he, Varn Tarl Sogan, had brought disgrace upon himself and all his house, upon the officers and soldiers who served under him.

In so doing, he doomed many others along with himself. His consort and concubines embraced their daggers, unable to bear the shame of his condemnation, that and the loss of the children they had borne him. All his offspring, sons and daughters, were slain to erase the pollution of his seed from their race.

His throat closed painfully. What had he done? He had given Thorne of Brandine her life. She was a fair and valiant world peopled by as fine and noble a race as the human species could hope to produce, but was anything, any mercy or right or justice, even the Empire's threatened honor, worth the price he had paid?

The former Admiral stopped himself furiously. What was the matter with him? His judges had been harsh, aye, and only their own anguish over the Emperor's surrender, their need to lash out some way, accounted for the savagery of the sentence they laid on him, but a war prince wielded enormous power and bore an equal weight of responsibility. A breach which would earn one of lesser rank only imprisonment or death inevitably called down something far darker on the few of his kind who chose to violate their code. He had known that. The choice had been his, and he would chart the same course were that same decision demanded of him again. He had no right to whimper over the consequences of it.

It angered and also puzzled him that he should do so. Beyond all right or expectation, he now found himself with work of importance again, yet still he played the coward, permitting himself to long for what was irrevocably riven from him . . .

Varn?

He straightened, tightening the shields he had instinctively set over his inner mind when this mood first began to sweep him. Islaen must not learn of this! *Here. By the flier.*

Sogan quickly slipped out of the machine and was half sitting, half leaning on it when she came into the hangar.

The Commando joined him. *I felt you leave your cabin and was afraid something might be wrong.*

There was, of course, but she knew from the tightness of the defenses he had raised that Varn would give her no explanation. He might even deny that anything was amiss at all.

Anger stirred in her, as it usually did when he pulled this on her. It hurt when he excluded her like this, but it was not something she could hope to alter in him. The Arcturian himself was aware of how often he reacted in this manner. He knew it wounded and irritated her and saw it as a failing of sorts in himself, but it was an integral part of him.

Sogan kept his face a mask. All he had gained had come to him through Islaen Connor herself or through the contacts she had opened for him with the Navy and Commandos. She at least had a right to believe him content in the life they had built and were continuing to build together.

Resolve firmed within him. He would be hard-pressed not to betray himself unless he could turn her attention from this until he had himself under tighter rein once more.

"Do you think this *Free Comet* will be able to carry through with her part?" he asked suddenly.

"She wouldn't have been chosen for the job if she couldn't," the woman said, responding in audible speech since he had reverted to that. She frowned in her own mind, fully angry now and worried as well. He wanted her out of his thoughts, then, and, apparently, in ignorance of whatever actually filled them. The last time they went into a mission with him so ridden, he very nearly wrecked it. She was not about to risk that again. "What's wrong with you?"

"I would merely be more certain of her abilities if she had a more normal crew."

Islaen's eyes flashed like a pair of discharging blasters. "What's that supposed to mean? If you're referring to the mutants, you might do well to recall that you're one of them yourself, mind reader!"

"I am not likely to forget that!"

Varn slumped back against the flier. He had succeeded in provoking his commander, but he found he lacked the spirit or energy to continue. He did not want her anger on him.

I am sorry, Islaen, he said in thought, apologizing both for his remark and for the canker it had been meant to screen. *I cannot simply cast aside everything that was bred and trained into me,* he added defensively, *not even all of that which is patently false.*

Her head lowered. *We're both guilty of that fault. Noreenans are quick to anger, and so I jump you too readily.* Her eyes met his. *Even when I know that's precisely what you want.—Varn, please let me help*.

He turned from her. *No one can help, nor is it a matter worth your trouble, not with real work before us*.

The Colonel started to go. Her defeat was a weight bearing down on her spirit, and shame and remorse smote Sogan.

He went to her, lay his hand on her shoulder to stop her. *No, my Islaen,* he told her quickly. *It is not lack of trust, but there are things which I must work through myself, at least to the point of understanding, before I can open my mind even to you*.

She faced him again. *I know,* she replied sadly. *Whatever my motive for it, my impatience must be harder for you to endure at times even than my temper*.

Her consort smiled. *I have no complaints*. His fingers brushed her cheek. *I think I have said once before that I am glad you are a woman, Islaen Connor. I should find it difficult to work with a goddess*.

He gently closed her in his arms. Suddenly, the full awareness of all his love for her, of all she had come to mean to him, swept over him, and his hold tightened. *Never let your light fade from my life,* he whispered almost fiercely. *All else I can endure, but not that loss*.

Islaen looked up at him. She said nothing but opened her mind to receive him.

She felt him touch her, softly, tenderly, in a manner that told how much he wanted to come to her, but Varn withdrew again, leaving only regret and the assurance of his love behind.

She rested against him as the pressure of his arms once more increased, trying to give him what he needed of her and wishing with all her being that he would permit her to do more.

They remained thus only another moment before the Arcturian recalled himself to their situation and released her with a quickly muttered apology. The siren freeing their comrades would soon be sounding, probably within the next few minutes. When it did and they began the task before them, there must be no sign of weakness or uncertainty on him.

SIX

THE FOLLOWING MORNING, Marta Florr described over the ship's intercom the *Free Comet*'s mission. She detailed its importance to the young colonies of the Sector and stressed the fact that they would be operating almost blind. No ship had encountered the cause of the mysterious disappearances and escaped to tell of it.

She emphasized as well that even the role they might expect to play was uncertain. The Patrol cruiser could carry the brunt of whatever was to come, or she might only provide transport and support for the four Navy soldiers they had taken aboard. The *Comet*'s mistress stated flatly that they had no cause to resent a minor part should that be their lot and went on to recount their passengers' record, drawing on a wealth of detail that told the thoroughness of the briefing Ram Sithe had given her when he assigned his team to her vessel.

It was late afternoon before the Navy party had an opportunity to observe the effect of that introduction. The task before them was enormous, and all four spent the day closeted in the exploration wing poring over the materials supplied them concerning their target region and the nine planets under heaviest suspicion.

They could not hope to learn everything, not even a small part of it all, before they penetrated the area, and they sought desperately to assimilate what they could of the most important detail, that and seek for clues, any clue, that might point to one of those worlds as a stronger prospect than the rest or eliminate one or more of them from the list.

Only when Islaen found their tempers growing short and their minds dulled did she order a break and the change of scene the crew's cabin would afford.

The loud buzz of multiple conversations ceased as they came into the big room. Their team's exploits were already well known throughout both services, but the detail Commander Florr had supplied earlier was sufficient to raise something like awe even in her battle-hardened hands.

The talk resumed again almost immediately, although many curious eyes followed them as they made their way across the cabin to one of the quieter booths.

The Colonel gave a wry smile. Their fame had served them well in this respect anyway, she thought. The place was packed, and this was a choice location. It would not ordinarily have been left vacant even for those commanding the *Comet*.

She slid into the seat. Her eyes sparkled, and she kept them lowered as Varn moved in outside her. She could read his disapproval. He disliked the noise of the room and even more the sight of officers and Yeomen jostling each other for space at tables and game boards. To one bred to the rigid Arcturian caste system, the general democracy pervading the cabin was jarring, to say the least.

The war prince felt her amusement and looked at her questioningly. She only smiled, however, and settled herself more comfortably. The seats were well designed, she noted, and encouraged long, easy conversation.

"Shall we eat now?" she asked.

"Let's wait a bit," Bethe Danlo suggested, "a few minutes anyway. I'd like a chance to get accustomed to this crowd first."

"Aye," Jake agreed, "and let them get accustomed to us. We're still coming in for a lot of attention."

"I know," Islaen answered. "They're transmitting strongly. It's all friendly, though. Just curiosity.—Are the four you ran into before here?"

"At the third table north of that chess game over there. They haven't taken their eyes off us since we arrived."

The Commando-Colonel's eyes half shut as she tried to concentrate on their patterns above the myriad of others clogging her mind receptors but had to give it up.

"They're not sending particularly powerfully," she said in the end, "or anything much different from what the others are feeling."

Once more, the flow of conversation altered at the tables

nearest them. That, the Colonel had engineered. The booth itself was reasonably dark, but she had told Bandit to flit around its outer edge as if moving from one to the other of them. Whatever Jake's skill in passing it off, the question of Varn's likeness to the Federation's recent, bitter enemies had been raised, and she wanted to snap the point of that dart before it penetrated too deeply into anyone's mind. The sight of him dining in company with the tiny Jadite mammal and showing her the same care and attention as his comrades did would be a subtle declaration that he could not be one of the would-be conquerors. It was well known that Arcturian warriors, the only caste with which her own ultrasystem had any real experience, scarcely acknowledged the existence of most nonhuman creatures and that none of them had been known to take an animal as a pet.

Her thoughts softened. This man who was her comrade and her husband was the exception in that, as he was an exception to so much else that formed the stereotype image the bulk of the Federation's people held of his kind.

She felt him stiffen beside her and glanced at him.

His head turned slightly without any show of haste or alarm. *Those Yeomen. They are coming over here, I think.*

She nodded. The four young men had indeed risen and were looking intently in their direction.

Easy, she cautioned, then switched to verbal speech. "I'm picking them up now, I believe. They're nervous, probably about the reception they'll get, but I can't find anything unpleasant."

"Perhaps," Sogan agreed without conviction. "All the same, Colonel, it might be wise for you and Bethe, at least, to have your blasters ready. You are on the inside, and they will not be seen until they are needed."

The demolitions expert's brows raised. "Come, Admiral, you underestimate us! We already have them covered. Right, Islaen?"

"Naturally.—Quiet, now. They're almost within earshot even in this din."

The Patrol agents saluted smartly when they reached the booth.

Islaen Connor returned it. "At ease. There's no protocol in a crew's cabin, or there jolly well shouldn't be." She smiled. "What can we do for you?"

Graff glanced at Varn. "We want to apologize, Captain Sogan. Your rank aside, we were out of line."

"Forget it," the former Admiral told him. "No harm came from it."

The shipman was carrying a small package. This he carefully set on the table. "We wanted to make a peace offering, sir," he explained as he deftly lifted out the contents.

Karmikel eyed the rectangular flask with interest. "Hedon distilled. Two hundred proof," he remarked. "The *Free Comet* is singularly well supplied."

"Well, sir, we were sort of hurried when we had to pack up after our last planet leave, and this, um, must've just been slipped in with everything else in the general confusion. You'll be doing us a favor by helping us get rid of it." He grinned. "It would be classed as contraband, but it'd be a real shame just to pour it down some drain."

The Commando-Colonel chuckled. "You do seem to have a problem. We'll be glad to help you out, Yeomen—that is, if you'll count me out on the actual disposal detail."

"And me," Bethe interjected. "I only like that stuff in lots of hot water and laced with a heavy sweetener."

"You're talking sacrilege, woman!" Jake told her in mock horror. "Very well, you're excluded."

Cowards! Varn grumbled.

The trials of diplomacy, Admiral, his consort replied. *This one's your problem.*

Sogan nodded with apparent pleasure. "Are you four off duty?"

"Aye, sir, just before we came here."

"Then we accept on condition that you join us."

Aste quickly secured glasses for them all. Bandit hopped forward eager for her share of the golden bounty but stopped short at the sharp verbal and mental negatives from both her humans.

The newcomers laughed, and Graff, following the direction of Bethe's finger, went to a neighboring table and deftly lifted the remnants of a slice of cake from a surprised comrade's plate. To his delight, the little hen accepted his offering eagerly.

After that, he carefully poured out the liquor. Islaen surreptitiously watched Varn, barely repressing a laugh when she felt his mental shudder at its harsh, fiery taste. Arcturian officers rarely drank at all and then only fine wine, but he sipped it in seeming appreciation, and when he had finished, he set the empty glass down carefully, as if with proper respect, a gesture she realized he had copied from Jake.

"What are your posts?" he asked the Patrol agents. None of the *Comet*'s crew wore badges indicating responsibility, a practice common on larger vessels where the places and capabilities of the many hands would not be individually known by all who might need to command them in an emergency.

"Actually, they're pretty mixed," Graff answered. "The Commander wants everyone able to handle another's specialty as well as his own and maybe a couple of others. Sort of a backup."

"Smart," Sogan agreed. He had insisted upon that himself, originally an unorthodox policy for the Arcturian Navy but one soon adopted by most of the other commanders when they observed its efficiency.

"Aye, sir," the other replied proudly. "She's that, right enough.—Anyway, I'm officially on the weapons banks, and Charl and Nels work in the drive room. Aste's one of our computer people."

"Not very glamorous work, I fear," the mutant said almost apologetically.

"All the courage and skill of the fighters could count for nothing without competent technical staffs to back them and the quick access to information that a well-managed memory bank can provide," the former Admiral observed.

"Aye, sir." Aste straightened a little. No one actually doubted that, but the *Free Comet* was as much a warship as any in the Navy fleets, and those hands assigned to combat-oriented duties were the ones most greatly admired and envied by their comrades. It was good to hear his own quieter post praised now and then, especially by this man who had so dramatically proved his courage and abilities.

The Yeomen remained with the newcomers a few minutes longer, then returned to the table they had vacated.

Islaen's fingers brushed the Arcturian's hand. *Thanks, Varn.*

His shields had been only lightly raised, and she had been fully aware of his revulsion. It had cost him a struggle to keep it from becoming visible, but he had not betrayed any sign of it. *Would you have had me order him off?* he half snarled. *He deserves something better than contempt,* he added more quietly.

Aye. She glanced at the galley entrance. "We'd better collect some supper, I suppose."

"Bethe and I'll go," Jake volunteered. "Any preferences, Colonel?"

"None for me," she said.

"Sogan?"

"No. Anything will serve."

The Arcturian scarcely noticed the food when it came, and he ate mechanically. He had forced his mind back to their mission in order to drive less welcome sensations from it, and the difficulties facing them soon gripped him.

He could see no way to resolve their questions before they reached Quandon Sector, and he did not like at all the prospect of letting the *Free Comet* blunder blindly into whatever had taken those other ships. She was strong, but she would still fare better if she had some foreknowledge of who or what her opponent might be.

Sogan himself was convinced they were dealing with a conscious agency, an active foe. The disappearances had apparently begun fairly suddenly about a decade ago, and there was no pattern in them to indicate a natural upheaval or phenomenon, although, space only knew, the Sector had been so lightly explored that its starlanes could hold many a dark surprise.

He scowled. No. All his instincts went against that. Something more sinister was at work.

If he was right, it was rather to their good than otherwise. A sentient foe could be fought. Be it human or some equivalent species, it was finite and capable of taking defeat at their hands. That might not be possible if they were forced to deal with one of the mindless, awesome forces generated in the functioning of the universe itself.

His frown darkened. They needed information, at least some indication of a location, if they were to fight effectively. Even some kind of pattern would be something. It seemed impossible that there was nothing to be discovered in the wealth of data they possessed . . .

"You're certainly full of talk tonight, Admiral," Jake Karmikel remarked in a slightly louder tone than he had been using.

Sogan brought himself back to his comrades. "Sorry," he apologized. "I was trying to figure some way to narrow our search a bit. I cannot help but feel that there must be some indication somewhere if we only knew how to winnow it out."

He stopped speaking suddenly and straightened. "There may

be a way to shorten the hunt, at least," he said softly, as if to himself.

"What do you have in mind, Varn?" Islaen asked quickly.

"Can we make use of the *Comet*'s facilities, her computers?"

"Aye, of course, depending on what you want to do, naturally."

He turned to the place where the four Yeomen were sitting, but they were engrossed in conversation with a couple of their comrades and were no longer watching the booth.

"Bandit, get the mutant for me. Aste," he added, seeing that she did not recognize the former term. The gurry did not care what had happened to a person's genes. She was interested only in whether he was friendly to her and her party.

Bandit will bring him!

She sped across the big cabin and landed on the table directly in front of her target. He started at her sudden appearance and stroked her with a bony forefinger.

The hen allowed him to continue for a few seconds, then she licked the finger and, taking hold of it with her supple toes, began gently tugging him in the direction of her company.

He laughed. "All right! I get the idea! Let's go talk to your friends."

Aste saluted the Navy officers and, at their invitation, slid into the seat beside Jake so that he faced the other two. He was certain it was one or the other of them who wanted to see him.

"Aye, Colonel? Captain?"

Sogan shifted a little so that he would not seem to be holding himself so stiffly. "I was wondering what the *Comet*'s computers can do."

"A lot, sir!" the Yeoman replied in quick pride. "What do you need?"

"It is a nasty job, I am afraid. I do not doubt your capability, but the time involved and the volume of work may be too great to warrant the effort."

"Try me."

The war prince leaned forward. "I want the course of every victim plotted. Start with what is known for a fact. Go from there to their planned routes, if any were filed, and to likely detours. Once you have that, let me also have any other possible flight plans that the vanished ships might have taken plus those anyone intercepting them would have used. I want to know if and where either the victims' or the aggressors' paths might have crossed, in any combination."

He eyed the Yeoman. "Can it or any part of it be done? Within the time frame we have?"

Aste was silent for several long seconds, then he nodded slowly. "It can, though an analysis like that won't be easy to set up. Or done fast. Our system isn't exactly the equal of a battleship's, and the *Comet*'s own demands are heavy."

"Do what you can. There may be no correlation for you to find, but anything you can pull out will be of help."

The mutant frowned. "I'll put together a program to speed up the integrating process. The retrieval itself should be no problem. I'll get the rest of my squad on it as well." He glanced at the door. "I'd best get started, sir. This'll take a lot of thinking through, and I want to start putting down a few notes as soon as I can."

Jake waited until the crewman had gone, then leaned back and fixed his blue eyes on the Arcturian. "You're not to be trusted, Admiral."

"In what way?" Sogan asked, falling in with the other's mood.

"You're not two full days aboard the *Free Comet,* and here you are commandeering her crew already!"

The war prince smiled in answer. "I am commandeering my own crew as well. Finish up quickly, and let us be getting back to quarters. There are a few things I want to try with our data."

Islaen listened to them with amusement. She liked to see this mood on Varn, even if it did mean that he would be working them, and probably half the *Comet*'s crew, into the lower decks until they reached Quandon Sector.

She roused herself at the sound of Karmikel's much exaggerated groan. "Have a little mercy, Admiral. Besides, you've been with us long enough to know we'll get a lot more out of Jake if we let him enjoy his second cup of jakek in peace."

"I am always merciful," he retorted, "especially since I want to plot out our hunt before we actually begin it anyway.—Will you come now, or do you prefer to stay here for a while longer?"

She gulped down the last mouthfuls in her cup. "I'm finished. You've got my curiosity up, friend. Let's get at it."

They came to their feet. Sogan glanced at the flask still standing prominently on the table. "Dispose of that," he told the others. "It might not endear us to the Commander if it were found." Had he discovered the like on any vessel of his, he would have clapped its possessors in detention for the voyage and probably taken whatever they had of rank as well.

Jake gave him a broad grin. "Aye, Admiral. Don't worry on that score."

The Commando-Captain held up the flask once he and Bethe Danlo were alone. "Not two drops left," he grumbled. "It might have been rather pleasant obeying that order."

"Never mind, you space tramp!" she retorted. "You know full well what he meant by disposal."

"I know. The man has no taste in some matters."

She eyed the remnant of the crewmen's gift. "I fear I agree with him in this case."

"Neither of you has any taste."

"I've more or less chosen you, haven't I?" the demolitions expert countered.

Karmikel scowled. "Have you? You won't even say you'll marry me."

"Right," she affirmed calmly. "We've been through that. I'm not making any move in that direction until we've had more time working together. Otherwise I might find I'd leaped feet-first and eyes shut right into a black hole."

"A flattering comparison!" he muttered.

The woman smiled. "Relax, space hound. You might as well. Every woman's entitled to a decent courtship period, and I don't intend to get rushed out of mine.—We'd best be finishing up. Our two comrades will be getting very impatient if we don't show up soon."

"Aye, Sergeant," he agreed none too eagerly. "Brace yourself. By the look of it, our Admiral's going to be driving us on all burners for the foreseeable future."

SEVEN

TIME PASSED QUICKLY for the Navy unit, thanks to the massive search in which they were engaged. The *Free Comet*'s computers brought them new information with every passing day, suggesting possible correlations, effectively narrowing the prime hunt area, but still no definite answers or even real clues, however vague, had surfaced. They learned immeasurably more about the starlanes and colony planets of the frontier Sector than would have been possible had they been forced to depend upon their own materials alone, but none of the suspect worlds had yet been eliminated.

With the Patrol cruiser rapidly approaching Quandon Sector, Islaen Connor demanded ever greater effort from her team. There was sound reason for pressing them as she did, apart from the direct demands of their mission. She herself was growing nervous, as she always did when her sharply honed warrior's instincts told her the possibility of action was near, a tension multiplied several times over by her relative helplessness, her uselessness, while they remained in deep space. It was no different with any of the others, and whatever she could do to keep all their minds from the uncertain future was to their advantage.

The Commando-Colonel woke to find the air still chilled to the sleep-period level. She lay in her bunk awhile. A glance at the self-illuminated face of her timer told her it was indeed very early, but the sleep had left her, and at last she rose and dressed, quickly, as habit dictated. If she was awake anyway, she might as well be getting started.

She would not be at it alone for long. Tension was high in them all, and none of them slept much, no more than their minds required to counter the effects of the stress and efforts they put on themselves each day.

The corridor outside her cabin was quiet, but she found the other three already in the hangar and at work when she got there.

"Morning, Colonel," Jake drawled. "Decided to sleep late, did you?"

Before she could answer him, the intercom crackled.

"Maintenance crew to hull. Repeat. Maintenance crew to hull."

The Colonel felt a surge of alarm. What was wrong? Routine maintenance details were not sent out by direct order from the bridge, much less over the general ship frequency, yet they had encountered no turbulence whatsoever during the voyage to cause damage, nor had there been any sudden strikes by the odd pieces of interstellar debris which were a constant hazard in any of the galaxy's starlanes.

A glance at her comrades told that they were as puzzled as she. More than that in Sogan's case. The tightness of his expression and the readings she was receiving from him revealed his resentment of the role he was being forced to carry.

Once more, the intercom sounded. This time, it was Marta Florr herself who spoke. "Commando-Colonel Islaen Connor to the bridge with your unit, if you please."

Her eyes met Varn's as their thoughts linked. A request, albeit one not to be refused. There was nothing terribly amiss, then, or the summons would have been worded differently, but why the call for them at all at this stage? They should be nowhere near any of those nine planets yet.

The former Admiral gave a mental shrug in answer to the questions they both shared. *There is but one way to find out, my Islaen.*

Bandit, who had perched on the back of the flier's driver's seat, her normal post during these work sessions, now fluttered to Islaen's shoulder.

The woman started to tell her to remain in their quarters this time, but the shadow of an idea rose in her mind, and she relented.

"All right, love," she said. "Come with us, but keep yourself very quiet and out of the way until we learn what goes."

Bandit will!—Bandit can help? she added, having detected

that there was a purpose of some sort behind the human's change of heart.

Maybe, Islaen replied in mind. *That's for later if at all, Little Bandit. Let's just concentrate on what's ahead of us for now.*

The bridge of the *Free Comet* was very quiet. Little of the ordered activity generated in the running of a Patrol cruiser was in evidence, little movement of any sort.

The concern Islaen Connor had felt since the call for the maintenance crew sharpened. What could be wrong? There was no sign of danger, nothing that suggested mechanical failure, yet she saw now that the starship had been halted and was anchored in the depths of space.

Marta Florr saw them enter and motioned for them to mount the command dais.

"I thought our preparations might interest you," she said as she switched on the hull scanners.

Even as the Colonel watched, the smooth lines of the *Free Comet* disappeared beneath the shell of metal plates. They were pitted and scarred. Solar steel, she decided, rather than any of the titanone compounds. They would no longer be traveling as a military vessel.

She turned to Marta for confirmation. The Commander smiled and nodded.

To all appearances, the *Comet* was now a freighter of uncertain age plying the starlanes on the outskirts of the Federation where competition from younger, faster vessels was not so keen.

"What do you think, Colonel?"

"Any pirate fleet within range will attack. I only hope our pletzars and screens will function through all this."

"No need to try them. It's blown off as a shrapnel bolt when the fighting begins. If we can strike before our opponents can raise their screens and hit the tubes directly, we can sometimes end a confrontation that way before it half begins.—Our strategy meets with your approval?"

The guerrilla nodded in appreciation. "The Commandos should have recruited from your service's higher ranks. You would've been an asset to any unit."

The Commander laughed. "Return to your wing now, Colonel. I wanted you and your team to be aware of what's going on when we engage the enemy. It's a difficult enough experience for those having no active part even with full knowledge of our tactics." She sighed. "You're probably all too well aware of that already. I'm only sorry I can't do more to ease it for you."

Islaen Connor returned to the exploration wing. She had understood Commander Florr's words right enough, and although she appreciated the unwonted courtesy they had been shown, she did not look forward to the time just ahead of them.

The *Free Comet* pierced the outer border of Quandon Sector soon after their summons and, several hours later, the target area itself.

A fierce tension rose throughout the starship. The only certainty now was that danger lurked somewhere in the void beyond, perhaps even at this moment watching, waiting for them to draw only a little closer. All realized that attack might come at any moment, either by a single vessel or by a wolf pack of unknown strength—or by some mysterious force of the natural universe which no tool of humankind could hope to combat or withstand.

There was nothing to be done at this stage save to monitor the instruments carefully and keep in readiness to meet whatever finally came against them.

Commander Florr remained on the bridge almost constantly during this period, leaving only for rest or food. She hoped the inevitable attack would hit soon. Battle itself would be a release for her crew and for herself.

The four Navy soldiers found this period of waiting even more trying. They endured all the pressure driving their Regular comrades without even the prospect of being able to render useful service once the challenge was before them. They were confined to the exploration wing or the crew's cabin, and they visited the cabin only infrequently, chiefly to eat or to meet with Aste, who had little other time to discuss his discoveries with them while the alert was in effect.

They drove themselves hard with the work they did have but derived little satisfaction from it. No major breakthrough occurred, and the minor, steady progress they made was not sufficient even to encourage them, much less give them any feeling that they were laboring equally with the Patrol Regulars around them.

Varn Tarl Sogan suffered most acutely during this period. For nearly the whole of his adult life, he had risen or fallen through his own decisions and the orders he had issued, and this inactivity, this dependence upon the skill and commands of an almost unknown officer, who was not even a member of the Federation Navy, was well-nigh as killing to him as the purposeless existence he led in the first years of his exile, before his meeting with Islaen Connor.

The Commando-Colonel was well aware of the emotions rending him, as much from her knowledge of the man as from the occasional indications he let slip through his shields. The last did not occur often. He was too much part of his caste to whine over a distasteful situation, particularly when he recognized that his companions were no happier about it than himself. He would not add to their burdens by drawing down his own.

Islaen wished that warrior code operated with less force within him. This was something she knew well herself from the past. She had traveled aboard various Navy battlecraft en route to her assigned targets during the War under conditions similar to these and perhaps might have been able to help ease this passage for him, but he would give her no opening even to try. She had no choice but to let him struggle on alone unless he himself chose to at least admit her to his mind.

She squared her shoulders and put those thoughts away from her as she approached the hangar. Varn had hit upon an idea last evening just before they broke off. It was promising, the most promising they had come up with yet, but she knew the implementing and testing of it would require careful, detailed work. She could not afford to come to it with her mind half filled with other, personal matters.

She felt no surprise at finding her husband already inside. Even without the excitement of what might prove the road to the answers they sought, Sogan always started before the rest of them each day to check over the reports sent up by the computer night shift and coordinate them with their own previous work before they were ready to begin themselves. She sighed to herself. He usually stayed here very late as well.

He was deeply engrossed that morning, and she had to touch her thoughts to his before he became aware of her presence.

The Arcturian looked up, his eyes and mind brightening as they always did at her approach. *Islaen, welcome!*—"Aye, and you as well, small one." He glanced down at the bench he was using for a temporary desk. *Take a look at this.*

The woman felt excitement in him and quickened her pace.

He had spread out a starmap of Quandon Sector and laid a

transparency over it. The latter was crossed with a complex webbing of fine lines drawn in varying colors. His finger circled a large region where they appeared to congregate. *It was simple enough once I thought to try it this way,* he told her. *I think we are getting near to pinpointing a real target at last.*

She shrugged off the self-reproach in his tone. *It was too simple an idea. That's why none of us came up with it sooner.*

The Commando nodded in satisfaction after studying the map for a few seconds. *Down to three star systems, five planets,* she remarked. *That'll make things a hell of a lot easier for us all. You've done some job here.*

This is not the half of it, he answered, pleasure coloring his response almost despite himself. *When I get the rest of the routes plotted, we should have a single world for a focus, or two at the most.*

Better still.—I'll give Commander Florr what we have now, though. You've given us a prime region, and we might as well concentrate our efforts there.

Aye. The sooner the better.

Sogan flexed his shoulders. The movement was slight, but something in it proclaimed the weariness that was on him, and she guessed that he must have been here most or all of the previous night.

Her fingers brushed the back of his hand. *Take it easy, Varn. Let us help you with the rest of this one.*

He sat down on the edge of the bench. He felt tired now and disheartened, and he lowered his shields, allowing her to read the full of his frustration. If the *Free Comet* were his command, she would already be en route to the area he had outlined. Even now, time was being lost, and maybe other ships would die as a result, vessels and crews which might have lived had they moved at the moment he made his discovery.

The Colonel frowned. Sogan was right. Marta Florr would doubtless follow through immediately once she was given this information, but a certain amount of delay between pinpointing the area of highest danger and their reaching it was inevitable.

Is it always this way? he demanded abruptly. *Was it like this for your teams during the War?*

While aboard ship, aye. It's very different on-world, as you well know. There, the skill is ours.

He nodded glumly. Hers and Jake Karmikel's. His place and his real superiority was in space, on the bridge of a fighting ship, but this time, he was proving little more than so much animated cargo.

Islaen watched him somberly. His thoughts were easy enough to follow despite the fact that he was broadcasting none of them. She hated to see him feeling so down, so helpless. She hated feeling that way herself.

She looked up as the sound of voices announced the arrival of Bethe and Jake. She thought they seemed subdued this morning as well, although they, too, had known of the track the Arcturian had begun to follow and had every reason to anticipate real progress at last.

Their commander glowered. If only they had some better idea of how they were actually faring, even if they could know their relative position, all this would be easier on them.

The Commando-Colonel straightened. An idea which had tickled her mind earlier returned to her, and with it came the decision to act.

"Bandit," she said suddenly, "I want you to start spending time on the bridge. Draw Commander Florr and the other officers to you, several at least on each watch. Let them get used to seeing you there."

Sogan read her intent and stiffened. "Islaen! Are you mad?" he demanded, aloud since the others were present.

"Not in the least. I've been wondering if she could handle long-term espionage. Now's a good chance to find out."

"For no greater reason than our mental comfort?" he snapped. "What if she is discovered?"

"How could she be? No one knows what lies between us and her. Besides, better to fail on the *Free Comet* where the only penalty will be the Commander's anger than among enemies where death would probably be our share."

She stroked the little hen, who had flown to the bench and was perched there, her feathers extended in excitement.

"Are you willing to take this on, love?" she asked. "It'll mostly be a lot of dull watching away from us, even if you'll be with other humans who'll like and probably spoil you."

Bandit will help! Everyone's unhappy now!

"That we are, love. Thanks.—When you're on the bridge, you'll link now and then with Varn, especially if something unusual seems to be happening. In the event of some real action, he'll join with me in turn, and I'll keep Jake and Bethe informed via our communicators. At least, we won't have to sit out a battle in total ignorance like so many statues."

The others were staring at her, but their incredulity was quickly replaced by open grins. The very audacity of the plan appealed to them in itself, and the fact that it seemed almost a revenge for their enforced secondary role made it seem all the sweeter.

The woman smiled at their reaction. She had guessed they would respond this way. "Go to it, Bandit," she told the gurry softly, "but take care, mind you. We really do not want you to be caught at this."

Bandit will be careful!

EIGHT

Two DAYS PASSED without incident save that Bandit was successful in her infiltration of the *Free Comet*'s bridge. The rise in the spirits of the Navy team was marked and immediate. The four humans were proud of the skill and daring of their strange little companion, and, illogical as they all knew it to be, they now felt more in control of the events shaping their fate.

The pace of their own labors did not slacken, a fact for which Varn Tarl Sogan was grateful. The ready access he had to the cruiser's bridge through the linking of his sense receptors with the gurry's was proving a distinctly double-edged benefit. He was as glad as any of his comrades for the sense of mental freedom their new knowledge gave them, and at last his curiosity regarding the management of a reasonably large-scale Federation military-type vessel was being satisfied in great detail, but all he learned and observed whetted his desire for a command, a real command such as he had been bred and trained to carry. It intensified with each passing hour until it became an almost physical ache within him. Had it not been for these other demands on him, he feared he might spend most of his time vicariously on that bridge, knowing that he could never expect better than that again.

Even owning that thought, much less acknowledging the possibility of his yielding to it, caused his color to rise and drove him to strengthen the shields screening his inner mind. He had no right to such weakness, no right to consider it, no right at all to continue entertaining it.

Clearing his mind of everything but the task before him, he bent once more over his well-worn starmap. He had his own work to do, and if he failed in it or delayed too long in completing it, the *Free Comet* herself and many a vessel after her might well die, and his would be the blame.

The quiet they had experienced throughout the long voyage continued into the afternoon, when an object, a ship, appeared on the perimeter of the *Comet*'s distance viewer. It soon became obvious that the strange vessel was pacing them.

Commander Florr's hand hit the siren.

"Battle alert! Repeat. Battle alert! This is not a drill."

There was little doubt as to the intruder's intentions. Since she was tracking them at a distance well outside the range of any commercial vessel's detection instruments, it was reasonable to assume that her own equipment and her purpose were military. With the *Free Comet* the only government ship, Navy or Stellar Patrol, anywhere within the vicinity of Quandon Sector, the newcomer could only be a pirate. Any merchantman so outfitted would have tried to speed away from them as fast as her tubes could take her while she herself remained undetected.

The Navy soldiers went at once to their cabins and strapped themselves into their safety nets. There they waited, tension firing every nerve, while their winged comrade hastened to take up her post on the bridge.

Varn's eyes closed. His heart was pounding as his body prepared itself for a battle he would not be permitted to wage. Seconds rolled by, interminable seconds, then the universe seemed to rock around him as the command dais of the *Free Comet* opened before him, giving maddening lie to his own senses.

As soon as his perceptions had stabilized, he opened his mind into Islaen's so that she, too, might experience all he saw and heard.

The gurry had chosen a good post. Out of the way, almost unnoticeable in that tense scene, she could still see everything on the bridge including the viewers and most of the instruments, and through her eyes, her humans were able to read them as well.

The bridge was strangely quiet. Only the voice of the navigator reading the distance figures with monotonous regularity broke the silence.

Then, with meteoric speed, the strange vessel began her approach. Soon she filled the near-space viewer.

She was a small craft, a five-man fighter, but very clean of line, trimmed for speed and maneuverability. An archetype pirate.

Marta Florr did not underestimate the fighter's strength. Such craft normally worked close enough to base that the amount of space required for supplies and replacement personnel was almost negligible. Even captured cargo was usually transported in a barge brought from base. A raider was free to devote every possible unit of space to weapons systems. By the look of this ship, hers would be more than powerful enough to attack almost any of the freighters plying Quandon Sector's starlanes.

Ship-to-ship flashed. The communications officer accepted the transmission at the Commander's signal.

"Hailing frequency open."

A thick, somewhat mechanical voice cut into his words. "This is the Captain of the *Minotaur*. You are outgunned, and you cannot hope to outdistance us. Kill your engines and do not attempt to resist our tractor. Your crew will be spared if you obey."

The channel closed at once, permitting no reply.

The *Minotaur*'s rear screens parted to allow the passage of the powerful tow beam.

Marta Florr flicked an intercom switch. "Weapons banks, fire shrapnel bolt."

A second. Less. The false hull exploded from the cruiser, its pieces converging and speeding with incredible force through the breach in the pirate's guard. Her laser banks responded immediately. They were extraordinarily strong, but they glanced harmlessly off the Navy-standard screens of the Patrol vessel.

The Commander smiled in satisfaction. The *Comet*'s bolt had struck true. The *Minotaur*'s tubes had been severely fouled, to the point that she would not maneuver so easily or quickly now, a disability that would much favor the larger government battlecraft.

"Ship-to-ship.—This is Patrol-Commander Marta Florr of the Stellar Patrol ship *Free Comet*. Surrender yourselves and your vessel at once or face destruction."

Her ultimatum was met by a fresh flash of laser fire. None of this space scum permitted themselves to be taken while they could still fight. The penalty for piracy was death, and little leniency was being granted to such renegades by Federation courts in these troubled times.

Varn Tarl Sogan frowned. Both vessels had their screens firmly in place now. It must be obvious to those vermin out there that they could not hope to penetrate the bigger ship's defenses, and they must realize what would happen to them once she chose to reply to their fire. It was well known throughout all the ultrasystem that Patrol battlecraft, like their Navy counterparts, were mounted with pletzars as well as the conventional lasers. No screens not specifically designed to withstand that wild brand of energy could do so for more than a very few seconds, yet the *Minotaur* was making no effort to break and flee. What was the matter with her master? Pirates were not normally fools.

Why had he shown so little caution in managing his assault against a vessel that so outclassed his? The former Admiral himself would have been most reluctant to take this on had other options been available to him, and he had made his reputation both in the Empire and now in the Federation's service as a daring commander when the need for that was on him. Freighters went well armed. Even had their opponent been fully confident he could take the *Comet,* prudence would have demanded very different conduct throughout the entire confrontation.

Marta Florr was about to order the *Free Comet*'s reply.

Not yet! his mind shouted desperately. There was something wrong with that ship, something very wrong. They must discover what . . .

The cruiser's pletzar banks discharged.

The pirate's screens buckled under the impact. She did try to flee now, but the damage wrought by the original shrapnel bolt had made her slow and difficult to manage, and much of her energy was being drawn into her fight to maintain her failing defenses. Only moments remained to her now.

In his despair, Sogan called out to his consort. *Islaen, try to get to her crew! Any of them!*

The woman wasted no time in reacting. Her mind shot forward, reaching for those manning the doomed starship.

She just found them, or found the indication of life, rather, when all creation filled with blinding light. A wrenching scream tore from her throat, and she threw her hands before her eyes, although it was not through them but in her mind itself that the explosion struck.

Islaen's consciousness fled back, severing the nascent contact so rapidly that she feared for a moment that she had left some part of herself in the pirates' dying minds. She reached the Patrol cruiser once more and the shelter of her own being, then strain and shock overcame her, and she was aware of nothing more.

The *Free Comet* shuddered as the waves from the exploding *Minotaur* struck her screens.

The turmoil soon subsided, and all became very still. The incandescent ball of dust which had been the pirate fighter slowly thinned and dissipated, and the velvet blackness normal to space flowed around the victor once more.

Islaen!

The Commando-Colonel emerged from the mists into which she had sunk, slowly at first, then more rapidly as she became aware of the Arcturian's frantic call. *Varn? —Varn, I'm all right now. Just shaken.*

Praise the Spirit of Space! I feared I had slain you.

No. I pulled out in time. There was no point in trying to minimize the experience. Sogan had been with her through it all, though she, as the actual seeker, had borne the brunt of the backlash. *I'm only sorry I failed you. I moved too late to effect any real contact.*

Better that than your death or the blasting of your mind!

The terror he had felt moments before was sharp in that, and Islaen's thoughts instantly reached out to touch with his on a level deeper than mere speech. *You wouldn't have asked it if it hadn't been important,* she told him gently. *Let me rest awhile, recover a bit, then tell me what troubled you so much about that ship. We may be able to figure out the answers we need some other way.*

He was quiet for a moment, but then he submerged his guilt and the shadow of his fear for her. *I shall be in the hangar. Link with me there when you are ready, or join me if you feel up to it.*

Aye, she agreed, successfully concealing the weariness even this brief contact had cost her. It was but a reaction, a rebellion by a sense not yet fully over the shock it had taken, and would soon pass off, but the knowledge of it would only have put more worry and reproach on the war prince.

The Commando marshaled her will and forced her mind out once more. She was met by an aching void where she had touched life but moments before.

Islaen withdrew altogether and lay very still until the trembling of her mind reached her limbs. By forcing her body back under her control, she was able to bring her feelings under her will as well.

She had known the dying of fellow beings and had shared in that dying by reason of the incomplete contact she had achieved. It had not been an easy experience and could have been deadly in every sense. Only by the will of fortune and of whatever gods ruled her life had she managed to escape without sustaining serious injury to her mind. As it was, the sensations of death still held her in a cold grasp, a grasp she had to struggle hard to release.

The Commando-Colonel remained in her cabin until she could be certain of her control, but then she rose and hastened to join Sogan in the hangar.

She was technically breaking alert. They both were. No order had come from the bridge easing the emergency state, but Varn did not seem to believe they had the time to wait for that now, and Islaen put her trust in him.

NINE

THE FORMER ADMIRAL'S dark eyes seemed to bore into her, and Islaen smiled softly. This deep concern, the care and gentleness of it, still surprised her when he permitted her to read it and never failed to move her.

She slipped into his arms, glorying as always in the strength and tenderness of his embrace. *I'm truly all right,* she assured him. *I used my talent to run a check on myself, and there aren't any aftereffects.*

Small thanks to me. I should have known it was too late to try such a move.

I very nearly did succeed in picking up some surface readings, she reminded him.

You got nothing?

She shook her head. *Nothing at all beyond confirming the existence of intelligent life. I could not even number the crew for you.*

She stepped back hastily and turned to the door as Jake all but exploded through it. Bethe Danlo arrived moments later showing an almost equal degree of anxiety.

"You're breaking alert," their commander told them mildly. Neither responded.

"Never mind that!" the redhead snapped. "What happened, and what's going on? First, you just about shatter our eardrums with that shriek, then you keep us hanging, and finally you tell us you're going to the hangar and will meet us there as soon as the release is sounded, as if nothing occurred at all!"

"If you'll quiet down enough to let me get a word in, I'll explain."

Islaen went on to describe her aborted attempt to pick up some sort of readings from the pirates before death overtook them.

Karmikel glared at the Arcturian when she finished. "Have you gone completely mad, Sogan?" he demanded.

There was enough real threat in his tone that the Colonel put herself between the two men. A glance at Bethe's steel-hard eyes was enough to tell her that for once Sogan had an enemy in that quarter as well.

Her head lifted a trifle. Whether he had been right or a damn reckless fool, she was not going to have Varn jumped on every side. "Break off!" she commanded sharply. "Varn Tarl Sogan never ordered anyone into peril without good cause, and you well know it. He felt this was important enough to warrant my taking the chance."

"I should hope there was something more concrete than feeling behind it," Jake replied coolly, completely unmollified.

"Perhaps there was not," the war prince told him.

Varn turned from the others when their eyes fixed on him. His head lowered. "It seems so insignificant now, laughable were it not for the possible consequences to Islaen, but everything within me said it was important. Despite all reason, I still feel it is."

The Commando-Colonel whirled on Jake. "No more out of you!" she snapped to forestall the outburst she felt rising in him. "And you stop cutting yourself down, Varn. That instinct of yours has been right so often that I've wondered before if it mightn't be part of your talent, like my ability to detect damage or illness is part of mine."

Sogan looked at her sharply. She could read his surprise and denial and raised her hands quickly. "Maybe aye, maybe no, and granted it isn't under your control. What matters now is that you did detect something in the *Minotaur,* and you'd best let us hear about it."

The demolitions expert nodded, entering into the discussion for the first time. "She's right, Varn. If nothing else, you've a commander's way of looking at things, and I know right well that you wouldn't take chances with Islaen's life without damn good reason, whatever you might be willing to try with your own now and then. What struck you amiss about the *Minotaur*? Jake and I couldn't see her, remember, and even our good Colonel didn't seem to catch it."

He sighed and spread his hands. "Everything was wrong. Her

whole manner. She was very powerfully armed and screened
right enough, capable of taking down nearly any normal target,
but by no turn of thought or dream would a hundred-class vessel
fall into that category, whatever her age and appearance. All rim
freighters are minor battlecraft and have been for decades. They
could not have survived otherwise. A major wolf pack, even a
small fleet, of such fighters should have been most hesitant
about coming against us, much less a single ship."

"So her arrogance bothered you?" the Commando-Captain
asked, speaking quietly now, thoughtfully.

He nodded. "Aye, and it was arrogance. Her whole approach
reeked of it. Some of my own people might have shown the like
under these circumstances, assuming they were ignorant of a
Patrol ship's armaments, but even at that I could not see it in any
ranking officer. In the case of the space scum they purported to
be, it is inconceivable. They know better."

He fell silent for several moments as he retreated into his own
thoughts. When he recalled himself to his companions again, the
frown already marring his features had darkened still further.
"Even that transmission . . ."

Islaen's breath caught. "Varn, no one was on the other end!
That was a tape talking!"

"A tape?" Bethe Danlo echoed.

"Aye. I didn't recognize the fact at the time, but as I recall
now, no emotion came with it. I should've been able to pick up
plenty from it—triumph, hope, greed, the lust for blood—but
there was nothing at all to be read."

"You could be right," Sogan agreed, "but there was more
wrong with it than that. The voice itself was—off." He looked
about him helplessly. "I am sorry. I cannot identify what there
was about it that struck me as it did. —You noticed no
strangeness in it, Islaen?"

"Aye, now that you draw it down, I think I did. There was an
odd quality to it."

"Mechanically or electrically generated?" the Noreenan man
ventured.

"Perhaps, but I doubt that is it. I have heard both, and this
seemed different, as if it came from a human throat and yet did
not."

"A mutation or nonhuman? Both exist in plenty throughout
the galaxy."

"Maybe. I just do not know." Varn pressed his fingers to his eyes. "So many small things, yet if we had the answers to them, I feel to the very core of my being that we would have the answer to this mystery of vanishing starships as well." His face hardened. "If only I had realized sooner, made a move sooner!"

"Probably it would have availed nothing," his consort said quickly. "I can't read other minds, remember, only pick up emotions from them."

Her eyes were blazing, and her body had tensed in the way it always did when she was preparing to set herself against some challenge. "We lost our chance there, if it ever was a chance, but that attack has given us plenty, even without what we might have learned from the *Minotaur*'s crew. I think Varn's right, that she was tied in with those lost ships. With the figures we now have from her approach and those we've been adding to our chart, we should jolly well have ourselves a target. —Comrades, let's get to work! Our speculations just now will have to stay within our company, but if at all possible, I want something to put before Commander Florr at the postcombat debriefing. That only gives us a couple of hours at best."

The Navy team worked with feverish haste. The computer would have helped them immensely, but they had no hope of accessing it for the next several hours, not until long after the alert was lifted. They were lucky in that they had much of the work already done, all of it really save plotting the *Minotaur*'s probable course. They were now certain of their own, thanks to Bandit's productive visits to the bridge.

An hour and a half slipped by with only an occasional comment or question breaking the silence in the hangar, then Islaen Connor gave a crow of triumph. They had their planet at last.

She picked out the appropriate file from among the suspects' records and slipped the spool capsule accompanying it into their tape reader.

"Omrai of Umbar," she announced. "Not exactly one of the Federation's glory spots, but we can't expect everything in a target."

"Caves?" Jake Karmikel asked suspiciously. They had split the studying of the nine files, and Omrai's had fallen to his commander's lot.

"Probably, but they should be of no concern to us."

"Her gods be praised for that!" he replied with great feeling. "I think I'd have deserted had you answered the other way."

"I should have joined you," Varn Tarl Sogan told him.

The Colonel was hard-pressed to cover her surprise. Sogan's experiences in Mirelle's underworld were such that she had not imagined him capable of jesting about them.

She answered quickly herself. "I shall abstain from making any comment. A CO mustn't give bad example to her troops."

She instantly became serious once more and reached over to activate the tape viewer. The image of a blue-green planet filled the screen, a water world as most of the Terra-normals were.

She opened the file. There was little enough in it, only the initial discovery and survey reports. These were very old. They had not aroused enough interest to warrant further study, and the planet had not been visited again.

Omrai followed an elliptical orbit around the sun-star Umbar. She was small, a mere 5,000 miles in diameter, and over 80 percent of her surface was submerged under an ocean of hydrogen-oxide composition. What dry surface existed was very mountainous and was not suited for agriculture on a commercial scale, although the soil gave every indication of fertility and supported abundant vegetation. The planet's minerals were concentrated almost entirely in her core with no significant solid ore deposits whatsoever. She had no native population, but there was a reasonably rich fauna, all the species classified in the lower intelligence ranges.

Both reports ended on a similar note: Suitable for colonization, but no action recommended while more economically attractive planets remained plentiful.

That, in summary, was all the Federation knew about Omrai of Umbar.

A summary was not sufficient for a guerrilla unit which might have to live and fight there and was certainly not sufficient for the officer who had to command them. Fortunately, a great deal of detail was available. If these reports were not as extensive as those on some of the other worlds within the Federation ultrasystem, they still held a large amount of fact, and the four settled down to assimilate as much of it as they could in the short time remaining to them.

They were still deep in the reports when the alert was at last lifted, and Marta Florr summoned them along with her own officers for debriefing.

They did not have long to wait before the conference room was filled and Commander Florr dimmed the lights.

All of them watched attentively while the tapes of the *Minotaur*'s approach and the battle were run. When the lights once more raised, Sogan felt his comrades' eyes on him. They, too, had seen what he meant and could no more explain the strangeness of the pirate's behavior or the subtly but decidedly distorted transmission she had sent. The abnormality of that last was so obvious to them now that they wondered how the Regular service officers around them could be oblivious to it.

The Commander gave her report of the encounter, but before she could enter into any discussion of her conclusions or propose a new course of action, Islaen requested the right to address her.

Marta was surprised, but she yielded readily. "Aye, Colonel? You have some contribution to make?"

"In a sense, Commander. This assault has confirmed our target for us. I want to planet my unit on Omrai of Umbar as quickly as possible."

The *Comet*'s officers stared at her, and she smiled. "We've been plotting the disappearances, as you know. This encounter supports our figures completely."

"In that event, with the *Minotaur* blown . . ." The man who had spoken stopped himself. The raider might have been responsible for the missing ships, but there were still many questions to be answered. What had she done with them? Why had she seized them in the first place, since no part of their cargos had ever to anyone's knowledge surfaced for sale?

"You're certain it is Omrai?" the *Comet*'s mistress asked.

"As sure as we can be without checking her out."

Marta Florr nodded. "Go as soon as you're ready, Colonel. If you'd like any help from us, you need only ask it."

"Thank you, Commander," she replied with sincere gratitude. The other meant that offer. "I think we're well set. We'll make our approach from the attack site in the flier. That way, we can claim to be survivors from a battle that took out both ships if we should be captured."

Something in the way she said that caused the Terran's eyes to narrow. "Just what are you expecting to find on Omrai?"

"We don't know," she replied frankly. The Commando-Colonel hesitated a moment, then resolved to go on. "If we fail to meet you by your third sweep, or if you think you have to bring the *Free Comet* in for any reason, contact the Navy. Tell them to get out here on all burners, that there's something big, maybe very big, starting up on Omrai, then break contact before they can question you. The call can be canceled later if nothing develops, and I'll take full responsibility for issuing it.—I do have the authority under certain circumstances," she added when she saw the Regulars stiffen.

"You believe those conditions to be in effect here?" the other woman asked quietly.

"I couldn't swear to it, but the possibility's strong enough that, alone as we are, we have no alternative but to act on that premise."

"Very well, Colonel. I know what your unit has accomplished in the past, and I'll take this on trust now, since you're patently unwilling to share what you know or what you saw in those tapes that we missed."

"I saw the strangeness of the *Minotaur*'s behavior," she said quickly. "The rest stems from discussions and studies we've made already." Her mouth twisted into a grimace. "A lot of it's pure conjecture, I very much fear."

Marta sighed and shook her head. "I'd need more than that to send officers of mine out at all in that toy vehicle of yours, much less after space only knows what in terms of foes, natural or human." She sighed again. "My orders are to aid and transport you, Colonel Connor. I, we all, heartily wish you the best of luck. I would we could do more for you than that."

"You've done quite enough, Commander. As for those wishes, I have a feeling we'll be needing all the fortune they can draw down for us."

Varn fell into step beside her as they left the conference room. *You put your neck out in there. The whole team is doing that. I just hope I am not sending us wrong . . .*

His consort smiled. *Have a little more confidence in your instincts, Admiral,* she told him with good humor. *We all agree with you. Besides, unless our whole theory's way off, Omrai's our logical target anyway, quite apart from your suspicions about our recent opponent. If I overstressed the seriousness of the situation, that was my doing, not yours, and it'll be to our good if I'm proven wrong in that.*

TEN

THE COMPANY WAS not long in readying their supplies once they returned to the exploration wing. They had assembled them early in the long voyage, and now all that remained was to place them in the cargo space of the flier.

Food concentrates and water were loaded first, followed by the tools and general survival equipment customarily taken on surplanetary missions, and the medical kits were supplemented to counteract the few known dangers that might be encountered on Omrai. Each one, of course, saw to his own pack and arms.

Before slipping it into her pack, the Colonel checked the renewer to make certain it was fully charged and sound. Its power to heal almost immediately even severe injury to most parts of the body save the organs of the chest and abdomen had saved them on more than one occasion.

At last, they were ready. They took their places in the flier, and Sogan slipped the space seals into place. He maneuvered the little craft into the air lock.

His hands tightened on the controls as the door closed behind them. It would not be long now before Commander Florr gave the signal to launch.

He activated the engine and signaled for the suction vents to be opened. Almost immediately, the pressure in the cabin dropped as its atmosphere was drawn back into the depths of the *Free Comet*.

All four watched the instruments carefully. Any irregularity now would terminate the launch. Later, if it went undetected, even relatively insignificant trouble might well mean their lives and the failure of their mission.

"All systems go."

The Arcturian kept his voice steady, almost mechanical, betraying none of the excitement racing through him. He was experienced in space and experienced now with this vehicle through the intensive training he had given himself with it, but off-world travel in it would always be new and marvelous for him.

Soon now. Very soon. The familiar sprays of tension played along his nerves, but he was eager to begin.

The atmogage outside read zero. The yellow warning light abruptly ceased its rapid blinking, replaced by a steady, piercing red glow. The hatch slid back.

A touch to the controls, and the tiny Commando vehicle eased through the narrow opening into the infinite void beyond.

Sogan's breath caught. No other craft, not even the *Fairest Maid*, could give him what he found here. The flier was small and fragile, aye, and no one, he least of all, would choose to make even a simple interplanetary journey between the worlds of a single sun-star in it, but its very lack of bulk intensified the sensation of oneness with the universe beyond. The transparent canopy certainly seemed no barrier at all between him and those fair, far stars which had held his love for as long as he could trace memory back.

Out of the corner of her eye Islaen saw him smile, and shifted her position slightly so she could watch him.

She smiled as well. He was at ease, open in mind and expression as she had rarely known him to be in all the years since she first saw him, then the chiefmost of her foes on Thorne of Brandine. He was sitting back, his hands caressing the controls, his eyes slitted in pure pleasure as he gazed upon the starfield ahead.

She longed to share this with him but made no attempt to reach out to him. Indeed, she endeavored to mask her thoughts lest they touch and distract him. Too few such moments came in his life, and she wanted no part of wrenching him away from this one.

The man's own mind turned to her. He read her desire and opened himself to receive her.

They remained thus joined together for only a few moments before he regretfully withdrew into himself once more. Their mission was before them, and responsibility for this phase of it lay with him. The last few seconds had been his to use as he

would—his comrades had been little less powerfully affected, he
knew—but now it was his to begin in earnest.

He looked down at the gurry snuggled on Islaen Connor's lap.
She was gazing up through the canopy in apparent wonder but
was perfectly at ease, neither showing nor transmitting any trace
of fear.

"Are you ready, small one?" he asked her. "We have a long
way to go, but we should have nothing to fear provided we are
not seen."

Bandit's not afraid! Varn's a good pilot!

He was at that, the Commando-Colonel thought, so good that
there had been no more question about his taking the flier's
controls in space than there had been about giving him charge of
it on-world, but then she had yet to see him encounter any
vehicle he could not quickly master.

Sogan was proving that skill now. He wove the little Commando craft among the twisted shards of metal which was all
that remained of the *Comet's* false hull after the shrapnel bolt. It
was tricky work, for although the pieces were still fairly tightly
packed, the intergalactic currents had begun sweeping them
apart, and a great many of them were more than large enough to
seriously damage a vehicle of this size.

Despite that threat, they had all agreed that they would do well
to make their approach directly out of this area. The fragments
were still readily detectable from a fair distance and would
remain so long enough to help substantiate their story, if
necessary, that they were survivors of a battle which had claimed
both antagonists. They could thus hope to protect the secret of
the *Free Comet's* presence in the Sector for a while longer and
maybe even win themselves enough time to complete their
mission.

Once he had left the congested spot behind him, Sogan sent
the flier streaking forward at a speed which caused Jake
Karmikel to stiffen involuntarily in the rear seat. Whatever his
respect for the abilities of the small machine on-world, he knew
it was at best a tolerated alien in the starlanes. He would never
have pressed it like this in deep space, and if that dark-eyed
demon up there were any less of a pilot, he would have soon put
a stop to this race. As it was, he resolved to hold his peace, but
he would keep his eyes on the instruments. Should any of the
readings begin to look sour, he was prepared to act very fast
indeed.

The Commando-Colonel, too, was well aware of the speed at which they were traveling but felt rather easier about it. She had trained Varn with the guerrilla vehicle and was accustomed to his handling of it.

In truth, the war prince did display a brand of daring when at the controls of any relatively small personal or semipersonal carrier, that differed markedly from his management of a command, on-world or in space. Had there been anything at all of a boy in him, she would have been concerned enough to refuse him this work, but Varn Tarl Sogan was fully a man, one in whom she knew she was justified in placing implicit trust.

The Arcturian himself was unaware of their thoughts as he concentrated on the task before him. This little craft of his former enemies was versatile in the extreme, but it had never been designed for voyaging great distances through space. Its instrumentation was not the best suited for that purpose, even with the adaptations it had undergone, and he knew he would have to manage it carefully if they were to reach their intended target, navigating and flying almost completely manually.

That notwithstanding, there was no pause, no hesitation in him. He knew this machine, and he had studied their course too well over the last few hours to allow for any uncertainty now.

The flier navigated without flaw. Sogan kept it at its top space speed, and in a shorter time than even he had anticipated, they entered the planetary system of the sun-star Umbar.

He rapidly approached the small, blue-green world holding the fourth orbit out from her sun, but he slowed quite suddenly and stopped altogether just beyond the outermost fringes of her atmosphere and held them there as if frozen on the edge of true space.

Varn watched the still-distant planet intently for several seconds, then turned and smiled at the questioning look in the eyes his consort had fixed on him.

No problem, Colonel. I shall explain when we planet.

Fair enough. Take us down whenever you're ready.

He glanced at Omrai once more and then at the closely written figures on the chart he had fixed above the control panel.

"Get set," he told his comrades. "We are going in."

Sogan opened up the drive once more and began maneuvering the flier carefully. When he had at last gained the obviously predetermined position he desired, he sent his vehicle hurtling toward Omrai's surface.

The Arcturian made a minute change in their course. It would be very ill if they came in so close to what he hoped was their target that they were sighted and taken. His intended error would cost them time when they planeted, but it could well save the mission and their lives.

His companions quietly braced themselves for entry, a precaution not really necessary in the Commando vessel. He could all but feel their curiosity, but they held their peace, knowing this was a task that demanded the full of his attention.

The first wisps of the atmosphere rose around them, turning the flier into a glowing star.

Varn cut their speed drastically. This was the most dangerous stage of the entry. He wanted to remain in the air for as short a time as possible, but if they came in too fast, they might end up fired like a meteor.

At last, they skimmed the surface. Water. The ocean.

His instruments indicated a large landmass close by, and the Arcturian adjusted their course for it.

Minutes later, the shoreline loomed up before them. It was mountainous, but the lower slopes at least were well weathered and supported a thick growth of vegetation. There would be fine cover for their activities.

Sogan brought his vehicle into the shadow of the trees but did not set it down. He wanted better shelter than this, just in case their approach or planeting had been detected.

The same thought was in Islaen's mind. He could feel the energy streaming out from her as she sought for any watchers or potential watchers in the vicinity.

He skimmed along the mountainside until he found what he sought, a deep, well-concealed cave in the side of a steep slope.

The former Admiral passed it without slowing. Once they were well away and his commander confirmed that they had not been seen, he stopped the flier and lifted the space seals, although he was careful to leave them attached. They might yet have to make a hurried retreat back into the void.

Without a word, Islaen Connor slipped out and backtrailed to the cave. After a few minutes, she returned, signaling that all was well.

Varn Tarl Sogan slowly drove back to its mouth, all the while seeking with his own mind, even as the Commando-Colonel sought, save that he hunted for any animal life that might directly or indirectly work their grief.

The touches he made were many and varied, but he considered none of them a threat, and at last he guided the machine into the dark space looming before it.

Once inside and after his eyes had adjusted to the reduced light, the Arcturian looked about him curiously. The chamber was larger than he would have thought from its narrow entrance. It was obviously of natural origin and showed no sign of having been disturbed in the recent past; there appeared to be no other exit from it.

"What now?" Bethe Danlo asked as she slipped from the flier and gratefully stretched her limbs. The journey itself had not lasted terribly long, but now that it was over she realized how rigid the tension had kept her. One bred in the starlanes knew the dangers of space. A great many things might have happened to them out there, and had just about any one of them occurred, the fragile little Commando vehicle would very probably have become their tomb.

"We get our bearings and decide what to do next," the Colonel replied. "By the time we're ready to move, we should know if anyone nearby has put out an air search for us."

"And we'll be long gone before any ground parties reach us," Jake agreed lazily. "Nice thinking."

He leaned against the flier and gazed about him with no great pleasure. "More caves," he muttered. "At least this one's small enough and doesn't seem to go anywhere."

"Perhaps we shall be wishing for a few good passages before this is over," the Arcturian responded gloomily. "We do not know what we are going to have to face here or what help or hindrance Omrai will be."

"You're a cheery soul!"

"Merely practical, friend."

The Commando's blue eyes ran over the other man. "Tell me, Sogan, why did you keep us sitting out there like a perfect little target? I doubt you were merely having a case of nerves."

Bethe glared furiously at him, but Varn's ready smile told her Jake had touched no sore spot, as she now realized that Karmikel had known full well before he had spoken.

Sogan's dark eyes seemed to dance for a moment. "A still object of the flier's size is less likely to attract attention than a moving one if it remains in the same general vicinity over a period of time. I wanted to see if I could spot our enemies' planeting site."

As he had anticipated, the other stared at him.

"All right, Admiral," Jake said. "I yield. Just what do you mean?"

"Well, since Omrai has no native populace or established colony, those we seek would have to be off-worlders originally and ignorant of her features."

"Right. So?"

"According to our reports, there is supposedly only one place, a natural clearing, broad and flat enough for a major port. I was hoping to see it from space, the way our opponents must originally have done."

"Unless they're insiders, traitors or renegades, and had access to the same materials we have," Islaen cut in. "Remember Thurston Sandstone."

"Aye" he agreed grimly. "I considered that as well. It is possible, though I think it less likely than my first premise. In any event, the base we seek should be in the same location."

"Were you able to see it?" the demolitions expert asked eagerly.

He shook his head. "No. The flier's instruments are not powerful enough to pick it out from that distance. It might be different with a true starship, particularly if she were closer. We did not have the luxury of a long search from many levels. We had to come down somewhere, however, so I brought us as close to the clearing as I dared."

"You'll make a Commando yet, Admiral!" the redhead told him, not concealing his admiration despite the lightness of his words.

He grew serious again in the next moment. "I read about that spot, too. It's a good place to start. Where are we now in relation to it?"

"Several days' walk to the west of it." Sogan glanced at the Colonel. "The flier would shorten that if you want to risk taking it."

She thought for a while but then shook her head. "We don't dare. According to our information, these forested places occur only in fairly well defined patches. Most of the countryside is pretty open."

She drew out the case of maps the *Comet*'s computer had

generated for them before her team's departure and quickly selected the one she wanted. This she studied intently.

"Assuming an acceptable degree of accuracy in this and the clearing lies where it says, we'll be crossing a lot of pretty bare terrain to reach it. If those pirates or whoever they are do any patrolling, we'd be painted targets for them in any vehicle, at least until we have a better idea of what we're doing. The distance isn't far if this is right. Let's leave it here and take a look at the base. We can come back for it if we need it to make our move."

Her hand brushed the machine's side as if it were a living thing. It should be safe enough here, she judged. Commando fliers left no sign of their passage, no trail to betray them to would-be trackers, and she would take great care to remove all traces of their ever having been near the cave.

Their equipment was another matter. She would not leave any of that and ordered auxiliary packs made up to transport it.

No one received that command with any pleasure. Omrai might be classified as a Terra-normal planet, but her gravity was slightly stronger thanks to her heavy core. Until their muscles had adjusted to it, they would find the going difficult enough without the bulging packs they would now have to carry.

None of them complained. They had brought only what was essential with them, and they might well have more to regret than weary bodies if they had need of these supplies later and lacked them.

"Colonel!"

Something in the demolitions expert's voice caused all three of her comrades to look back quickly in her direction.

"What's wrong, Bethe?"

"I was just giving the flier a final check. It's been antimagnetized, hasn't it?"

"Aye, of course," she replied, frowning.

"What would it take to break through its guards?"

"Plenty. Why?"

"We've run into that 'plenty,' apparently. Take a look at these readings."

The others crowded around the blond spacer.

Jake Karmikel whistled. "I've never heard of anything like this. —What about you, Admiral?"

Sogan shook his head. "Never."

"I haven't, either," Bethe said, "but I may know what could be responsible. The theorists have been claiming for decades that powerful magnetic eddies might well exist in the galactic currents. If these readings are true, Omrai lies within such a turbulence zone."

Varn Tarl Sogan felt a chill pass through him as his eyes seemed to fix of their own accord on the flier's instrument panel. Fortune had been with them this day. There had been no inkling of this earlier. Had they made their approach only a few hours later and been caught in the fury registered on these dials, they would never have made Omrai's surface.

Islaen looked once more at the instruments, then resolutely turned away from the machine. "We'd best be starting," she told the others.

The off-worlders camouflaged the cave, and the two guerrillas set guard alarms both on the entrance and on the vehicle itself. Finally, they prepared traps outside that would signal a visit by an intruder or the possibility of an ambush when they at last returned.

That done, they shouldered their packs and set out in search of the mysterious threat they believed had taken root on Omrai of Umbar.

ELEVEN

ISLAEN CONNOR TOOK the lead. Varn had brought them down well to the west of the clearing. Now she set an eastward course to what she hoped would prove to be their enemies' base.

They kept a fast pace despite their heavy packs and the strong pull of gravity. There was a definite slope to the land, but the ground was free of excessive undergrowth and was reasonably smooth so that little impeded their progress.

There was no need for extreme caution. While they remained under the cover of the trees, it was highly unlikely that they would be spotted from the air, and their own natural wariness coupled with the Commando-Colonel's ability to detect others of their kind would take care of any ground parties that might be searching this remote place.

The off-worlders were glad of the strenuous pace their commander set. The exercise helped warm them. The air was cold, colder than it should have been. Umbar was bright in the sky, but little warmth seemed to come from the star. The forces raging through Omrai's space must be absorbing a good part of her heat.

Their route paralleled the ocean, so closely that it was visible at times through the trees. A constant, sharp breeze blew inland, deepening the natural chill of the air. It carried with it a smell that, while pleasant enough in its own way, was not the clear scent of Thorne's seas. The ocean wind of Omrai was too heavy with the odor of growing things in all the varied cycles of their lives.

They could have made better time on the water, but none of them were willing to risk exposing themselves on the open sea, no more than they had been willing to take out the flier. They would simply be too easily seen from the air or from observation posts on any of the coastal mountains.

Even had they wanted to chance it, they would have been hard-pressed to find the materials to build a craft large enough to carry the team. Few of the trees in this section of Omrai's woodlands were suitable for such a purpose.

Islaen looked about her. Plant life was abundant here. There were many species of shrubs and trees, all of the same blue-green color.

She plucked several of the curiously thick, pulpy leaves and almost without thought tested them. They were edible and nourishing, containing large quantities of proteins and hydrocarbons as well as enormous amounts of sugars of varying degrees of complexity.

The leaves were covered with semimicroscopic bristles, hollow tubes like hypodermic needles. The Commando-Colonel wondered at this almost universal trait but could think of no logical reason for it. She resolved to investigate the problem once their mission had been completed and temporarily put it from her mind.

She found little else to hold her interest. The planet seemed to be the child of a tired nature. She showed none of the strong sweeps, the masterpieces that wrung awe even from the cold hearts of inner-system residents. No proud forests grew here. The woodlands consisted of scrub trees, twisted, thin, and small. The mountains, from what she saw of them, were fairly low and were merely harsh without showing anything of the grandeur her heart almost ached to see. There was no drive, no roar, in the ocean, and the quiet surface was choked with a thick layer of minute plants.

She soon forgot about the dullness of her surroundings. The guerrilla felt uneasy. The forest was quiet. Too quiet. The survey reports indicated a reasonably abundant fauna, yet she could detect no obvious signs of animal life anywhere.

Varn, are you picking up anything? she asked; the Arcturian could read animalkind the way she did humans and might be expected to detect any nearby creatures. *I can't find the native wildlife that's supposed to be here.*

He nodded and linked his receptors with hers.

Immediately, a flood of sensations swept into her, the sendings of a vast number of a great variety of beings. Their transmissions were confused and indistinct, and she started to withdraw again, fearing her presence would distract the Arcturian from his efforts to learn as much as he could from them.

He stopped her. *Stay,* he said, whispering as if he feared his thoughts would somehow startle those animals he was struggling to understand. *Be still, but remain with me. It is better that we share whatever information I can glean. Your wilderness knowledge is greater than mine, and you may be able to deduce things where I would fail.*

Sogan tried to calm his mind, to empty it as much as possible of extraneous thought. The creatures around them were of low intelligence and alien to him. There was no hope of actual communication with them, not like he knew with Islaen or Bandit, but emotion, instinct, were basic to all life on a level he was able to reach. He could receive feeling from the countless silent beings native to these woodlands. That could tell them much if they interpreted it properly.

There was no lack of subjects to study. The area teemed with life, probably to a far greater extent than even this massive inpouring indicated. Many of the contacts were marginal, barely within the range of possible reception. This would have to be so. Omrai was a fairly primitive planet. Her fauna was still very much in a state of rapid development, and it was reasonable to assume that a number of other creatures existed here whose patterns were below his ability to receive.

No matter. Those coming to him were more than he could even satisfactorily manage, but despite the confusion caused by the enormous number and variety of them and by his lack of familiarity with any of Omrai's denizens, Varn Tarl Sogan did learn a great deal.

Some of that knowledge disturbed him, although he realized he should have anticipated this. *They fear us,* he said at last. *They have been hunted, I think.*

Aye, she replied. *Our kind has been here.*

The other two off-worlders remained unaware of their leaders' silent exchange, although they knew full well the watch both were holding. They had enough to occupy them in maintaining their own guard as they fought to keep up their pace against the numbing weariness that was eating into their reserves of strength.

The hour was late. Umbar had been low on the horizon when

they planeted and was now set. Omrai's moon had taken her place, a small, pale satellite casting little light, just barely sufficient to permit them to continue their march.

The Commando-Colonel searched the gloom for a suitable camping place. Perhaps they could go farther, but she did not judge the slight gain in distance worth completely exhausting them all.

They finally came upon a spot that was sheltered from the sea wind by a low cliff and was close by a small, fast stream. It could be easily guarded and offered more than one avenue of escape. Fuel was no problem. There would be no fire that night.

Jake broke open a packet from their rations and quick-fried it on his plutonium disk. When it was ready, he divided the food among his comrades.

Sogan ate in silence, feeding Bandit from his portion, then he slipped away from camp. He felt utterly spent and more than a little disoriented after hours of nearly constant contact with the surplanetary creatures and wanted a little time to think quietly before trying to settle down for the night.

He continued walking until he came to a high place from which he could watch the ocean without being visible himself.

The man stood gazing at the water for several long minutes, then he sighed and lowered his head. It was shallow, tame, a far cry from the wild, clear seas of Thorne, yet it woke in him such longing . . .

The Arcturian stopped himself in surprise and shook his head, as if to clear the strange feeling from it. Surely he could not be developing a world wish? It was a minor and usually harmless weakness but one which he could not afford. He would never again be free to return to his own place, to the star systems he had been born to rule. Did he imagine some Federation planet could take the place of that loss—or that he would ever feel comfortable enough or love another world strongly enough to permit one to do so?

His dark eyes raised to the star-bright night sky. So many of those brilliant sparks were suns, nurturing planets and the life that nearly inevitably arose on them.

Alien worlds and alien stars. In that moment, he ached for a sight of his own ultrasystem, the more so because he knew that no part of the Arcturian Empire was visible from Omrai's surface. The better part of the galaxy lay between Quandon Sector and the nearest of those loved stars, so great a distance that, to his knowledge, no fighting had ever taken place here during the War, certainly no serious fighting, despite the basic vulnerability of the undeveloped Sector.

There had been little to attract his people to it. Similar weak spots peppered all the Federation's rim, areas with desirable targets just beyond. Even at the end, when any good target was welcomed, it was hardly surprising that Ruling Command had not elected to squander precious fuel and matériel against this backwash.

Thoughts of war vanished again as his mind envisioned the familiar configuration of the star systems he had once ruled. Had the great conflict gone differently, he might even now be governing their planets and training his son to take up that work from him when the time to do so at last came.

His eyes closed. The others had all been young, but his heir-son had been less than a year away from active service and the official manhood that would have shielded him from automatic destruction upon his sire's disgrace.

Only a few more months, and that fine young warrior would have lived. He should have tried to draw it out, he thought dully, struggled to appeal and delay the sentence against him instead of yielding to the inevitable . . .

His head bowed. It would have been useless. He had known that. At best, all he could have gained was a couple or three weeks and probably not even that, time more painful than quick execution for everyone involved.

Sogan straightened. The soft brushing of Islaen's mind against his announced her arrival, and he turned to receive her, carefully checking his shields as he did so.

They were strong and had been since he came out here, and he did not believe he had broadcast any of his actual thoughts. Mood was another matter. He was rarely successful in concealing real heaviness from his consort when it lay hard on him, and he doubted he would be able to mask it now. Perhaps he could pass most of it off as a reaction to weariness and the uncertainty of their future course.

The gloom shadowing him did not lessen the pleasure in his greeting when he saw Islaen. Indeed, the sensations of loneliness and loss which had filled him moments before intensified his awareness of all she meant to him, his wonder that she had entered into his life, and he saw and felt her brighten in response.

His eyes darkened, and his own concerns vanished. The Commando's face was white and pinched. Even her body seemed less erect than usual, as if it were costing her some effort to hold herself straight. *You look tired*, he said gently as he went to her.

He put his arm around her. A number of big, yellow-brown boulders lay nearby, and he urged her toward one which was broad and flat enough to permit both of them to sit comfortably. *Rest here for a few minutes*.

The woman complied, but she smiled. Sogan did not look as if he had spent the day at ease himself.

He read her thought readily enough and gave her a rueful smile. *I worry about you, Colonel, not myself*.

That's quite apparent.

Seriously, let me take this first watch for you. I am awake anyway.

That's apparent, too. —You should be out cold, Varn. Is something wrong? If any of the readings you've been receiving are bothering you . . .

She knew full well that this was not so, but the question gave her an opening. Because it involved their work and their safety, he would at least have to answer her.

The Arcturian shook his head promptly. *No. I should have told you that at once*.

A sharp whistle stopped any further explanation he might have made. *Varn's not happy!* the gurry interjected.

"I'm tired, and the Spirit ruling space only knows what lies ahead of us before we can leave this place," he said quickly.

The man rubbed Bandit's head, the only part of her extending from beneath the Commando's jacket. *It is cold for her*.

She'll be happier under a blanket, Islaen agreed. *Take her back with you when you knock out*.

She laughed softly at his expression. He could be as stubborn as Jake at times. *I'm fine*, she assured him patiently. *This was not worse on me than on any of the rest of us. Except maybe you*.

Sogan felt her worry. It was deep enough that he could not leave it unanswered. He could at least tell her what had sent him out here in the first place without lessening himself.

I wanted to put my thoughts together. It was something of a strain dealing with all these unknown creatures for so extended a time.

You're all right? she asked sharply.

Aye. It was not that sort of trouble, mostly just a little unsettling. I merely needed some quiet for a few minutes.

His head turned toward the ocean. *Watching that did the job.* He sighed. *It is very different from Thorne's,* he remarked a bit more sadly than he had intended.

The memories which had tortured him earlier returned with blistering force, but another thought rose up which smothered them. This woman had a homeworld as well and a happier situation with respect to it. Her kin lived, and no blighting shadow rent them apart. *What are Noreen's seas like?* he asked suddenly. *I saw nothing of them when we were there.*

Similar to Thorne's, though not as extensive or nearly as deep. None of my people live anywhere near them.

A pity. His tone told that he felt it was strange as well.

You're forgetting how flat Noreen is, Admiral. Our highest country consists of gentle hills, and they're located far inland. The coastal areas lie only on an average of eight feet above the year's normal highest tide, and we are blessed with a great number of very violent storms. All such territory frequently winds up under deep water. No one's going to situate himself where he's going to have his home, crops, stock, and family washed off several times in the year. Besides, the richest grazing lands are in the interior. We've kept our population small and have no need to take the poorer stuff.

All very logical, he agreed.

The war prince studied her somberly. *You have not been back since well before you were sent to Visnu save for those few days we had after our union.*

There'll be time later, the Noreenan replied in surprise.

Do not let yourself grow away from your kin, my Islaen. You are fortunate in them, and you would lash yourself should fate sever you if you wasted the opportunities you now have to be with them.

Islaen Connor's breath caught. Was this what had set that cloud on him which both she and Bandit had felt so powerfully? She had sensed that his thoughts often traveled back to his old existence and those who had peopled it, but it was not a subject he would ever discuss or share with her. Only once before had he ever opened to her any memory of his life before he was commanded to conquer and hold Thorne of Brandine, when they melded their souls right after their work on Hades of Persephone had been completed. He had never alluded to it again, and only his concern for her, his fear that she might someday have to suffer similar torment, made him do so now. *You miss your own, don't you?* she whispered.

He looked away from her. *There are few to miss,* he answered almost harshly. *You know how my first consort and my concubines died, and their children . . .*

I'm sorry, Varn, the woman said quickly. *I'd no business raising a question like that.*

The tips of his fingers brushed her hand, although he still did not face her. *No. I value your care, Islaen Connor. —Do not pity me in this. It is to my good rather than my ill that I have so few ties left in the Empire.*

His hand fell away again. *My parents are long dead, fortunately so. They saw my star's ascent and did not have to endure the rest. I had no brothers, and my sisters, of course, I never knew, not even she who is consort to the Emperor's heir-son. Of my more distant kinsmen, some fell and some survived, but I never had a chance to learn the fate of a number of them.*

He looked out over Omrai's ocean without seeing it. *I am sorry for that. Many were sound friends. The men of my house never sired many offspring in any generation, and because we were relatively few, we have always tended to be rather closer than is usual among the members of an extended blood group.*

For the first time, he faltered. *I never had the opportunity to know any of my own small . . .*

His shields closed swiftly as he fought to maintain the controls he had set on himself.

Islaen said nothing. She could not help him with this battle and could only wait quietly for him to go on or to withdraw.

After a few seconds, she felt his shields draw apart enough to permit communication to continue, although she had to school herself to give no reaction to the strength of them when her thought touched with his again.

Varn took a long breath. *Even had I violated no order, I should be one set apart, I suppose,* he said slowly. *Perhaps my children were fortunate to have died so early. Had they taken my-talent from me and somehow revealed their possession of it, they would have suffered. It is a mental rather than physical mutation, but still the response to it would have been harsh.*

The woman looked at his averted face in alarm. She had known something of the pain and the weight of guilt he carried, but only now did she realize that this other harpy might still be rending him as well. *Varn,* she asked softly, *are you ashamed of what your mind can do? Or ashamed of yourself because you possess such power?*

Sometimes. Aye, sometimes even yet, her consort replied tonelessly. *I cannot forget that no other of my race is able to do this.*

He faced her suddenly. *Logic or will has a very small role in any of it, Islaen. I cannot explain what makes me shrink now and then from what has given me so much. I do not condone it in myself, and I assuredly do not expect you to understand, but never, never at any time do I see you as less because something in you gives you the power to meld your mind with mine or send it forth to discover and read the feelings of others. That you must believe!*

Of course I believe it. I think I'd know before you did if it weren't true. Her eyes raised to meet his. *I love you far too much not to be aware of your response to me.*

He put his arm around her and drew her close. *I little merit it sometimes,* he said ruefully. *You have enough to carry at the moment without my throwing more on you.* The war prince glanced at her. *I was serious about not wanting you to sever your contacts with Noreen, Islaen. I know what exile means, and I would not see you take that upon yourself needlessly.*

No fear of it! she answered him. *We Noreenans are much too clannish a lot to permit that.*

The woman studied him carefully. He seemed only tired now, as if the cloud had lifted from his spirit, although with his shields still so tight, she could not be entirely certain.

Varn got to his feet. *I have not changed my mind about wanting to take this watch.*

Not on your life!

You are stubborn, Colonel.

Right.—Go on back to camp and keep Bandit company if she hasn't given up waiting for you and bedded down with one of the others. She laughed at his surprise; he had not realized until then that the gurry had gone. *She knows when to give us privacy and took off as soon as our conversation turned serious.*

Sometimes I think she knows a far sight too much, he muttered.

Sogan gave up his struggle to take over for the Commando,

knowing it to be useless. He glanced back in the direction of the camp and then east toward their distant target.

Rest well when you do retire, Islaen Connor. I very much fear tomorrow will be considerably worse than today. At the very least, we shall have a good many more hours of travel ahead of us.

TWELVE

Dawn found the off-worlders already on the move, walking single file as they had the evening before and traveling steadily eastward.

The Colonel pressed on in the lead, assurance as to the rightness of their course growing ever stronger within her. Varn reported an increasing intensity in the fear radiated by the still-invisible creatures of Omrai, a sure indication that they were heading toward human haunts.

It was well that they had this encouragement. They were not making as good time as they had the previous evening. The trees were no longer as thick as they had been, and the way had become more rocky and grown over with underbrush. Greater care was necessary to compensate both for the rougher footing and for the rapidly lessening cover, and they had to slow their pace accordingly. Their spirits would not have been long in dropping had these other signs been ill as well or hinted that their efforts might only be wasted work.

The company had been traveling for less than an hour when both Commandos froze. There was a subtle change in the route they were following, one they recognized all too readily.

Humans had taken to this natural path, making of it a road for their own use. They did not come frequently or in any great number—the wildness of the way gave testimony to that—but this trail was used by members of their species or one very similar to it.

The four slowed their advance still further so that they might keep a better watch on the surrounding countryside. There was no immediate fear behind their care, but they all appreciated the value of moving with caution through the territory of very probably hostile strangers.

Islaen Connor swore softly in her own ancient tongue. Even in this short time, the woodlands had thinned significantly. The trees were fairly sparse now, and a jumble of low bushes choked the spaces between them, catching at their feet if they attempted to leave the increasingly well defined trail.

The cover was not likely to improve that day or even the next. According to her map, they were skirting the broken coastline of a long peninsula. The land was exposed to whatever Omrai's ocean could throw against it, and it was worn far beyond the more sheltered region they had seen the previous day.

The whole nature of the countryside had changed. The mountainsides were weathered. Rocky spikes of hard stone remained where most of the softer materials which had once surrounded them had long since eroded away.

These cliffs of notched stone became a more frequent sight as they continued eastward, and the landscape became rougher, more difficult to negotiate.

The ground fell away in places, rose sharply in others. Fissures, some of them miniature canyons, forced frequent detours. The level of the land dropped until they walked beside the quiet water or, more commonly, on a narrow ledge a very little above it.

In places, the vegetation gave way altogether to small, rock-strewn beaches of dark gray sand. Although none of them were more than a few yards across, the Federation party soon grew to hate these bare stretches. Cover was sparse and unevenly placed or, occasionally, absent entirely, and the irregular coastline made it impossible for them to scan very large sections of either the ocean or the sky. If luck went against them, danger could be nearly upon them before they became aware of it, whatever their leader's gifts, and it was always with a sense of relief that they gained the foliage again.

The only comfort the team could take was from the fact that no craft, no sign or work of humanity except the path on which they walked, had presented itself since their arrival on Omrai of Umbar.

The off-worlders kept to the trail, first by necessity, later most willingly as they came to realize it followed the best available cover, twisting, doubling back to avoid exposing the travelers any more than necessary. Experiment proved it to be invisible to anyone standing two feet beyond its course, a seeming disappearance none of them could believe was a coincidence.

The Commando-Colonel began to feel more secure as the day wore on toward noon. Thanks to the carefully chosen route, her unit was reasonably well hidden. Discounting the brief episodes on the beaches, they could be seen only from a very few places on the higher slopes, and then only by chance for a few seconds at a time. The worst threat to the party remained an air search, and they should hear or sight any craft before they themselves were in danger from it.

Varn Tarl Sogan was less at ease. Other things were beginning to worry him besides a possible attack by pirates.

His receptors were wide open, but he was receiving few impressions. The creatures whose patterns he had touched the previous evening and earlier in the morning seemed to shun this more open country. There was little life in the brush-veldt, or little that he could reach.

Some of those contacts he did make were far from reassuring. One major pattern from individuals of a single species predominated among these. They did not come often, but when they did, they ripped into his mind, lashing him with the strength of their confidence and hatred for his species.

A particularly close and powerful transmission struck suddenly at him. Despite himself, the Arcturian started to radiate fear. The response was immediate—triumph, even contempt, mingled with a new surge of confidence.

Sogan threw up his shields, still leaving his receptors open. The victory feeling waned, tainted a little by puzzlement.

What manner of creature was this? He knew it was a lower animal. There was crude cunning in its pattern but no actual intelligence, yet it could feel him as readily as he did it, could read his fear and did not fear itself. What weapon, what defense or offense, gave it this freedom from the dread of humanity, this feeling of superiority over his kind, that was so alien to the lesser beasts of other worlds and, with this single exception, of Omrai?

The hatred hit him again, this time so near and so malignant that he shuddered openly. It took an act of will to pass the place that seemed nearest to the hidden watcher.

Varn, break off!

He started at the unexpected, welcome human contact but answered immediately. *Not yet! Not here.*

They traveled nearly a quarter of a mile farther before that vicious mind ceased to drive into his. Sogan relaxed at once, but still he hunted lest the other was merely laying a trap for them . . .

Stop searching, Varn. Now!

Islaen's small, strong fingers clamped on his arm like a living vise. *You've had enough for a while. Keep your receptors open so we won't get any surprises, but leave off active seeking.*

He nodded silently. She was right. The constant use of this faculty was draining, and he badly needed a rest at this point. On top of that, he had immersed himself too deeply in his hunting, to the extent that he had not even noticed her stop or return to him. Such oblivion could get him, or all of them, killed.

Jake and Bethe had come to a halt as well.

"What's wrong?" the Commando-Captain asked in a low voice.

"We're taking a break," the Colonel told him tersely. "We're all tired, and we could use some food. This cliff gives us good enough shelter for that."

Karmikel frowned. "Can it, Islaen! You're both ghost white, and I know by now when you two're involved in some kind of mind discussion. Let's have it."

Her head lowered. "You're right. Sorry, Jake. —Varn's been picking up some readings that have properly spooked me. Whatever's sending them seems like really bad news and certainly has no love for anything human. As for stopping now, this spot's clear of the creatures, so we're in no immediate danger from them. Varn has to have some rest. So do I, for that matter. I've been hunting for enemies of our own kind. You can only push our talent so far, and we've been at this constantly since before dawn."

The other nodded. He glanced at the Arcturian. "My apologies, Admiral. I've been with Islaen long enough that I should've realized you might be getting overworked. You two just sit back and relax. Bethe and I can manage to unwrap our lunch without help, I think."

Sogan was glad enough to accept the offer. He let the wall of the cliff, whose slight overhang was sheltering them from both an air search and Umbar's surprisingly strong rays, take his weight. His eyes closed. There was a dull ache behind them which he hoped would soon vanish.

Is the bad animal gone?

He roused himself as Bandit alighted on his knee. She peered into his face, obviously anxiously awaiting his answer.

"For now, small one. Forever, I hope." He held out his slightly cupped palm to her and curled his fingers protectively around her when she came to him. "I am sorry, Little Bandit. Those transmissions were not for you."

Varn couldn't help it, she answered serenely.

That was true enough. He had not linked with Islaen, since she needed her receptors free for her own searching, but neither had he been able to go shielded, since it was necessary to share the information he was receiving, especially with potential danger near to them. Both woman and gurry had suffered as a result.

He stroked the Jadite creature absently. She was shivering, and he slipped her into the front of his jacket.

The hen gave a contented purr as she settled herself. *Jade's nicer than Omrai! Thorne's nicer, too!*

The war prince smiled. "Agreed on both counts."

So many ugly things here! Not like gurries or goldbeasts!

The man stiffened as a pang of guilt shot through him. "Would you rather be with the other gurries, Bandit?"

Nooo! Bandit belongs with Varn and Islaen!

"I know, small one," he assured her hastily as he felt her claws begin to dig into his tunic and the flesh beneath it, "but you might like to live with gurries, too."

Nooo, she replied, he thought a little sadly. *Bandit's different now. They live for goldbeasts. Bandit has her humans.*

"Some gurries have adopted settlers," Islaen Connor reminded her as she joined them.

The Commando-Colonel was frowning. She had overheard this conversation, and she, too, was upset by it. Had they wronged their little companion by allowing her to accompany them into the starlanes?

The gurry hen wriggled free of the Arcturian's jacket. Her feathers were fully extended. She looked furious, and the anger she was transmitting confirmed that she was. *Islaen and Varn are special!*

The woman relaxed. She had meant that.

Sogan felt easier as well. For good or ill, the tiny mammal's happiness was now bound with them. That he could understand. Was he, too, not making his life among strangers?

"We are not as special as you, small one," he told her in voice and, with greater feeling, in mind.

A shadow loomed over him, and he looked up to find Karmikel standing above him.

"I agree with that," the redhead said. "Has she added handing out compliments to her other endearing traits?"

"We were discussing her separation from her own kind," the Colonel told him. "She was explaining why she doesn't mind it."

"I'm glad she doesn't," he replied seriously as he squatted down so that he could run his finger along the gurry's back. "I wouldn't like to think she was unhappy."

"Neither would we, friend. That's why Varn raised the question."

Jake handed them a couple of packets he was holding. "Your rations, quick-fried by my own able hand. Eat them while they're hot. —Come on, Bandit," he added. "You're dining with us. These two'll probably get involved in some depressing discussion that would spoil even your appetite. Ever since you saved my life back on Hades, I feel honor bound to look after your interests."

"Varn had some small part in pulling you out of that crawlway, too," Islaen reminded him.

He turned to the other man. "Sorry, Admiral. It's not that I mean to slight you, but you're simply not as cute as she is."

Sogan laughed heartily. "It would be a foolish human who would try to compete with a gurry on that score. —Go on if you are planning to feed her. I would feel like some sort of savage to start eating myself without giving her anything."

Karmikel returned to the demolitions expert, who sprang to her feet in delight when she saw Bandit.

"Come on, pet. I don't have any chocolate for you, but you can have some of this."

Both humans sat down. They ate quickly in the manner of all spacers, then Bethe glanced over her shoulder at their comrades. "They seem all right now," she said in a voice low enough not to carry.

"Sure," he answered. "Islaen's right about not being able to push that power of theirs too far, but the recovery seems to come fairly quickly."

He scowled. "She was spooked!" he exclaimed in a voice thick with sarcasm. "It was plain enough that he was hit just as bad or maybe worse!"

The Sergeant shook her head in mock disgust. "You weren't exactly slow in picking up the cue she tossed you, I noticed." All of a sudden, her expression changed. "Those transmissions must've been something pretty extraordinary."

"They stayed just transmissions," he pointed out. His voice was quiet and serious, and as he spoke, his hand covered hers. Surplanetary perils could loom very large in the mind of one bred to space as this woman had been. "They'll warn us if an attack is imminent, and we're armed to take care of just about anything."

The spacer gave him a weak smile. "Sorry, Jake. I guess I got spooked myself there for a moment."

He sighed. "You're entitled, Sergeant. Considering some of the adventures we've had in the past, we're all entitled."

THIRTEEN

WHEN THEY STARTED out again, all four had their blasters loose in their holsters and already set to kill.

Varn Tarl Sogan kept his receptors wide open as he sent his mind out, seeking, ever seeking. If one of these dark, violent beasts were to attack, the first warning, perhaps the only timely warning, would have to come from him.

Hate! Fury! Sogan recoiled as if he had been struck. Hissing a warning to his companions, he threw himself to the ground.

Islaen, who had shared reception of that transmission, froze, momentarily standing as one paralyzed, before dropping down herself. Instinctively, her wrist snapped, activating the powerful spring mechanism that sent the slender knife strapped there flying into her waiting hand.

Surprise, pain, horror rushed into her in rapid succession. A man in death trouble. Close.

The antagonism was gone in a moment. Pain and growing fear remained.

A low moan gave her the victim's location. She realized with some surprise that this was the first sound to be uttered since the attack began.

She remembered Jake and Bethe Danlo. They lay close beside them, their minds full of wonder and uncertainty. They had seen no indication of danger save their leaders' strange behavior. "A man," the Colonel whispered. "Close. Hurt."

They nodded and remained still, scanning the beach a little below the ledge where they had been walking. Nothing.

Most of the strand was hidden by a huge boulder, almost a

mountain in itself, that had rolled down from the peaks in ages
past.

Signaling her comrades to stay where they were and cover her,
Islaen Connor worked her way along the ledge, moving rapidly
despite her care. She soon skirted the boulder and was able to
observe the whole of the beach.

The figure of a man lay near the cliff wall. There was some
heavy, tall foliage a yard to his left. From the marks and the
blood on the sand, it seemed to the guerrilla that the attack had
taken place there and the Omrain had then dragged himself to his
present location.

Islaen dropped lightly to the strand. She was at the Omrain's
side in a moment. She knelt to examine him, nodding as she did
so to acknowledge her consort's warning that the creature which
had done this was still near and still filled with the lust for death.

The man—boy—was unconscious or very near it, incapable
of aiding himself. His left leg was badly swollen. It was
punctured in two places, and the area around the wounds had
taken on a sickly greenish hue.

The Omrain had apparently seen his danger and had tried to
avert it. He had applied a tourniquet fashioned from the leather
thong that had been his belt to his leg and was bringing a knife
to bear on the limb when his strength had failed him.

Working as quickly as she could, the Commando slit the skin
separating the punctures to encourage the flow of blood. She
called to Varn for help but knew she could not wait for it to come
if the boy was to live.

The Colonel frowned. There was but one suction cup in the
venom kit she had removed from her medical supplies, and that
was not nearly large enough to cover the two punctures. The
poison would have to come out of both immediately. Judging
from the Omrain's condition, any further delay would be fatal.

She placed the cup over one of the wounds and put her lips to
the other, sucking at it as Noreenans had done with nathair stings
since her ancestors first planeted there.

Islaen!

She whirled in the direction Sogan's warning dictated, bringing her knife, which had never left her hand, to ready.

A large, gray-black beast, fully as high at its shoulder as she
was tall, stood at the edge of the foliage. It was powerfully
muscled and supported itself on four pairs of legs, each pair

slightly longer than the one before so that the head was considerably lower than the spined tail.

It glared at her out of small, deep-set eyes. Its muzzle was sharply pointed and revealed a double row of wicked-looking teeth when it drew its gums back in a soundless snarl.

The Omrain creature held its attack for a moment, perhaps surprised that she had become aware of its presence in time to meet it armed, but then it dived at her with marvelous speed and force.

The attacker used only six of its limbs to carry its charge. The Colonel saw with horror why. The front legs had been adapted into giant pincers, and these even now reached out to grasp her. Drops of clear liquid glistened on their tips.

Too late, her hand darted toward her holster.

The discharge of a blaster and the creature's death gasp came almost simultaneously. Varn Tarl Sogan lowered his weapon and broke into a slow run as he hurried to inspect his kill. He stopped beside his commander, his eyes resting on the knife Islaen was just then preparing to resheathe. *Those claws will not always serve, Commando.*

The Colonel flushed. Her error was a serious one, and she deserved the rebuke, although she recognized that his fear for her had sparked it.

She glanced at the carcass. *I'm in your debt for that.*

No, never that, my Islaen. We stand together, or we surely fall.

He made himself answer quietly despite the strain still on him. She did not need him to ride her after that attack, nor had he any right to condemn her. He had failed to locate the beast or to name the moment of its moving before it actually began its assault, although he had been fully aware of its proximity. He shuddered in his very soul at the memory. Even as he released his bolt, he had been sick with the certainty that it would strike its target too late.

Bethe and Jake Karmikel were kneeling beside the injured boy. Islaen joined them. She studied the stranger closely for the first time.

The Omrain was young, no more than the equivalent of sixteen Terran years as nearly as she could judge, and short in stature, although it was likely he would be a big man once he completed his final growth.

His body was obviously adapted to meet the demands of

Omrai's climate. It was solid-looking with a trunk made almost shapeless by thick deposits of fat beneath the skin. This was not the flab seen on some inner-system weaklings but solid insulation such as was found to a greater degree on a number of sea-dwelling mammals throughout the ultrasystem. It was nearly absent from the muscular arms and legs.

The impression of squareness given by the body was emphasized by the shape of the head, which was particularly flat with a large, prominent forehead and a strong, heavy chin. The ears were small and set close to the head, minimizing the chances of cold damage during severe weather. The features were chiefly flat and not actually unpleasantly formed, although none of the off-worlders found them attractive.

The nose was an anomaly. Long and both very straight and very thin, it seemed to have been fixed to the rest of the face in error or in jest. The very strangeness of it worked to confirm the youth's essential humanity in all their minds. His hair was a nondescript, muddy brown, and his skin had an ugly yellowish cast now, but his natural complexion appeared to be a clean coffee-beige.

The Omrain's clothing consisted of leather breeches and a vest-like garment of natural fur. Despite the chill, the last was sleeveless and left much of his chest bare. On his feet were heavy leather boots that were crude in design but looked serviceable.

"His chances?"

Jake shook his head. "Poor. Too much of the poison had already entered his system before you got to him."

"An antidote, quickly."

"We cannot identify the toxin in time."

"Try!" she commanded sharply as she sent her mind into the youth's body, desperately seeking the answers that could save him. She would not be able to identify the actual substance, but if she could learn enough about how it worked, they might still be able to do something for him.

The boy was gasping now. That he had held so long spoke well for his strength.

The venom was marvelously potent. He could not draw breath at all, although his chest heaved mightily for it. His muscles seemed sound. The fault did not lie with them.

"Neurotoxic!" Islaen exclaimed suddenly. "Hitting the lungs.—We can treat the symptoms if not the specific poison."

The other hesitated. If she was mistaken, the Omrain would die.

"Try it. He's done anyway if we don't act."

Karmikel nodded and prepared a large syringe. He held it a second, then injected the full of it without further delay.

They waited for several minutes. The boy's breathing seemed to come easier, and Jake sighed with relief. The antivenin was taking.

A sharp breeze caused the Commando-Captain to frown. Umbar was well past her zenith now, and the night would bring a drop in temperature. "We must get him to a more sheltered place. It's too exposed here."

The Colonel scarcely heard him but somehow forced herself to reply. "Whatever you think."

Her voice sounded distant, strange even to her own ears. Weariness was doing it, she supposed. She was deathly tired and felt queerly detached from the scene around her.

The redhead glanced up at his commander in alarm. "Sogan, grab her!"

Islaen felt arms come around her. They lowered her to the sand. Moments later, her jacket and then her tunic were pulled, almost ripped, open . . .

The mists that had enveloped the woman's mind began to clear. She struggled to sit up, but a firm hand forced her back, and she quieted once more. She lacked the strength to fight the pressure.

Varn?

I am here, my Islaen. His fingers twined with hers. His mind touch had been steady, but she could feel a tremor in his hand.

Varn, what's wrong? she asked in alarm, once more trying to rise.

Again, he forced her to stay down. *Gently! Lie still a moment. Give the antivenin a chance to work.*

Antivenin? Of course. She must have absorbed some little part of the poison while treating the Omrain. Both Sogan's nod and Bandit's excited whistle confirmed that surmise.

The boy? she inquired after a moment.

He sleeps, as you should. We-almost lost you, too. He gripped himself. *We have decided to set up camp here.*

Islaen started to protest, but the other merely shrugged. *The Omrain is too ill to travel far, and you are little stronger. This boulder will give us some protection from the wind, but be that so or not, here we shall stay.*

The Commando-Colonel was forced to agree with that decision when she finally got to her feet some time later. She had been nathair-stung once on Noreen and had thought that bad, but this venom was more potent still. She could have ingested only a very little of it, yet that slight trace had been enough to carry her to the brink of death.

She moved from behind the shelter of the rock and started for the Omrain creature's hiding place. The wind struck her so sharply that she gasped and retreated behind the boulder again, shivering violently. Islaen sighed. Her temperature must still be very high for her to feel this cold. A glance at her comrades revealed that they seemed equally affected. The chill was considerably deeper this evening than it had been during the day or on the previous night.

The woman felt rather than saw the Omrain stir and hurried over to him. The others were beside them in an instant. The boy's eyes were open, staring. They did not see. The fear had returned to him, and he struggled to rise.

"Sea-cold . . . death . . . Cabin . . . s-safety . . ."

The off-worlders exchanged puzzled glances. He had spoken Basic. His pronunciation was archaic but not to the point that they had difficulty in identifying what he said.

Their expressions were grim. The urgency in the Omrain's voice had been too clear for them not to realize that some new peril threatened them. What was the danger? The words themselves might have been intelligible, but their meaning was not.

"What can he have meant by that?" asked Jake Karmikel in some exasperation. "Islaen, can you make any sense out of it?"

"Not much in itself, but his fear's as sharp as when that wretched thing attacked him. We won't do well to ignore any cold that can put this kind of fright on a citizen of a planet normally as chilly as Omrai of Umbar seems to be."

"We shall have to find shelter, then," Varn Tarl Sogan said calmly, belying his own concern.

"He mentioned a cabin," the demolitions expert interjected. "Can you find out from him where it is, Colonel?"

"No! I can't read minds!" It seemed like the millionth time she had to say that since she first discovered her talent and turned it to her colleagues' service.

The Commando made herself think calmly. "I can't find it," she said softly, "but maybe Bandit can!—What about it, love? Do you think you can locate this shelter for us? We can't even tell you what it looks like."

Bandit will try!

The gurry took wing and was quickly gone from their sight.

FOURTEEN

It seemed a very long time to the shivering off-worlders before Islaen and Varn straightened in the same instant.

"She's spotted it!" the Noreenan woman exclaimed. "It's near the crest of that mountain above us. —We'd best start at once. It won't be an easy climb with full packs and a wounded man to lug."

"Are you well enough?" Bethe asked doubtfully.

There was reason for concern. Even under normal conditions, the spacer would have disliked facing the mountain with night falling and the party tired from the efforts of the day. Islaen's added disability took on an ominous aspect in the light of their general poor condition. If she could not complete the climb herself, her comrades might not be able to bring her up, not quickly enough.

"We have no choice."

The Colonel started up the slope, forcing the others to follow. She paused again so that they might properly ready themselves for the long ascent.

This they did quickly. Jake Karmikel's comrades bound the Omrain to his shoulders. It would be for the duration of the climb. He was by far the strongest of them, and none of the others would be able to take this burden from him.

Bethe wordlessly lifted the redhead's pack and her own and signaled that they were ready to begin.

The Commando-Colonel took the lead, following after Bandit, who went slowly, allowing for the handicap the humans' lack of wings put on them. Even so, it proved a complex path to trace, and the Noreenan frequently entered the little hen's mind to confirm their course.

At first, the slope was gentle, requiring little of the off-worlders, but they knew that would not last long and conserved themselves for what was to come.

It was well that they did. Soon the ground was steeper, the way rougher, and they found it necessary to turn more and more of their attention to the mastering of the ascent.

It was not particularly dangerous, nor did it require any specialized training to scale this face of the mountain. The grade was very steep, in some places nearly seventy degrees, but the ground was rugged and supported a forest of low bushes whose roots clung tightly to the rocky soil. These offered excellent handholds. Falls were few and the chance of serious injury almost nonexistent.

The mountain did demand the full strength of anyone who would scale it. This was a contest of muscle and stubborn will against a too-strong gravity and a land whose harshness put a limit on the amount of time they could take to complete the climb. It required a physical stamina and a resiliency Islaen Connor's worn body was hard-pressed to provide.

Despite the antivenin, she was still very much aware of the dose of poison she had taken. Even automatic movements were acts of will. Omrai's gravity alone demanded too much. Her chest seemed heavy, paralyzed, and she had to fight for every breath. How much longer would she be able to continue waging this double battle? How long did she have before her body failed her entirely?

They were more than half through their ascent, but the Colonel did not signal a halt. Only one was scheduled, and that brief, before they began the last, most difficult phase of the climb. She knew they never would be able to take that final stretch without a rest.

Islaen forced herself onward almost blindly. It was her mind rather than her eyes that kept them on the rugged trail. Her physical senses had long since failed.

An hour passed, an eternity. Suddenly the ground rose sharply to a slope of more than eighty degrees. The Commando eased the heavy pack from her shoulders and threw herself on the ground.

She lay that way for what seemed a very long time, trying to draw air into lungs that were all but unable to accept it. Gradually, the scarlet flashes that seared her brain came less frequently and with less violence, and she looked about her.

Her comrades had already recovered themselves, but she took a perverse satisfaction in noting that they showed small inclination to press on. Islaen raised herself a little from the ground. She caught hold of the sward with something of a shock. She might have been standing upright or looking over the edge of a narrow ledge, so steep was the place on which she sat.

They had come a remarkably long way since beginning the ascent. The slope was much sharper than she had thought even while scaling it, a discrepancy in perception that was understandable. The guerrilla had been concerned only with the individual hurdles then rather than the whole course of the climb.

The shadows spreading over the beach below and a sudden, sharper blast of the already high wind reminded Islaen that they could not remain where they were. She slowly got to her feet. The others rose as well and took up their packs. Sogan and Bethe Danlo helped raise the Omrain to Jake's back and fastened him as securely as possible.

Islaen marveled at the redhead's strength. Despite all—the Omrain gravity, the exhausting climb, his heavy burden—he moved with scarcely less smoothness than he showed that morning.

The Commando-Captain caught her slightly envious expression, and his lips curved into a grin.

It vanished almost as it was born. "Is it much farther, Islaen? I doubt he can take a whole lot more."

"Not according to Bandit, but the way's very steep." She shivered. The cold was becoming intense. Their sweat-soaked clothing would soon begin to freeze. "Hurry," she said. Islaen reached for her pack, but Varn's hand stopped her.

This is my task, I believe.

Varn . . .

One word of protest, Colonel, and by all your ultrasystem's gods, I shall take you up on my back the way our redheaded friend has that Omrain.

That'll be the day space turns white, Varn Tarl Sogan! she snapped, but she read the real determination behind his words and yielded to his will. When she started off again, it was to the sound of his laughter ringing in her mind.

* * *

That phase of the climb proved harder than the first. There was no easing whatsoever in the slope now, and the off-worlders took full advantage of the handholds offered by the hardy blue-green brush that still covered so much of the mountainside even at this altitude.

The Arcturian remained close to his consort. Islaen welcomed his strength on occasion but found that she had to depend comparatively little on it.

Her team was finding this last stage more difficult than the first, but not so herself. She seemed to have sweated out most of the venom, and the brief rest had refreshed her. She suffered chiefly from a natural weariness now, and she could handle that easily enough after the intense struggle she had undergone.

FIFTEEN

IT WAS ALMOST fully dark, and the temperature was dropping rapidly. With the biting cold to goad them, the Federation party increased the pace of their climb.

At last, they scrambled over the ledge and stood on a flatter stretch of ground, a plateau the size of a small field.

Islaen looked about her. This was the location of the cabin according to Bandit's report, but she saw nothing that remotely resembled a dwelling.

There could be no mistake! There must not be! With irritation and an increasing despair, she scanned the cliff that rose from the opposite end of the field to the high peaks far above.

The Colonel smiled suddenly. "There!"

The other three peered at the place to which she pointed. Sogan's thought touched with hers, affirming that he had seen it as well, more the result of her mind instructions than of actual sight.

His comrades lacked that guidance. Bethe Danlo switched on her raditorch. The beam was shielded, and little light escaped from the bright streak she directed against the stone.

Now they saw the narrow windows cut into the seemingly solid cliff wall.

It was a cunning piece of camouflage. The building was set in a shallow cave, whether natural or excavated they could not tell from where they stood. The cliff face had been built up around it so that it blended perfectly with the rugged natural formation of the whole. Only those darkened window slits and the nearly invisible outline of the door betrayed the deception, and then only to the most practiced eye. The gurry had done a remarkable job of scouting to discover it, and she purred happily under the praise they poured into her despite the cold biting savagely at her.

"From Patrol cruiser to cave," said the demolitions expert in mock dismay.

"It's easily seen how you passed the War," observed Jake in an equally low whisper. "To Commandos, a cave was the ultimate in luxury. At least, shallow ones were," he amended, recalling their own more recent history.

The other arched her brows. "I would've volunteered to check it out, but since you're so much more experienced than I . . ." Even as she spoke, she dimmed the light.

The Colonel laughed softly. "Quiet, you two! I'll do the exploring. Cover me while I go in."

"Gladly, Colonel," Karmikel told her. "Just don't run into any more Omrain monsters."

"There are none," Sogan told him tightly, "at least none I can detect."

"No humans, either," Islaen announced. "This shouldn't take too long."

So saying, she crept forward. She was receiving no signals from the cabin, nothing that suggested it was occupied, but caution was too much a part of the guerrilla for her to openly approach any strange building in possibly hostile country.

The Commando tested the door and found it unlocked. She eased it open, standing back as she did so.

When all remained quiet, she entered the structure. A cursory search confirmed that it was indeed empty.

Islaen Connor returned to the door and signaled for her comrades to come ahead, then went back inside to better explore the dwelling.

At first, she had been conscious only of the blessed warmth in the room. Now she realized that it was not entirely dark. A fire still burned on the hearth. It was from here that the heat came and the pleasant glow.

The Colonel looked about her. The room was rugged and primitive but comfortable enough, certainly more so than she had reason to expect.

The furnishings were sparse, a table and several chairs. Most of it had been constructed by hand from the natural wood of Omrai.

There was one exception: an ancient flight chair, as obsolete as the starship it had once outfitted.

There was no way of determining its exact age. That pattern had been in use for a very long time, and the synthetics that went into its construction had been developed to last. Years or even centuries would leave little mark on it.

There had been a crash. The chair had been set on a wooden frame, but some of the original metal supports yet remained. They were scarred and warped in a manner that suggested great stress.

Islaen wondered absently whether the occupant had survived. If not, then who had transported it here? What was the Omrain boy's connection with it?

The remainder of the team was inside now. The room was quite dark despite the fire's glow, and Jake swept his torch along the wall until he located what appeared to be some kind of crude lighting device.

He examined it curiously. Its mechanism was simple, utilizing a liquid fuel drawn up by the capillary attraction of a wick. He took a sample of the oil for testing before touching a spark to the wick.

A soft light of rather surprising purity filled the room. There was no smoke or odor. The oil burned cleanly, leaving no residue in its wake.

The newcomers examined the dwelling in much the same manner as had their commander.

"By the Spirit of Space!" Bethe Danlo touched the flight chair in disbelief. It was as incongruous to this setting as it would have been aboard Jake's *Jovian Moon*.

"It was the master's seat," Sogan observed, pointing to a dim mark on the back that Islaen had missed in her less exacting examination. "I cannot read the ship's name."

"How did it come here?" the demolitions expert wondered aloud.

The Colonel repeated her deductions about a wreck and met with no challenge. It was a theory supported by the meager evidence available to them.

Jake returned from the small sleeping chamber to the left of the central room where he had settled the Omrain.

"How is he?" There was concern in the Colonel's voice. The journey had been hard and long for one in the boy's condition.

She feared they might lose him even as they found safety themselves.

"The antivenin worked. He should be coming round in the morning sometime."

Varn's dark eyes fixed on the door. "What do you make of him, Islaen?"

She shrugged. "Little enough. He's been unconscious through most of it, but I can say this much: I got no shadow of evil or violence from him, nothing that usually marks pirates or their supporters.

"As for anything else, it's pure conjecture. He's a local, I'd say, probably a descendant of those who came down with that ship. To judge by the old Basic he used, I imagine she crashed just after Omrai was studied and rejected for colonization."

Jake nodded in agreement. "Instruments weren't very good back then, and a lot of ships were lost. There wasn't any radiation immunization, either," he added. "The changes aren't extensive, but if our foundling's typical of his kind and assuming they've sprung from basically Terran stock, Omrai's citizens would definitely qualify as mutants."

"I haven't seen anyone resembling him during my travels," Bethe agreed.

She yawned. "We'll probably find out most of the answers tomorrow. Why not see if there are any hidden treasures around here and try for some sleep ourselves?"

The off-worlders were not long in scouting the central room of their refuge. They found it to be well supplied with the basic necessities.

A box of branches was set near the fire. There were only a few pieces in it, but apparently that would be sufficient for a fairly long siege. Only a single sliver burned on the fire now, but it oxidized slowly, throwing off tremendous amounts of heat and light. This one stick was keeping the dwelling at its pleasant temperature.

A huge barrel of water stood against a wall near the rear corner of the room. A bucket sat beside it on the floor.

Jake tested the flags near it as a matter of course. One sounded hollow. He looked closer and soon lifted out a slab about one foot square, exposing a stream flowing beneath that section of the cabin.

Only one thing remained. Islaen set her comrades looking for a storeroom. It seemed unlikely that all this would have been provided and no thought given to food.

Karmikel located the stockpile a few minutes after beginning the search, in a small chamber carved from the cliff at the rear of the dwelling.

He shivered when he went inside to inspect its contents. It was cold. The heat that did reach the planet's surface did not penetrate far. In a chamber cut into the heartstone of a mountain and insulated against the warmth of the house, the temperature would rarely, if ever, rise above freezing.

An enormous quantity of foodstuffs was stored there, enough to last a team like theirs for several years. There was the flesh of many species of land and sea creatures. Also represented were a large variety of roots, seeds, pods, and a few forms of fruit. The latter seemed to be in relatively short supply, and he suggested that they not touch any of these when he made his report.

As he had imagined she would do, Islaen decided to use the more plentiful of the Omrain supplies to help conserve their own. There was no danger of depleting these stores during the short time they expected to remain on-world.

"I suppose it's pretty pointless in this case," the Colonel told him, "but test the stuff thoroughly anyway, all of it if you can, but at least whatever we'll be using. Bethe can give you a hand with that."

She glanced over her shoulder at the door to the room where the Omrain lay. "I want to check on the boy. —We'll probably be bedding in that big chamber below ourselves. Varn, give it a once-over and bring our gear down if it passes muster. I should be with you in a few minutes."

Jake Karmikel began the familiar testing process immediately and had already finished with the first slab of meat when the demolitions expert joined him.

"It looks like we've found ourselves a nice little nest," he remarked with considerable satisfaction.

"We could've done a whole lot worse," the woman agreed. "Camping outside wouldn't be very pleasant tonight."

He chuckled suddenly. "Staying here might be almost as bad for some of us."

"How so?" she asked in surprise.

"That young mutant in the room above is obviously our host, assuming he's friendly or at least neutral. It should be good watching our Admiral deal with him in these close quarters for maybe a prolonged stay."

"Varn'll handle himself just fine!" Bethe snapped.

"Take it easy, will you! I was only joking."

"You joke too much about some things," she said sourly.

He scowled. "And you fly too fast to the defense! —Unless perhaps he's given you good reason for a proprietary attitude. Maintaining a harem was a way of life with him."

The spacer's head snapped back as if he had physically struck her. "Well, it's not mine! I told you before that I won't be anyone's shadow, not even Islaen's, and I'm telling you something else right now. If you think I'm joining up with a jealous, arrogant, ignorant boor like you, then you're hallucinating worse than a raklick user on a roar! —I'll buy that maybe you've given over your old feeling for Islaen, but you can't forget that Varn Tarl Sogan took her away from you, or that he can fly orbits around you in space!"

The door of the larder flew open and slammed back against the wall with a force that silenced the furious response he had been about to make.

Islaen Connor swept into the room. Her face and eyes were blazing. "That will be enough out of both of you!" she snarled. "I don't know what's setting you at each other's throats, and I don't care if you kill one another once you're back on the *Jovian Moon,* but I had a lifetime's fill of infighting in my company on Hades, and I won't put up with it here! Now shut up and get back to work!"

She glared first at the Sergeant, then at the man. Without giving them a chance to reply, the Commando-Colonel left the pair alone once more.

Jake flushed hotly. He should have known emotion of the intensity they must have been emitting would draw their commander down on them in short order.

Islaen was right, too. This was no time or place for such squabbling, not in a unit where survival itself depended on the cooperation of its members.

He faced his companion. "I'm sorry, Bethe. I was way off the charts."

"We're both tired," she responded curtly. "Let's finish up here and knock out. Our watches'll roll around all too soon as it is."

Karmikel nodded but made no reply. A feeling of doom hung

over him. Bethe had neither softened in her manner nor retracted any of her statements, and he dared not question her regarding them. He feared too much that she would confirm her intention of breaking from him, whatever truce they might forge for the duration of their work on Omrai.

Islaen Connor took hold of herself once she returned to the cabin's central chamber. She was angry with herself now as much as with her companions. She should not have reamed them so hard. They were all spent, and it was probably that more than any real difference which had touched them off.

Still, she could not let the argument pass, either. She had felt the violence of it. Only a rare kindness of fortune had prevented Varn and their surplanetary guide from killing one another on Hades and killing their mission and some 300,000 innocent people along with them. She could not expect to be shown similar favor a second time.

Bandit's anxious whistle drew her out of herself. "It's all right, love. They're quiet again."

The woman sat next to the gurry on the flight chair and lifted her gently, cuddling her in her hands.

She should join Sogan, she supposed, but she wanted to give herself a few minutes to be sure of her own temper. He was still in the lower room, unaware of the bitter altercation between their two comrades. Fortunately, her mind had not been linked with his when she detected it, and she wanted to keep that added worry from him if she could, that and shield the others. They had a right to some privacy.

Her fingers caressed the purring hen, but Islaen looked down at her somberly. Bandit had suffered cruelly from the cold during her search for this place and even more intensely, to the point of real danger, while she guided them back to it, yet she had never whimpered and never moved to seek shelter herself until she had seen them safe. "You're the most valiant one of all of us, Little Bandit," she whispered softly.

The purring increased, but the bright, black eyes raised to meet hers. *Bandit's not brave! She has to take care of her humans!*

"That's a very large part of courage, love."

The Commando lay back. The ancient flight chair was surprisingly comfortable, at once yielding and supporting. Perhaps technological progress was not always to humanity's advantage, she thought wryly. Nothing like this existed on present-day starships.

It was pleasant in the cabin. The fire filled the room with its warmth, and its crackle made a cheerful contrast to the gale howling through the night outside.

When she closed her eyes, the slight glare disappeared, and only a faint glow pierced her lids to tell her the lamp was still lit.

She allowed herself to draw a little farther from the present . . .

SIXTEEN

A COOL LIGHT struck her eyes, and the Colonel awoke. She was in the larger sleeping chamber, the one the off-worlders had chosen for their own use, although she had no memory of how she came to be here.

Islaen lay still a moment to further orient herself. The pallet on which she rested was merely a sack made of soft-cured hides. The packing was probably fine wood shavings. She had slept on similar often enough in the past to recognize the feel of them now. Two spider-silk blankets covered her, her own and another. Varn's. He must have draped it over her when he got up himself.

The other two were gone as well, she saw, and she was quite alone in the room except for the gurry, who was nestled against her side, buried beneath the blankets, rather than lying at her shoulder as was her usual wont.

A jar of washing cream and a towel had been placed on a low stool near the pallet and fresh clothes from her pack were neatly folded beside them.

With a regretful sigh and much to Bandit's annoyance, she pushed aside her coverings.

She shivered violently when the air struck her. The chamber was cold. Even the light that filtered through the window was cold. The Commando-Colonel frowned. There should be no light. The blinds should never have been removed while they remained within the cabin.

She went over to the window to set the crude but efficient shutters in place again. She stopped short. An obstruction of some sort covered a large part of the viewing area. She had to strain to her full height in order to see over it.

111

Islaen Connor stared. The whole world, from what she could see of it from this high place, was thickly covered with a blue-white, glinting mass. Ice.

Scant wonder her comrades had set out the washing cream, she thought with a shudder. No one would want to face water, even very hot water, after a look at that, and she very much doubted any such luxury as the last was readily available in this place.

The sight of the glimmering glacier gave strength to her already active sensation of cold, and the Commando hurriedly washed and dressed and hastened to the central chamber and the fire.

Her three comrades were there before her, although they had apparently not been up very long themselves. Sogan was still bent beside the fire, readying their morning's rations, work he did not welcome but which he performed competently when the turn fell to him.

His eyes brightened when she appeared in the doorway, but they immediately fixed intently on her. "Better. Much better," he judged critically.

His mind's relief was more pronounced. She felt both embarrassed and pleased by his concern but made no direct response to it. "Why did you let me sleep through last night?" she demanded.

The Arcturian smiled. "It was fair payment for your doing that to me on Mirelle. Besides," he added smoothly, "you were so out of it that you would not have been of much use to us anyway."

"I fear he's right, Colonel," Jake agreed. "You wouldn't have noticed a full invasion in progress two feet from the door. —Did you take a look outside?"

She nodded. "Quite a sight! Little wonder Omrai wasn't recommended for immediate colonization. I wouldn't care to first ship down to meet this."

"It'd be an unpleasant surprise," agreed Bethe Danlo. "The surveyors have a strange sense of humor, that's for sure. They didn't make any mention of this in their reports."

She moved closer to the fire. "It's a marvel that our ancestors succeeded so well with the Federation itself plotting their fall. I, for one, won't put much trust in the Settlement Board's descriptions and assurances if I ever decide to join the ranks of the planet huggers."

Islaen laughed at the very thought of the Sergeant, of any of her team, settling on even the wildest colony world. They were space hounds, all of them, and once the stars claimed a person's heart, he could not again be content with the narrow confines of any single planet, even the one he acknowledged and loved as his homeworld.

"How long will it last?" the redhead wondered aloud.

His commander shook her head. "There's no way of knowing. It's still very early. Perhaps Umbar will melt some of it off."

Islaen Connor was worried. They could not move with the ice like this, and she had to know what the chances of a repetition were before she could risk taking to the open again. It was obviously a common enough experience, since the boy's half-delirious mind recognized the signs of it so readily the previous evening.

There was so much more that the off-worlders must know if their mission was to succeed. She smiled grimly. They did not even know for certain that there was a mission at all on Omrai of Umbar.

One person could give them all this information and more, and she found it more and more difficult to control her impatience. Islaen was eager to question this young Omrain who spoke Basic and furnished his cabin with material from a dead starship, eager to know how he came to be here, in an obviously long-established residence, on a supposedly uninhabited planet, eager to learn his connection, if any, with the *Minotaur*.

She glanced at the door. He was transmitting nothing as yet to indicate imminent awakening. "How long more?" she asked of no one in particular.

The Sergeant shrugged at the exasperation in her tone. "Soon I'd say. I'll wait with him if you wish."

The auburn-haired woman nodded. "Thanks, Bethe."

Islaen Connor roused herself once the spacer took her leave of them. "We might as well put this time to some kind of use. —Varn, pull that map out. I want to go over it again in light of what we've learned thus far. Jake, check out our weapons. All of them. We may be needing them soon. The other gear, too."

His brows lifted. "Aye, Colonel. I think I know that routine by now."

She laughed at his wounded tone and bent over the map Sogan brought to her.

They both reviewed it carefully, using the information they had already gleaned to update it and trying to plot out alternate routes to their target. There was no telling yet what the consequences of their meeting with the young Omrain would be.

In the end, they sat back, still looking at the chart but knowing they could do no more with it without further data.

The Arcturian glanced curiously and with some concern at Karmikel, who was sitting on the floor before the fire working on one of the blasters, Islaen's, in total silence. The Noreenan man had not spoken at all since beginning his labors.

What has happened? he asked his consort. *There is something amiss with both our comrades . . .*

That's their business, not ours.

Her response had been quietly, almost casually spoken, but there was no missing the command in it. The man stiffened but did not protest. He preferred his own affairs kept close, and Islaen Connor went to considerable lengths to guard his privacy. He would be a fool or worse not to realize she would show equal consideration for the other members of their unit.

He scowled then. The break between the pair must be a serious one or she would not have warned him off as she had. *I am sorry,* he said somewhat stiffly, at the same time sending a not entirely friendly look in Jake's direction. *I had hoped those two would marry.*

The Colonel shot a sharp glance at him which she took care to conceal. She knew full well that Sogan still regarded the Commando-Captain as a kind of rival and that he saw himself, with some justification, as showing poorly against Karmikel in most of their surplanetary work. He would of a certainty like to see another step put between the redhead and herself.

It was not a subject she wanted to broach with him, not at this time, and so she merely shrugged. *Don't give up on them yet,* she replied casually. *It's not hate or indifference that I'm picking up.*

To Islaen's relief, Bethe Danlo appeared in the doorway of the Omrain's room and signaled that he was at last stirring. She quickly went to the entrance but remained concealed outside so as not to frighten or overwhelm him as he awakened. The Sergeant's presence might be enough of a shock for him at first.

The boy's eyes opened. They were a pale brown. He started in very real fear when he saw the demolitions expert.

"Easy," she said softly. "I won't hurt you."

He relaxed. "No. Your comrade would have left me to die if you wished that."

"My comrade?"

"She who helped me. —I saw her dimly before the poison took full hold. She had different eyes. And hair."

"You see a lot, lad."

Islaen Connor entered the room. They would have to be careful with this one if they were not to betray their true mission, she thought, and she was determined to hold that secret until she knew considerably more about the on-worlder and conditions in general on Omrai.

"To live, we must see much."

He studied the Commando-Colonel with intense interest but without his earlier fear. "How came you here, starwomen?" the Omrain asked, no longer able to control his curiosity.

The guerrilla introduced herself and Bethe. As they had agreed from the outset, she explained that they and their two comrades now in the room beyond were survivors from a blasted Patrol vessel.

The Omrain boy looked at her in surprise. "Pirates?"

"One ship, the *Minotaur*."

"They made no attempt to pick you up?"

"Both vessels were destroyed."

His eyes flashed in the exultation pouring from his mind. He was not one of the pirates at the least. "You were very fortunate. Your fate would have been hard had you been taken. —You are welcome to Omrai, starwomen. I am Barak, Commander-in-Exile of this world since my father's death."

"I'm very curious about your presence here. Our briefing didn't mention an inhabited planet in this part of Quandon Sector."

Islaen had been trying to glean what she could from the boy's mind since the interview began but with remarkably little success. He was transmitting only a small part of what he was feeling, and she could not detect that unless she concentrated strongly on him save in those moments when really powerful emotion gripped him.

What she did receive was sufficient. There was no hostility or deceit in him, and she thought she felt a positive wish to help them.

In the face of that, the woman felt a rush of shame for her own duplicity, but wisdom demanded that she continue with that, at least for a while longer.

Barak's story was simple enough. His ancestors had manned the colony ship *Space Queen* out of Terra bound for Miskra. The Flynnal Nova had struck during the voyage, catching the fragile vessel in its powerful waves as it had hundreds of others.

The *Space Queen* weathered the violent series of shocks, but she had been driven far from her course into an utterly unknown section of space. Her automatic guidance system had been damaged beyond all hope of repair, and communications over the vast reaches of space, a space torn and ajar with the throes of a star's violent death, were impossible with their remaining equipment. Whatever was to be done to save the colonists would have to be accomplished by those aboard the ship herself.

Her master, whose descendant and heir Barak was, was skilled in astral navigation, an art more important in those older times than in the instrument-ruled present, and he might well have been able to bring them through to their destination. His passengers and crew had faith in him and remained calm, accepting the rationing of supplies and the endless unknown quietly and without complaint.

In the end, they entered a region which they were able to identify at least roughly, a part of the rim almost totally wild and unknown but which was the rim all the same and had known some initial exploration. From that point, they should be able to find their way to their destination or to the help they needed to reach it.

Then the ill fortune that seemed to ride them like a mara struck a further, irrevocable blow.

They entered the magnetic eddy that tore through Omrai's space. It was not quiet then but boiled in a vortex that no vessel, not one with ten times, a thousand times, the *Space Queen*'s strength, could hope to ride out.

She held a few seconds, then began to break apart. The planet's gravity caught the helpless vessel, and the *Space Queen* hurled toward her surface.

The master and crew were helpless before the forces that ruled the dying ship. All they could do was try to brake their descent with whatever power remained and pray that they would come down on some inhabitable place.

The crash was terrible, crushing the engines and communication system as if they were paper. More than half those aboard

were killed outright or died shortly afterward, but by some
miracle, those on the bridge, those best fitted to lead the
castaways, escaped with only minor injury despite the almost
total destruction of the equipment surrounding them.

After salvaging what they could, the colonists took stock of
their situation.

It was obvious to all that the *Space Queen* would never again
lift. All hope of bringing help had died in the wreckage of the
interstellar transceiver.

What did remain was more important. They still had their
supplies and the equipment with which they had hoped to win a
hold on Miskra, and they had the courage and determination that
had sent them from their safe homes to begin new lives on a
strange world.

The *Space Queen*'s tapes survived the crash. From them, with
the help of some shrewd calculation and deduction, they learned
the identity of this planet and what little was known about her.
One fact above all the rest restored the hope to their hearts:
Omrai of Umbar was Terra-normal. If fortune and her unknown
gods were with them, they should be able to claim her for their
own.

". . . It was difficult, very difficult, those first years. Many
died, but we established ourselves, and we flourished. We would
never be rich as some worlds measure wealth, but Omrai had a
fine hope of becoming a strong planet and a good one on which
to live until the Big Ship came."

Islaen's interest quickened. The hatred in the boy's mind was
as sharp as the bitterness in his voice. "The Big Ship?"

"Storms like that which brought the *Space Queen* down are
not rare to Omrai's space. They come frequently in this season,
always accompanied by the sea-cold here. Our wise ones were
able to determine that much while some of the old equipment
still worked."

Again the hatred, this time so strong that the Commando was
forced to withdraw a little. "About ten years ago, the Big Ship
passed through our space and was caught up in one such storm.
Since she crashed, we have become a hunted, terror-ridden
people, dreading the weapons of the shipmen, weapons against
which we have no defense except our cunning and our knowledge of Omrai, dreading the doom they have brought with them.
I can scarcely remember a time now when freedom and high

hope and a long, peaceful life were but the accepted right of every Omrain," he concluded furiously.

The Colonel turned away to conceal how deeply the youth's pain affected her. She felt it as sharply as if it were her own. It was not difficult to imagine such a disaster striking her beloved Noreen, not after her experiences on overrun worlds during the War.

There was no need to ask why the strange ship had remained so long. Her engines must have been severely damaged even as the *Space Queen*'s had been. Omrai was a poor planet in both services and the materials needed to repair a starship.

Piracy might give the crew what they needed if their victims could be taken more or less intact. It would be a slow process. Few vessels came to this part of Quandon Sector at all, and most of those would fight hard. It is far easier to destroy than to capture a craft manned by those certain of either a cruel death or slavery if they should be taken.

Those captured faced the latter fate, according to Barak. The Big Ship had suffered heavy casualties, and those who remained were occupied with the guarding of their base despite the patent weakness of the surplanetary populace and with the more delicate repair work on their vessel. They wanted slaves to handle the physical labor of the camp and the basic tasks of stripping their victims and restoring the hull of their own craft.

Those workers were chiefly captives from trapped ships, who seemed better able to survive the treatment they received. Native Omrains died very quickly under the off-worlders' rule, so quickly that they were now simply burned down when the opportunity presented itself and were not brought back to the base at all.

The Colonel asked Barak for more specific details regarding the damaged starship. His description should tell her enough for her to deduce the pirate's class and allow her to make some sort of realistic guess as to how she was armed and, most important of all, how best to move against her.

To her surprise, he possessed almost no concrete information about this enemy from the stars. "Have you ever seen the Big Ship?" she demanded.

The Omrain shook his head emphatically. "No. To approach her is to die. The invaders take or slay almost everyone who comes near. —I have seen the other pirate several times, though, once very close."

"What was their relationship?" the Commando inquired, trying a new course. "Did the *Minotaur* crash with the Big Ship?"

"She did not crash. Perhaps she witnessed the Big Ship's fall from afar and came in for an easy kill when the storm ended, but whatever drew her, she soon fell victim to the Big Ship, the very first one, and became her tool. —I have little knowledge about any of this," he finished apologetically. "I was very young at the time, and our people were in a state of chaos from the shipmen's hunting and killing. I am truly sorry."

"No need to be," she told him gently. "You've told us a great deal."

Islaen Connor faced the ice-choked window for several minutes, her eyes staring unseeing at the frozen vista beyond.

She turned once more. "I must see that ship."

The boy blanched. The intensity of his terror was such that it gripped the woman's own fear centers with a force she had to struggle hard to quell before she could expel it from her mind. "I only ask that you direct us," she told him quietly.

By a seemingly superhuman effort of will, Barak drew himself back under control. "No. I will guide you. I do not know much about the Big Ship, but my knowledge of Omrai will at least ease the way for you, and the escape, if escape should prove possible."

A flash of hope ran through him. "You will destroy the Big Ship?"

"With what?" the Commando-Colonel asked.

The boy's joy faded. Islaen sighed and dropped her eyes. Shame once more seared her, although she had often before been even less open in her dealings with surplanetary leaders. "We'll do what we can," she promised, "but I must know more about this Big Ship before I can decide on any course of action."

Barak nodded. That was hardly unreasonable. "Wait one more day. The ice will be gone by then, and I will have regained my strength. We must have nothing against us when we begin."

SEVENTEEN

THE OFF-WORLDERS LEFT him to rest and rejoined their comrades.

Islaen reported what she had learned, chiefly for Jake's benefit, since Varn's mind had been linked with hers throughout the interview and had shared both the information she gathered and her perceptions of it.

"He was honest?" Karmikel asked.

"Aye." The woman's eyes shadowed. "Or he seemed to be. I couldn't pick up much from him unless one emotion or another was really riding him. Then he transmitted quite strongly." She frowned. "He appears to possess some degree of mental shielding, maybe as part of his mutation. It could have come to him along with his more obvious physical adaptations.—What do you think, Varn?"

The Arcturian did not answer for a moment, but then he nodded. "Aye. It seems likely. We did of a certainty get far less from him than I remember receiving any other time when our minds were so joined. As for why . . ." He shrugged. "Mutation is possible and probably racial. The Flynnal Nova cast a lot of that form of radiation, and as Karmikel says, there was no immunization at the time. I believe many such differences in Federation peoples began at that time."

He did not elaborate further and quietly withdrew from the conversation.

His face was set and grim. He had not noticed that absence of communication, not until Islaen called it to his awareness and memory just now. The lapse was no mere accident, the result of his relative inexperience in the interpretation of such transmissions. It had come of negligence on his part. Negligence and something else.

Varn Tarl Sogan had not wanted that contact with the mind of the young mutant. Although he had managed to conceal his repugnance from his consort, who would have had little patience with it, he had shrunk from accepting those transmissions, and his attention had been fixed more on his struggle with himself and with the distress the boy's touch caused him than with trying to comprehend the information he had received. In so much, he had failed his comrades, and he vowed that the like would not happen again.

He listened intently while the Commando-Colonel outlined her impressions of all Barak of Omrai had told her and Bethe Danlo.

She warned that they should not accept his tale of the Big Ship too literally. Although she was personally convinced Barak had told them the full truth as he knew it, they could not dismiss the possibility that much or most of what he said might well be nothing more than folklore built up out of fear and ignorance carefully nurtured or, at the least, encouraged by the enemy themselves. She judged it more likely that the Big Ship was simply the prime partner in a team of pirate raiders, the *Minotaur* being the other, whose masters were astute enough to use a people's weakness and terror to protect their base.

The former Admiral shook his head. "Why not believe the boy?" he demanded suddenly with some irritation. "He seems a steady, responsible youth. If he terms the pirate large, take him at his word. It is no inordinate claim. There are plenty fifty-class vessels in the galaxy's wolf packs and all too many one hundred-class. Why should the crashed ship not lie within that range?"

He stiffened at the look Jake bent on him. "You disagree, Karmikel?" he asked a bit sharply.

"No," the other said hastily. "You're right. We'd be fools to dismiss that possibility outright. Barak hasn't shown himself to be hysterical or a total barbarian, either, for that matter." He hesitated, then went on. "It just surprised me a little that you should be the one to judge him most fairly."

Sogan's head raised, but the memory of his earlier failure made him answer mildly. "Perhaps it is because I know I am too ready to misjudge and so must guard against doing so."

He felt the Colonel's gratitude, but she made no comment

even in her mind. There was work before them and little time, maybe very little, in which to accomplish it. They might not have all the answers yet, but their target was confirmed, that and the need for fast action.

Those pirates would have to be cleared out immediately. A pack of desperate, stranded killers could spell great suffering for a planet and a people that had already known too much of it.

In addition to their duty to Omrai and Quandon Sector, a second responsibility had been set on them as well. Barak's information had been very specific about the ice storms and their magnetic counterparts in space. The *Free Comet* was scheduled to make several sweeps of this area, sweeps that would bring her well into the danger zone and hold her there too many hours at a time. The first of these would come in less than a fortnight. As communication from the planet's surface was impossible with the equipment they had, she would have to be met in space and warned before entering the circle of peril.

They could not move yet. To do anything about Omrai, they must have some real information about the pirate starship and base, and Islaen began setting her plans at once to make an expedition to study them. She wanted to be ready to set out as soon as the ice melted enough to permit travel.

Once again, Sogan intervened. The necessity of the journey and the fact that a Commando must lead it could not be questioned, but he argued bitterly against her going alone in the Omrain's company. Whatever Barak's courage and goodwill, he was still a boy and was totally unaccustomed to the use of Federation weapons. By the on-worlder's own testimony, it was extremely dangerous to approach the enemy ship, so dangerous that the mere thought of doing so drove terror through him, and Varn insisted that another of their company be permitted to go with her.

The Colonel shook her head. "This promises to be real Commando work. Neither you nor Bethe could handle it."

"Karmikel, then!" He flashed a look of open appeal to Jake.

The other man was not slow in responding. "He's right, Islaen . . ."

"You're not thinking, either of you," she said in exasperation. "If I'm killed or taken, everything falls to Jake. He'll be the only one left with the experience to finish this off, if it can be done at all. We can't afford to risk both of us on an information hunt, however important it may be in itself."

Bandit will go!

Even as she spoke, the gurry shot from her place by the fire and settled on Islaen's shoulder. Her sharp claws gripped the woman's tunic and the skin beneath, threatening to close completely should any attempt to dislodge her be made.

"I don't know, love," the Colonel told her. "It'll probably be cold out there. Maybe you should stay here in the cabin while we have the use of it."

Nooo! Bandit's helped before!—Varn?

"She commands, small one. The decision must be hers." He reached out and stroked the hen with his finger. "You could give sound service even though she cannot share your senses as I do," he added.

"She can describe what she sees," Islaen Connor said none too happily. "All right, Bandit. I'd rather leave you here, safe and comfortable for yourself, but you might well be a big help. You can come with me, but take care not to reveal your talents to our guide, however much you choose to charm him."

The day passed slowly. All the off-worlders were intensely curious as to what their commander would discover on her expedition, and they found the waiting hard.

Barak's feelings were difficult to judge when he joined them in the early afternoon after declaring himself well enough to leave his bed. He did his best to help them by giving them whatever detail he had learned on or heard about the Big Ship and the *Minotaur,* but he kept his own thoughts to himself. If he still feared the journey to come, he concealed it well, but his original terror had been so powerful, so obvious, that neither Islaen or Varn Tarl Sogan could believe either that it had been abandoned or that it was grounded entirely in vague tales. They knew pirates, and they knew they were facing a real challenge on Omrai of Umbar.

The strength of the control the young Omrain displayed impressed the Federation soldiers, as did the ease with which he accepted their presence. Only Bandit provoked open surprise in him. He continued to stare at her, apparently amazed and quite puzzled as to her presence and purpose, until the gurry at last took charge of the situation in her usual manner by flying to him and whistling sharply for his attention.

A smile spread over his broad features. "What a strange, funny little creature!" he exclaimed. "What does it want?"

"For you to pet her," Bethe Danlo explained. "Just stroke her head gently."

His smile widened at the hen's answering purr to his clumsy effort. "What is she? Is she your pet?"

"Bandit's a gurry, a denizen of Jade of Kuan Yin. Islaen and Varn were allowed to bring her off-world with them after helping the settlers out there. We tend to think of her more as a comrade than a pet, though."

"I can see why. She is wonderful!" He paused, then went on thoughtfully. "Omrai has some fine little animals, too . . ."

He looked at the Sergeant suddenly. "Why are you watching me like that?" he demanded. "Are you thinking I may betray you?"

"No," she assured him quickly, "but you're taking all this very calmly. Visitors from other parts of the galaxy can't be that common an occurrence for you."

"No, but we of Omrai know other races exist." Barak raised his head, a touch of anger flashing in his eyes. "Just because we live primitively does not mean we are barbarians. We lack tools, machines, the means of making them, not knowledge. All of us have studied the *Space Queen*'s tapes very thoroughly."

"They're still preserved?" asked Karmikel in amazement. Such ancient material would make fascinating reading, and he could not quite restrain the eagerness that crept into his voice. "Where are they now?"

"Well hidden."

There was no need for further explanation. Those tapes, hopelessly dated as they were, were the Omrains' sole contact with the past and with the vast universe beyond their planet's atmosphere. Should they be lost or destroyed, the colonists would indeed revert back to the conditions of humanity's earliest years.

The ice melted with incredible speed during that day, and it had all but disappeared by the following morning.

Islaen Connor and Barak carefully gave their equipment a final check while waiting for dawn to begin, signaling their departure.

The woman watched until she found herself alone with the Omrain and then approached him. "You're under no obligation to do this," she told him quietly. "Only direct me. I'm trained for such work. You're not, and you needn't feel compelled to take part in it when the rest of my own team are holding back."

The boy shook his head, refusing the escape she was offering him. "You have given me my life, and you may yet give life back to Omrai. Had I no personal honor at all, I must still aid you to the full of my strength for my people's sake." He met the Colonel's brown eyes. "You understand?"

She nodded. "Aye, Barak of Omrai. I understand."

EIGHTEEN

ISLAEN AND BARAK set out when the first light paled Omrai's black night.

Both carried heavy packs. They expected this would be a journey of about a week's duration. Barak had said they might cover the distance to the base in two days' hard walking if the weather held with them, but he warned that this kind of speed would take most of their strength. They might well have need of that later, and the Commando had elected to keep to the slower pace he recommended.

The war prince watched until they were gone from sight, then slipped the blind back into place and turned from the window to stare sightlessly into the fire.

Bethe Danlo watched him. She knew what it must be doing to him to see his consort go into probable danger while he remained behind in safety, but there was nothing she could do to ease this time for him, and the offering of her sympathy would not be welcome, not to this man.

Her lips tightened. Islaen held so central a part in Sogan's life. She wondered what would happen to him if the Commando-Colonel did fall, as was all too strong a possibility in their work, and a chill passed through her because she knew the answer full well.

Her eyes fell. The spacer felt very glad in that moment that she would never mean this much to Jake Karmikel. No one should have to bear such responsibility for another.

A surprisingly strong surge of sadness welled up to flood her already heavy spirit. Maybe she no longer meant anything at all to him.

Fear seemed to grip every nerve in Varn Tarl Sogan's body, to poison every faculty of his mind, not panic or the sharp anxiety and more than anxiety that preceded and accompanied battle, but a dull, aching dread that he knew his will would not be sufficient to banish, not entirely. His memory of the Omrain boy's horror at the initial mention of this expedition was too keen to allow that.

He had expected this and had braced himself to do battle with it, but the Arcturian had not anticipated the intense loneliness which accompanied it.

The Commando-Colonel had been with him, physically and even more closely in mind, through all that had befallen them since their meeting on Visnu of Brahmin. Even in those times, which he now cursed, when he closed her off from all but surface speech, she was with him, trusting in him and ever ready to receive and welcome him. Now when he instinctively reached out for that warmth, to give to her or to receive, he found only a vast, cold void.

There would be no relief from that nagging emptiness until his consort returned, if she did come back. He doubted that their power to link mind with mind would stretch over any very great distance, but even if it could, he dared not try it. That restraint they had set on themselves almost from the beginning of their association, not to risk disrupting one another's concentration when battle or other similar crisis was near. Since he had no way of knowing how she fared at any given moment, it was necessary to assume a state of alert at all times and act accordingly. For that reason, too, they would not use their communicators without real need.

The former Admiral fought and finally chained his anxiety and sense of loss. He could not afford the luxury of wallowing in his own concerns. Jake Karmikel would have to lead any actual assault they made against the pirates in the event of Islaen's fall, but in all other respects, he held command in the Colonel's absence. There was work to be done which must begin at once, work which he must direct and do. It took no extensive guerrilla training to realize that they were not free to sit back and wait for their scouts' return.

Squaring his shoulders, he turned away from the fire and

ordered Bethe and Jake outside to examine the cliff for sign of another exit while he searched the cabin itself.

If either Islaen Connor or Barak should be taken, he wanted a faster and better-concealed escape route for the remainder of his company than the way they had come up.

There was little danger of a surprise attack in its strictest sense. Land, sea, and air were all visible for many miles from this high place, and it was impossible to approach the dwelling on its single blind side directly from the invader's base, but although any attack would be seen well in advance, they would still suffer if they had to go down that slope to avoid it. They would almost certainly be picked up by surface scanners or even by distance lenses, and they would never be down and away in time to be completely secure against mechanized pursuit.

The war prince was certain that there must be another, easier path if they could only locate it. The cabin was a fully contained unit designed to withstand attack or siege, whether by an enemy or by Omrai's own wild weather. That would have been obvious to any inner-system fop, but it was also a home, a place meant to shelter people in the daily course of their lives.

Varn could not imagine anyone, much less young children, coping with that climb regularly. It most assuredly could not be easily negotiated by anyone heavily burdened, as their own experience had proven. Reason insisted that there must be some way of rapid ascent, if only to permit the inhabitants a quick escape from the sea-cold.

He examined the central chamber with great care. Everything else was either located in or led from this room. Logic insisted that the hidden exit should as well.

The search proved fruitless. There were no hollows in the floor save for the one corner where the stream flowed.

That he rejected immediately as useless in anything but the direst need. There was no room to maneuver even the tiniest craft, and a man could not survive for longer than a few minutes in water of that temperature.

At last, he had to admit defeat. The others returned, also without success. They searched the two sleeping rooms and the larder with no better result and finally gathered before the fire to discuss the course they must follow.

The Commando-Captain glared at the chair from the long-dead starship. He was angry and frustrated by their failure. Now they would have to quit the cabin and chance the uncertain weather in the surrounding countryside. He was doubly loath to leave the comfortable dwelling because it meant losing the vantage of the high ledge, but there seemed little help for it.

His brows came together. Jake lay his hands against the wall behind the seat, then moved them to the side of it.

After a moment, he stepped back, smiling. He had always been responsive to sensory stimuli and was certain now that he had found something. The stone behind the flight chair was slightly colder than that of the surrounding walls.

The Noreenan ran his fingers over the surface. It was natural stone, corrugated and pitted with the wear of the ages.

One of the fissures was straight. He followed it, slowly because the craftsman who fashioned it had been cunning in his use of camouflage.

At last, he traced the full outline of the door. No handholds. It would open away from the room.

Karmikel placed both hands against it and pushed, steadily increasing the pressure. The stone would not give.

"Sogan, help me!"

They threw their joint strength against the barrier. It held, and they were forced to rest.

At the second attempt, its resistance broke, and the door swung back, revealing a long passageway that stretched beyond the limits of their torches. The light glittered and rebounded from the ice-sheathed walls. The door itself was of solid rock over two feet in depth. Scant wonder the Arcturian had been unable to sound the hollow place behind it!

Sogan nodded at the sight of it, satisfied that they had found what they sought, although, of course, the way would have to be explored to confirm that.

"Bethe, Karmikel and I are going down. Keep watch here. Let us know if anything looks suspicious," he added, touching the communicator on his wrist as he spoke.

The two men entered the tunnel.

The corridor sloped downward steadily but not too steeply. It had been formed partly by nature, partly by human working. Short flights of steps had been cut into the floor wherever the grade became too steep or where the ground fell away into a sudden drop. The stairs themselves were wide and low. The architect had taken the ice into consideration when he cut them.

The off-worlders were glad for that. The footing was not

impossible, but it was treacherous, and both moved with extreme care.

Despite the difficulties the ice caused them, their descent was rapid, and they soon stood in the small cave that marked the end of the tunnel.

The outline of another door, this one not concealed, was visible beneath the ice at its opposite end.

The glittering coating over it was light. Apparently, the outer wall was relatively thin and some of Umbar's heat penetrated to warm the interior. The ice probably vaporized completely a few days after the sea-cold retreated.

The caution evinced throughout the cabin held here as well, and the outlines of an observer's port, a spy hole, could be seen in the door. It would not be opened until the world outside was known to be free of intruders.

It was not speculation about the caution of the early settlers that drew the exclamations of wonder from them.

A needle-nosed missile some six feet in length was set before the door, as if ready to blast out when the long-sealed entrance was at last opened.

The off-worlders examined it curiously. The little projectile, a rocket of some kind, was under the cover of an atmoshield. Its casing glittered when the torch beam glanced off it. None of the moisture in the cave had damaged it, at least not in any visible way.

It was secured to an old-type unmechanized transportation sling, a sturdy device intended for work on a colony planet whose people had not yet won the ease to think of style. The wheel base was wide and strong, well suited for movement over rough countryside.

Jake gave a low whistle. "Late atomics! The *Space Queen* must've been one of the last ships to carry anything like this."

"Can it still fly after all this time?" Sogan wondered aloud.

The Commando shrugged. "Bethe will have to answer that, if even she can do it." He chuckled. "We'll have to put a time watch on her when we show her this."

Bethe Danlo reluctantly emerged after examining the rocket for nearly an hour. She strongly advised against using it, since she could not vouch for the stability of the active elements in its power cells after all this time, but she pronounced it perfectly capable of flight while the little life still present in its fuel core remained. She ventured that she might be able to restore its warhead, an atomic cannon, to firing order as well but would promise nothing definite on that.

Her report pleased the former Admiral. Their whole discovery did. Not only did they have a potential additional weapon for their limited arsenal but, of more immediate importance, they now had the reasonably secure escape route they had sought.

The Arcturian was well-nigh certain that the secret of the cave's existence was not shared by Barak. The boy had told them the cabin had not been lived in since the death of his great-grandfather and that he had come here only since the crash of the Big Ship.

The difficulty he and Jake had experienced in first opening the door tended to confirm long disuse. They had tried it several times since then, and it had always moved with ease.

Sogan resolved to bring their flier here as quickly as possible. This cave offered a better hiding place than the one where it was presently secured, and it gave them a base of operations within easy striking range of the invaders, unless their Colonel chose to send the vessel off-world immediately to warn the *Free Comet* to stay clear of Omrai's near-space.

He made his plans without further delay. Islaen's report would determine their course, and he wanted to have the little vehicle near, whatever role she decided it was to play.

The war prince cleared the ice from the exit with a quick burst at low power from his blaster. He tested the door, but it held firmly in place. It was more difficult to move than the one leading from the cabin had been, and it took the efforts of all three of them to free it.

The cave opened into a sheltered glen facing the ocean. Sharp fingers of rock protected it on every side. An intruder just behind the turn of the mountain would not see them there.

Nor they him, Varn thought in momentary concern. They could be surprised here.

The advantages of the place outweighed this single weakness. They would be all but invisible to any form of direct search during the rare minutes when any of the team would be outside the cave. The entrance was concealed in a natural hollow in the stone of the cliff. Although shallow, it was so set as to be permanently in shadow. The observer's port was so cunningly disguised that it could not be sighted even when fully open.

The first colonists were suspicious by nature, and since they had not known what to expect on Omrai, they considered every possible source of danger when they built their dwellings, a caution for which the Federation party now gave fervent thanks.

Sogan thought briefly about the best way to bring the flier, but the answer was plain enough.

To return to it on foot the way they had come would take time, perhaps too much if he met with any delay at all. Should the scouts return early and Barak see him with the machine, their deception—and their claim on the boy's trust—were dead, and he concurred with Islaen that it was still wise to hold both intact.

No, the sea would be his best route, and Varn had Karmikel construct a curragh, since that was work more in the Commando's line.

There were few trees in this part of Omrai and fewer still that suited this purpose, but the off-worlders finally located enough and brought them to the cave, first concealing as well as possible the signs of their handiwork.

The actual fashioning of the craft was a simple enough task, although it took the better part of the day to complete it. Jake had learned the art as part of his survival training and utilized it many times in the past. With the help of his two comrades, who worked under his close supervision, he trimmed the branches away from the felled trees and split the trunks into planks. These he shaped and fitted together. It took only seconds to prepare and apply the sealant they carried as part of their general supplies. Half an hour more, and the curragh would be seaworthy.

Once the final coating had been applied, the Arcturian left his companions. He wanted to ready his pack, and he had been growing concerned about the lack of a watch above. Their scouts had not been gone long enough for them to be in any real danger from the base yet, but they would still be safer for maintaining the discipline of a good guard right from the start.

Bethe Danlo remained below with Karmikel. She eyed the curragh critically. "Not a bad-looking job," she conceded.

"Thanks. —The Admiral's right about this being the best way to go. He's a bit off about the proper crew, of course, but I figure we can argue that out closer to launch."

The woman did not reply for a moment. "Let him go, Jake," she said at the end of that time. "According to Islaen, he's really good on the water, the match for any Commando."

"With a boat, aye, but there aren't any pirates hovering over

Horus' seas or Thorne's." He shook his head. "He's getting there fast, but he's not a Commando yet."

"He's no shooting star, either. Trouble may come to him like it seems to come to all of us, but he isn't one to seek it out."

"No, but he might well miss spotting it until it's too late, especially since he's worried sick about Islaen."

"That'll only drive him to greater caution. He'll never give in so far to himself as to let that rule him."

Her eyes held his. "You can't go, Jake. You're needed here. If Varn doesn't fetch the flier, then it has to be me. If I'm the victim," she added, "your boat-building was a wasted effort. I can't handle her well enough and will have to trek back overland."

The man scowled but nodded, knowing she was right. "Let it be the Admiral, then."

Bethe smiled. "Don't look so dark. As you say, he's worried, and this'll give him something constructive to do, not to mention getting him off our backs for a while. A nervous Arcturian isn't the easiest person in the galaxy to live with, and you know damn well that if he starts climbing walls, he'll have us climbing them right along with him."

He chuckled. "You reason soundly, Sergeant."

A sudden spark lit his spirit. This was the way it had always been between them. "Bethe . . ."

"Aye?"

His courage failed him, and he looked hurriedly at the curragh. "She's just about ready. Tell Sogan to be coming down, will you?"

NINETEEN

THE TWO MEN carried the small craft to the ocean, although the war prince could have handled the task alone. She was designed to be managed by a single person.

They settled the curragh in the water, and Sogan boarded her, taking care to avoid soaking his clothing. It would be an uncomfortable and dangerous journey if he were forced to remain in essentially the same position for hours on end in wet garments. Omrai was too cold a planet for that.

Jake put his hands on the vessel's side. "Umbar'll be setting soon. If you keep going through the night, you should be back here by early morning. We'll give you that much time again before hunting for you."

Varn nodded. He was more grateful for that assurance of a backup than he wanted the other to know. It was the unit's policy when circumstances allowed it, but still, the confirmation of it was welcome just then.

Of that, he said nothing. "There should be no problems. The only delay may be in scaling the cliffs."

"That's why we're allowing you so much extra time, Admiral."

The Commando released the boat. "Don't try taking on any armadas single-handed out there."

Sogan smiled. "I should not dream of it."

"Dream what you will. Just don't do it."

This time, the Arcturian laughed. "No fear of it, friend!"

The other stepped back, and he paddled a little way out from shore where he could test the curragh before actually beginning

134

his journey. Better to discover a serious flaw now and abort the mission than have her fail later.

Jake waited on the beach, watching while he put the boat through her paces and holding himself ready to help if any problem should develop.

Varn Tarl Sogan was very conscious of him. He felt that this was his own proving as much as the curragh's and stiffened under it until he was certain he was handling himself and his craft well, more than well enough to meet even a Commando's standards.

When he was at last satisfied that his vessel was both seaworthy and maneuverable, he began his journey in earnest.

Although the short, rather heavy planks they had been forced to use did make the curragh a little clumsy, it was not enough of a fault to cause him to hesitate. He anticipated no trouble as long as the ocean remained calm.

The former Admiral smiled. He had yet to see its still surface troubled by more than a wind-driven ripple.

Sogan did not fear traveling on the open sea, not while he moved in this direction. Barak had assured them that the invaders rarely left their base to trouble the coastal areas and never ranged as far west as he would be going.

For this reason, too, he had decided to wear his own clothing rather than the costume of Omrai's people. It would better protect him from Umbar's rays, and it was a great deal warmer, a matter of no small interest to one planning to face this world's biting night chill in a small, open boat.

Umbar slid below the horizon, but the Arcturian did not think to stop. He had made excellent time so far, better than he had hoped, and he wanted to hold his pace for as long as possible.

It was dark, but the dim moon and the starshine were bright enough to guide him. He could even see, or thought he could see, some color, although the sea and the more distant land seemed darker, bluer, than they were in the light of the day.

It was necessary to keep farther from the shadow of the shoreline than he really liked. Fingers of stone reached up from beneath the quiet water, eager to grasp at any boat passing over them. He could not trust he would see all of them in time if he ventured too far in.

Varn soon regretted his decision to continue through the night, but no suitable place to stop presented itself. His company had traveled at a much slower rate when they passed this way on foot, and the curragh had long since taken him parallel to the forests. The cliff face was sheer and sound here with few breaks and almost no beaches or places where he might moor the boat for the night.

The Arcturian had ample reason for worry. There was a phosphorescence in the water that was not present in the sea nearer their refuge and which had not been visible in the twilight. It was quite obvious now. His progress was marked by momentary flashes of brilliance where the curragh or his paddle disturbed the glowing vegetation which was the source of the eldritch light. Even the most casual of observers could easily trace his course from it.

At last, he brought his boat in under the shadow of the slightly overhanging cliffs. It was better to remain there and travel with less speed than to risk exposing himself to unfriendly eyes.

Varn Tarl Sogan was not concerned entirely with human foes. His receptors were open to receive any impressions originating on the shore or from the water around him. Omrai's night, though seemingly quiet, teemed with life. Even at the coastline and immediately beyond, there were many more and many more varied creatures than he had been able to detect by day. He knew it must be the same farther inland beyond the point where his mind could reach.

These animals were bolder than their diurnal cousins. Those who sensed him showed a wary curiosity rather than fear. There was caution in them, to be sure. They respected humankind and its tools, but they also knew that night was their domain, that they held the advantage here.

Barak had told the off-worlder as much and had described a few of the more common nocturnal species. He had said that most of them were innocuous, but that did not mean all were, and Sogan was well aware that he must depend for the great part on his own recently acquired skills and on this strange talent of his for his safety.

There were no waves of hostility at least. The multipode, as the boy had named the beast which had so nearly slain him, was a creature of the light.

Varn was glad of that. Hatred of that magnitude coupled with the potent venom and the cunning to use it well made a singularly horrifying combination to throw against a man alone on an alien world.

The Arcturian became aware of a growing restlessness in the creatures on the shore. There was a high wind, and he knew a moment of fear. Was the sea-cold coming in again?

No. It was not that kind of feeling, although the ocean was somehow involved.

Some of Omrai's denizens were moving back, away from the coast. Others were eagerly pressing forward until they were almost at the water's edge. He was receiving an entirely different set of impressions from those he had read earlier. There had been a complete and sudden change in the species representation along the whole of the coast. It was a voluntary movement, he reasoned. No mere territorial change would have been so radical; it would have come gradually, a slow blending of animals from the different areas.

He would have preferred to halt then and watch whatever was to come from some concealed beach, but that was not possible. The war prince kept every sense alert. Not knowing what to expect, he must be prepared to meet all things.

Varn Tarl Sogan still pressed on, not lessening his pace any further but striving to mask the sound of his passage as much as possible.

He came at last upon a place that might someday become one of the beaches that were a feature of the coast nearer to Barak's cabin. Now it was merely a shallow spot at the foot of the cliff. High boulders rose out of the water in a natural dam that held the sand in place.

Sogan hesitated only a moment before maneuvering his curragh through the narrow space between two of the rocks.

He was filled with a nameless relief. It was dark in there, and he felt secure for the first time since he noticed the changes in the onshore patterns.

He remained for ten minutes. Twenty. The excitement around him was reaching a fever intensity. Whatever caused it was not far distant now.

Varn froze suddenly and sat very still. Had he heard something? His ears strained, trying to catch again what had seemed to be a sound. Aye, there was something out there, something that lay just behind the horizon and seemed to reach past the full length of it.

His mind could pick up nothing. Either no living thing was responsible or it was beyond or below his ability to contact.

Sogan's breath caught. The sea along the horizon seemed to boil. The turbulence rushed inland with startling speed. He watched, fascinated, as the water turned from the dark blue of Omrai's night to blood red, lit momentarily from below by the ghostly glow of the already shredding vegetation.

As it neared, he realized this red tide was actually a hundred billion swimming creatures, all caught in the mad frenzy of terror.

The shallowing water slowed them. The school knew its danger, and a soundless wail seemed to rise from it, a wail the man was unable to receive but could almost physically feel.

A shriek! Black clouds swept over the horizon, and wave after wave of flying things filled all the visible sky. With them came a hunger, a single-minded urge to feed and the excitement of finding prey at hand such as he had experienced in the ravager horde on Visnu of Brahmin. This issued from minds many times higher on the intelligence scale, and as it smote into him, almost overpowering every thought and sensation of his own, he knew within himself all the dread of the school.

The airborne hunters hovered a moment over the terrified swimmers, then dived as a single creature.

The ocean writhed in the death anguish of the school. The man watched in a kind of hypnosis of horror as the water around him turned a deep pink from the vast amounts of blood suddenly released into it.

He shook his head, as if denying what was taking place in the sea before him. He had seen the violence of the wild in the past, on Visnu and in Mirelle's vile fungus, but never before had he witnessed such abandon, such an orgy of death, even when perpetrated by his own species.

A kill-maddened scream warned him of his own danger. He had a glimpse of a huge, scaled body supported by membrane wings, of gaping jaws filled with row upon row of ripping, crushing teeth, before he dived, flipping the curragh over his head for a shield.

The creature struck hard. It did not leave at once but tore at the strong, wet wood in its frustration.

By some miracle, perhaps because her size prevented the winged beast from bringing its powerful jaws fully to bear, the boat held firm.

After what seemed an eternity, the hunter gave up the fruitless work and returned to the richer harvest in the open sea.

Sogan's feet reached bottom, and he straightened a little. The water was only waist-deep here. By crouching low and keeping the curragh over him, he could watch the slaughter without again exposing himself.

To his relief, the writhing mass did not come closer to the shore. A few thousand individuals were forced into the shallows, but most of the survivors at last turned and fled back into the deeps.

His own refuge remained safe. The approach to it was narrow and complicated, and only a few of the exhausted creatures worked their way through to the place where he stood. Most of these were injured; many were obviously dying.

Finally, it ended. The school was gone, and the hunters followed it back over the horizon whence they both had come.

Varn Tarl Sogan stood up. There was an instant of marvelous agony as his muscles relaxed from the cramped, unnatural position in which he had crouched, and he allowed himself the pleasure of the release.

It was only for a moment. The strong wind of the earlier night was still present, and he was soon shivering violently. All sense of well-being left him. He must find shelter, must dry his clothes out at once, or die.

The Arcturian was frankly frightened. The elements would soon finish him, and if they did not, there were other perils to be faced, or there would be very shortly.

He was reasonably secure from another attack from the air now, but he was standing in a sea that must be a loadstone to every predator in Omrai's vast ocean.

He looked about him. The cliff was high here, but it was rugged and pitted, offering good holds to a climber. There should be caves beyond its crest or at least some hollow where he could build a fire.

Varn secured the curragh to one of the high rocks very near the cliff, knowing it would not be damaged in the tideless sea, then he turned once more to study the cliff. He was more thorough this time as he scanned the scarred stone, noting every possible hold. The worst part would be the first few feet where the stones were wet and overgrown, he decided. He could take a serious fall there.

The Arcturian settled his pack on his shoulders and sprang, putting as much of his strength as he could into the jump. The soft bottom and the water cut the force of his leap, and he did not gain much altitude. It was enough. His arms closed around a dry prong of stone. With the help of that hold, he was able to pull himself up beyond the wet area to a more secure ledge.

This was technically a more difficult ascent than the slope leading to Barak's cabin, but he found it much easier. The distance was considerably shorter, and he was now fully accustomed to Omrai's gravity.

Sogan soon reached the top and scrambled over it. A short search produced what he wanted, a low cave, sheltered and dry. He inspected it, first with mind and then physically, for sign of occupation. Finding nothing, he hurriedly gathered a supply of fuel and built up a fine fire. The heat from it quickly spread through the small chamber.

Varn Tarl Sogan relaxed for the first time since beginning the climb. He had made it, but just barely. His clothes were already frozen.

He stripped off the stiff garments and wrapped his blanket about himself while they thawed and dried. It was too cold to remain unclothed even with the good fire to warm his lair.

The former Admiral kept his weapons near him. The night had become very quiet. The excited touches he had received before the school came in were gone now. The creatures who had transmitted them had most probably moved to a gentler area where the cliffs were lower and where beaches of sorts existed.

He could not be certain all had done so, and he could not depend completely on his talent to warn him. It had failed him utterly with the school and with the flying things that followed it until they were all but upon him. The off-worlder had little liking for the thought of being discovered here, essentially trapped, by some creature or pack half mad with bloodlust. It was necessary that he remain within the cave awhile yet, but it could well be his death to be penned there without an escape exit.

He prepared a light meal from his rations and had begun to eat it when his heart leaped painfully. Another mind touched his, very curious and very close. Sogan looked up, his blaster in his hand and set to kill. A pair of bright eyes watched him from out of the night. There was no hostility here, merely puzzlement and even amusement at his startled reaction. He lowered the weapon.

Varn smiled despite himself and endeavored to project his

goodwill. The response was immediate, and a small animal moved into the circle of light. It was about six inches high and was covered with a short coat of soft cream-white fur. The hairs on the head and long tail were feathered and thick. These were of a slightly brighter shade of white than the rest of its small body.

It walked up to the fire without any hesitation and sat about a foot from the man, studying him with its bright, green eyes.

The Omrain animal apparently decided this stranger was to be trusted. It curled up into a tight ball, the whole of its body covered by its tail, and promptly fell into a deep sleep.

Sogan, for his part, was charmed by the delightful little creature. Until now, his experience with Omrai's wildlife had been less than pleasant, but this visitor caused him to revise his former judgment somewhat.

He tested his uniform. The material had dried, and it was now ready to wear. He dressed but settled down again. He had no way of knowing what the remnants of the carnage might lure in from the deeps, and he judged it wise to let whatever did come eat its fill before he ventured once more out on the water. The curragh would be scant protection against a really large or powerful attacker, and he was not so strong a swimmer that he could hope to outdistance a creature native to Omrai's sea even with the shore fairly close to hand.

The few hours of sleep would refresh him as well. He had long since learned to function on minutes snatched between phases of a mission or a crisis and knew they were not to be wasted.

The war prince lay down with his face to the mouth of the cave. It opened on the east, and he would be awakened by Umbar's first light.

TWENTY

Varn Tarl Sogan woke when the sun-star's rays touched his eyes. He ate quickly and doused the fire, scattering the cold embers throughout the surrounding area so that no one might trace him through this camp, a procedure he had learned from the two Commandos.

The Omrain creature was sitting up when he returned to the cave. It seemed annoyed to discover that the comfortable heat of the fire was gone.

Before he left, Sogan attempted to caution the friendly little animal. It would not always receive so cordial a welcome from his kind. He found there was no need. It apparently possessed a remarkable communicative ability. It had been drawn to him and had entered the cave only because of his welcome for it.

The off-worlder realized he must guard himself more closely. If one of Omrai's creatures had this sensitivity to his thoughts, so might others.

He shivered. The multipodes did, albeit to a lesser extent.

The descent to the curragh was not difficult in the daylight. The Arcturian dropped lightly to the rock to which it was fastened, automatically countering the slide of his body on the wet growth. From there, he released the moorings and boarded the curragh. Maneuvering it out into the open sea took only a few more seconds.

The water plants had suffered terribly during the night. They seemed to have been almost totally destroyed. The ocean surface for as far as he could see was clear of them. Only in a few sheltered places near the cliff did scattered patches remain to begin again the process of colonization.

Sogan noted with some surprise that Omrai's ocean was a vivid, crystal azure. He peered into it. The water was incredibly clear.

Nothing remained on the gray sand of all the creatures that had died here a few hours before.

He frowned slightly. The bottom bore still-fresh marks that seemed to indicate that long, heavy objects had been dragged— or had dragged themselves—across the floor of the sea.

No other sign of disturbance was visible, no mark of turmoil. Even those tracks could be the norm for the littoral seas of Omrai. He had never before seen the bottom.

The war prince had been moving for about three quarters of an hour when he came upon a tiny beach, merely a sandspit, jutting a few feet out from the base of the cliff. It was a vivid red rather than the customary gray, and Umbar's light reflected from it with punishing glare.

His curiosity aroused, he put ashore. The sand was littered with what appeared to be the shards of countless shells. They were very hard, and he trod with care. Even his service boots might not stand up against a sudden slice from one of the sharp, broken edges.

Varn examined several pieces. The breaks were fresh and had been purposely made. The signs of large teeth were plentiful— tokens of the flying things. There were other marks on the shells as well, marks left by teeth that depended on their keenness rather than on strength of jaw to pierce this very hard material. The shells were clean. Not a shred of meat remained on any of them. Now he realized how fortunate he was to have waited out the carnage in the water rather than on a beach and to have left the place almost immediately.

The man remembered with sudden clarity the eagerness with which some of the creatures had approached the shore the previous night. He could all but see them, small animals with sharp teeth to cut through the shell coating and strong, agile bodies that could climb down the steep cliff to the beach below.

He felt suddenly uneasy. How had his comrades weathered the carnage? Those in the cabin would have had no trouble, but what of Islaen and Barak? He could only trust in the Omrain's knowledge to keep them safe. He also wondered what his team's reaction would be. The strand before the cabin would probably be buried in shells. Would they think he was dead?

Speculation was all he had. He could not rightly break silence with the Commando-Colonel or even with those in the cabin merely to ease his curiosity or theirs, at least not until the time came when they might be growing seriously concerned about him.

The Arcturian returned to the curragh. Nothing more was to be learned here. Umbar was well up, and he wanted to continue.

Sogan pushed out onto the open sea once more. He made extraordinarily fast time. The ocean offered little resistance to the curragh now that not even the sea plants remained to hold her back. With the coming of daylight, he no longer had to keep down his pace for fear of missing landmarks or the partly submerged rocks.

It was not a pleasant journey. His position was strained and uncomfortable. The sky was cloudless, and the curragh was open to Umbar's rays, which the water reflected with punishing intensity. He would have taken a painful burn had it not been for the protective silicates Federation scientists had perfected to shield skin against light stronger than it had been prepared by nature to bear.

Shortly after midday, he spotted another sandspit, or the beginnings of one, that had begun to form on a flat, nearly submerged rock.

He hesitated. It was still over a sea mile from the cave where they had hidden the flier, much farther than that overland, but he also knew the coast became even more rugged as it approached the spot where they had set down. This might well be the only landing place anywhere reasonably near.

The war prince beached the curragh and studied the cliff. Ascending it would not be easy. What rock there was, was relatively smooth. The materials comprising the cliff were of a softer type than most he had seen along the coast. This section appeared to receive more shelter from the weather than was usual, and the process of erosion had been considerably slowed.

That could mean danger for a man trying to scale it. Soft soil would not bear weight as did hard stone. Even the rock here might be soft, rotten, ready to crumble under the first pressure. There was some evidence of past slides to lend force to that possibility.

The off-worlder took a length of rope from its place on his pack and fashioned one end into a slip loop. He cast it, pulling the noose tight around an outcropping. He tugged it. The rope held firm, and he put his full weight on it.

A crash. He leaped to one side as the decayed stone crumbled and fell to the beach.

Varn retrieved his rope and tried again, this time catching the loop a little higher than he had on the first attempt. This hold looked firmer. Beyond that point, he should be able to climb without aid. He tested it again, trying the ledge for stress. It held, and he began his ascent.

The Arcturian did not trust the rope, and he strove to remain as independent as possible of it. He succeeded to some extent, but he could not dispense with its help entirely. There were places where other holds simply did not exist, where he was forced to brace his feet against the smooth rock and work his way up along the line.

He came to the site of the slide. There was a considerable amount of loose, gray soil around the scar, and it was hard, tricky work getting over it, since it crumbled under any real pressure. He succeeded in crossing it in the end and gradually made his way up to the place where his rope had caught the outcropping.

His face hardened as his hands closed over it. Reaching this point represented a victory, but it marked the opening of a new challenge as well. From that point on, he would have to go up alone, with no aid or support should his own body's strength or his skill fail him.

The remainder of the climb was no easier than its beginning. The cliff face was rugged and treacherous, and Sogan had to use extreme caution in choosing his holds, particularly when the heartstone was covered. The overlying soil continued to be inclined to slide from him at the slightest pressure.

At last, he reached the summit. He dragged himself over the edge and lay there breathing hard for several minutes. When he was somewhat rested, he freed his rope and started his trek through the woodlands.

It was cool under the shadow of the trees. The touch of the shade felt good against his hot face, and he realized he had taken a burn despite the Federation's silicates.

* * *

It took less time than he had anticipated to reach the flier. Muscles accustomed to Omrain gravity and a foreknowledge of the country had given him greater speed. The Arcturian checked the area carefully before entering the cave. Finding nothing amiss, he went inside. Again, everything was in order.

After camouflaging his trail, he boarded the small vessel and turned back in the direction of the curragh. The flier covered the distance in a matter of minutes. He lowered it to the strand and loaded the tiny boat into it, then brought it up quickly and moved once more under the cover of the trees.

Varn Tarl Sogan did not hurry, although he kept the vessel at a good speed, and the afternoon was well on by the time he reached the mountain where Barak's cabin was concealed.

Here he halted and, activating his communicator, announced his approach.

Once Jake acknowledged his call and told him to come on in, he made the remainder of the run at high planetary speed.

The Commando-Captain was waiting for him at the entrance of the cave. The flier shot inside, braking even as it cleared the door, which was quickly shut behind it. Karmikel helped the newcomer settle the curragh against the hindmost wall and stood back to look at it.

He laughed. "Our fortunes have certainly risen over the past week. We were but baggage aboard the *Free Comet*. Here we command our own fleet."

Sogan's eyes ran from one vessel to the other, resting last upon the curragh, and he laughed as well.

The two men went up to the cabin where Bethe Danlo was keeping watch on the surrounding countryside. There the war prince described his journey and his experience with the red tide. "I see it reached here as well," he concluded. "The beach looked to be red with shells when I made my approach. Did you have any problems?"

The Commando shook his head. "None. We were safe up here, but I confess the thought of ravenous horde feeders of the ravagers' ilk did cross my mind. We certainly didn't envy you."

His words were light, but something of the fear he had felt for the other man touched his voice, enough to cause Sogan to look swiftly at him.

The Arcturian turned away again. "No word from the other two, I suppose?" he asked seemingly casually.

"Nothing." Jake glanced at the window, then back at the former Admiral. "The lack of news is hard on us, but it's probably an indication that they haven't gotten into trouble."

Sogan sighed. "Aye. We shall just have to assume that is the case."

And hope it was true, he thought with a mental shudder.

TWENTY-ONE

BARAK SET A fast pace. He knew this country well and wanted to make good time now, while the trail was easy and the danger light. Impatiently, he signaled for the woman to follow more closely after him.

Islaen smiled as she complied. The Omrain was still young enough to enjoy his temporary superiority over his far-traveled guest.

Their trail turned away from the sea. The inland country was more sheltered than the coastal areas, and the woods soon thickened until they were very much like those the off-worlders had seen their first evening on Omrai.

She welcomed the return of the trees and the cover they afforded. She would feel far more comfortable if they were well hidden when they approached the Big Ship's base.

Night fell, and they made a rough camp. Barak allowed a small fire but warned that they would have none the following evening.

They made their meal of tough dried meat and a hard waybread baked from a flour of finely ground nuts.

The Commando absently shared the last with Bandit, who devoured it with her usual eagerness.

Barak watched them for a few minutes and then timidly offered some of his own ration. To his delight and a little to his surprise, the gurry accepted it with every indication of pleasure.

He scowled then and glared at the Colonel. "You should not have brought that poor, harmless little thing here. It is not her fight."

Islaen shrugged. "She usually goes where we do. You'll find that she keeps out of the way."

She bent to rub the little hen. *You must do so this time, love,* her mind instructed seriously. *Leave us as soon as we reach the danger area. It'll be up to you to report back to Varn if we fall.*

Bandit will protect . . .

No! Your responsibility is to Varn and the others, and to Omrai and the Free Comet. You mustn't fail in that by trying to help us.—That's our work, Little Bandit, yours as much as any of the rest of us. Do you understand?

Bandit understands, she agreed unhappily.

A shadow filled the woman's eyes and more darkly still her mind. *You'll have to help Varn if I don't make it back. He'll need you desperately, no matter what he decides to do.*

Yes, Islaen.

He will see you settled first. Would you adopt Jake or Bethe or return to Jade?

Nooo!

Her feathers started to extend, and Islaen quickly reached out to soothe her. *It's important that we know, love. We're responsible for you, and we both could die. From many causes. It's best if you tell us what you want done.*

The hen calmed herself at the obvious cost of a struggle. *Gurries and goldbeasts both live long, but we can choose again. Bandit would take Jake. Or Bethe.*

Thank you, my Bandit. We'll tell them when we get back, or you'll tell Varn if I forget or can't.

Yes, Islaen.

Don't look so glum. You'll upset Barak. We just should've settled this before, that's all, and it's entirely my fault that we had to be on an active mission before I thought to do it.

Islaen Connor took the first watch. She stood a little way out from the camp, listening for any sign of disturbance in the night.

Her senses were alert, as receptive as was possible for anyone lacking Varn Tarl Sogan's gift. More receptive in one sense, for her mind sought for and could receive news of her own kind even if she had to depend on her lesser senses for information regarding this planet's wildlife.

She turned in the direction of their resting place and shook her head in admiration at the Omrain's woodcraft. She was only a few feet from the camp and knew full well where it was, but no sign of it betrayed them. The fire was so banked that none of its glow spread, and Omrai's wood helped them in that it burned without smoke or odor.

She shivered. The temperature had dropped rapidly once Umbar set and was only now beginning to stabilize for the night. It was not low enough to be a danger in itself, but she was not at all looking forward to the nights to come.

Her watch closed without incident, yet the Commando-Colonel was uneasy when she woke her companion. For nearly an hour now, there had been a constant scurry of living things through the woodlands around the camp. This was so strange for Omrai's normally silent creatures that she told the boy about it even before he was fully awake.

Barak frowned and motioned for the off-worlder to be still. He listened a long while. "The Death Flight comes," he said softly. "We have nothing to fear so far inland, but woe to anyone who ventures out on the sea this night."

Despite his continued assurances of their safety, the Omrain gathered a large supply of fuel and kept a strong fire burning for the remainder of the night while busy feet hurried back and forth on every side of them.

When morning came, Barak carefully broke apart the fire even as would a Commando and scattered its ashes among the roots of the trees where they would quickly be absorbed. Islaen finished the restoration of their campsite to its former state. They might be pursued on their return, and they could ill afford to leave any sign of their route behind them.

The day passed quietly. The woods were very silent now, showing no sign of whatever had disturbed them the night before.

The woman found herself wishing for Varn's company. The Arcturian might have told her why the animals were so still. Were they frightened by them or by the proximity of the pirates? Or was this quiet merely natural to them? The creatures of Omrai had given very little sign of their presence since her unit planeted, and someone less knowledgeable about the ways of wild things than she might well have thought no fauna existed here at all. Still, she could not explain their utter withdrawal now, and she would have sold a large part of a rich planet to know the answer to it.

* * *

Night fell, quietly, without tumult. Again, they made camp, but, although they were both tired, neither slept very soundly.

Barak was growing increasingly more nervous. He had never come this close to the Big Ship before, and all the terror in which he held her crowded into his mind. It spoke well of his courage that he bore his discomfort without complaint and made no suggestion that they turn back.

His unease communicated itself to the Colonel, and she, too, found herself listening for sounds in the night. Islaen Connor had seen too many worlds, had trodden too many strange and dangerous paths, to ignore feelings of this intensity.

She considered moving only after dark but rejected that course on several grounds.

Barak knew in general where the Big Ship was located, but he was unfamiliar with this area. A trail he could follow with ease during the day could be lost at night, and her own map, which she carried concealed, was not so detailed that it would bring them quickly and precisely to the clearing. Once in its vicinity, they would lose precious time and maybe betray themselves in searching for the wreck.

Even if they did find her, the vessel might be guarded by sophisticated alarms. Islaen could not be certain she would be able to discover and disconnect them all in the dark, coming in cold like this, and the young Omrain, although amazingly woodcrafty, knew nothing of such mechanical devices.

Lastly, she probably would not be able to see well enough in Omrai's black night to complete her mission satisfactorily. They would only be forced to wait until daylight, and every moment they remained near the base would increase their danger.

Morning found them already on the move. The Commando wanted to reach their destination and be away again as quickly as was humanly possible.

They were very close to the pirates. The woods were crossed by well-used paths created by men unversed in wilderness skills who felt no need to conceal their presence.

Through occasional breaks in the trees, they were soon able to discern what appeared to be a large clearing in the distance.

The two scouts approached slowly, carefully, from what they judged to be the least frequented section of the woods. Neither wished to be surprised by a work or hunting party while they spied out the pirate camp.

They moved with painstaking care until they lay at last on the very edge of the invader's base.

The Commando-Colonel's breath froze in her breast as she stared in silent horror. The clearing was indeed large, and most of it was filled by a deep-space vessel of immense proportions, a battleship, four thousand-class, one of the true space-permanent warships that were the pride of both Navies. Never before had she seen or heard of anything approaching this size on a planet's surface, and of a certainty, her master would never have set her down voluntarily.

More amazing even than her size was her design. She was circular and was crowned by a large command spike rising from her center. This last could be withdrawn into the ship's body during battle.

The Federation unit was fortunate—if the presence of this monster did not render that term laughable—in that there would be no problem in recognizing their targets when the time came for attack. The exhaust ducts and various firing positions were clearly visible on the hull and made excellent points of reference. Her unusual form did not alter that.

There was no shine left to the starship. She had been too long planet-bound for that, but the hull looked sound. Whatever damage she had taken in the crash had since been repaired.

Those injuries appeared to have been considerable. The entire section over the engine and drive tubes, from what she could see of it, had been covered with plates of a very different type from the original smooth skin of the battleship. These were pitted and scarred in varying degrees, solar steel from many different vessels, little if any of it first-rate.

The remnants of the cannibalized ships lay along the perimeter of the clearing.

Men moved around the vessel. Most were uniformed and represented somewhat less than three quarters of the ship's normal complement. The crash had indeed taken a deadly toll.

Others, not many of them, were working with the crew, alone or under their supervision, men clad in spacer's dress, most of it quite ragged. They looked well fed and well treated, as would have to be the case. Slaves were scarce here, if Barak was to be believed.

The Commando studied them. They seemed to work readily

enough and without the necessity of guards. Collaborators? Or perhaps they had merely given up hope, died in spirit. She had seen that tragedy before this.

She automatically pressed deeper into the shadows as a group carrying a heavy beam from one of the most recently captured ships passed near her.

Islaen Connor frowned. Their blank eyes and oddly lax faces told that this was not voluntarily labor, after all. The slaves had either been utterly broken, broken as she had not believed possible in anything still retaining humanity, or they had been heavily drugged, although that was not their captors' habit, nor did it seem likely that such supplies could still remain after a ten-year isolation from any re-outfitting. Such vessels rarely carried them at all.

Her mind tentatively reached out. There was no response, none whatsoever, from any member of the work party, which included none of the crew. A shiver ran through her spirit. It was as if they were in truth no longer human.

Suddenly, one of the captives jerked away from the others. "No more!" he croaked.

It seemed to cost him a tremendous effort to speak even this much.

No one made a move toward him, although several of the crewmen were near enough to hear him.

His face contorted, then his expression cleared, and he fell forward. Islaen knew instinctively, even before her mind reached out to confirm it, that he was dead.

She realized with an inexplicable sensation of horror that the episode had taken less than three minutes' time.

Barak's hand closed over her arm, pulling her away. The Commando went with him, fighting an almost uncontrollable desire to flee headlong from this place, fighting to keep low, to conceal the slight trail they left.

After an eternity, they felt they were well enough away to halt for a moment's needed rest.

"We could not have remained longer," the boy explained. "More of the shipmen would surely have come, and we would have been discovered."

Islaen nodded. "What happened to him?"

"The sickness. Sooner or later, it strikes all their slaves. Something they carry, I ween."

"All die?"

He nodded. "Every one. My own people are stricken within hours. That is why they no longer bother to take us alive when they chance upon any of us. We are not worth the trouble to them."

They did not remain there long. Anxiety pressed them on. Islaen Connor, especially, was driven by a deep urgency. She must get this intelligence not only to her comrades but to the *Free Comet* and to the Navy as well, and as quickly as possible.

She had been correct in telling Marta Florr that something very big might be building on Omrai of Umbar, but nothing in her maddest nightmare could have led her to envision the true situation. She trembled to think what might and would happen if that thing lifted before the Federation moved to defend the planets in and near Quandon Sector.

TWENTY-TWO

DESPITE THEIR HASTE, the scouts made little better time than they had on the previous day. The need for caution held them to a slower pace than they liked, but the delay had to be accepted.

They kept going all that night and most of the following day. By midmorning, the extreme fear of discovery could be abandoned, and they traveled normally after that through these more familiar treelands.

Twilight came, and clouds began to gather, gradually building until it seemed that the sky would break under their weight. The pair continued on as long as the light remained. When that finally failed, they stopped in the most sheltered place they could find.

The Omrain constructed a very low tent from the rough hide blankets he had brought with him. Its entrance faced downslope, and he weighted it in such a manner that no wind could take it. The Commando did not question him. If Barak felt there was need for this, and the ordered haste in his movements gave testimony to that, she could only believe him. Islaen took no active part in the preparations. This was obviously a familiar task to the Omrain youth, and she would better serve their cause by keeping a careful guard against pursuit.

When Barak volunteered to take the first watch, the woman accepted. She was tired to the depth of her being.

Although they had given no thought to their physical needs these past hours and little in the days before, she realized the weariness riding her was as much an exhaustion of spirit as of body. The knowledge she possessed—and must live to transmit—stayed like a white-hot spear in her mind. Even now, it held her awake and so restless that Bandit, who did not comprehend the intensity of the trouble on her human, protested sharply at the continued disturbance of her own rest.

At last, she used her will to calm herself and almost immediately drifted into sleep.

A searing flash of fire and an almost simultaneous explosion shocked the guerrilla awake. Islaen's hand grasped her blaster even as consciousness returned to her.

The slanting roof of their shelter buckled, strained at its fastenings, as it was struck by a great force of water.

Now she understood why Barak had been so careful about setting the entrance on a steep downward slope. The rough tent would have been flooded in any other position.

She lay back again. It was dry and reasonably comfortable in here. She would trust in the Omrain's skill and take her rest while she could.

A cold hand touched her, and Islaen sat up. The rain was still falling as heavily as ever.

Barak squatted beside her. He was soaked. Water ran from his clothing, forming rivulets on the ground.

"Your watch." His eyes were laughing. They became serious in a moment. "Wake me when the rain stops. At once."

The Commando crawled outside, leaving Bandit, who for once offered no protest at being left behind, inside the shelter.

The sound of the storm had not belied its fury. The rain struck her with such force that she had to struggle to stand erect and found it difficult even to breathe.

She located a place on the leeward of a large boulder. Here she could get some protection from the wind if not from the rain.

Islaen realized that, apart from her mental hunting, she could keep only a token guard under these conditions, but she took comfort from the fact that nothing else, human, beast, or machine, could move against them this night.

An hour passed. Two. The force of the downpour wavered, then it cleared altogether.

Islaen Connor waited a few minutes. When it did not start up again, she awakened her companion.

They immediately began dismantling the camp and concealed the evidence that it had ever been there.

Barak's movements showed a new haste. He explained that

the shipmen usually went out on patrol and ranged farther afield than normal after such storms, as if they feared that the violence of the elements might give cover to potential assailants. The Omrain wanted to be safely hidden in the cabin in case the interlopers should get that far.

The Noreenan woman needed little urging. They traveled at a killing pace, taking advantage of every natural path or break they could find, until they at last reached the foot of their home mountain a little before dark.

The Commando-Colonel sent her mind out in search of her consort and found him almost immediately. He had been holding himself open to receive such a call and welcomed her eagerly. *Islaen! Praise the Spirit of Space! What did you learn?*

Plenty, she told him grimly. *It's real bad, Varn—let it hold until I come up. I don't want to have to go through it twice.*

As you will.

She could feel the steeling in him, an instinctive girding for battle. He knew the tone she had used. *Keep a good watch,* she instructed. *Barak says patrols come far out after storms. We don't want to be spotted here.*

Aye, Colonel.

Islaen tightened the shields on her mind, all save those permitting communication. A new fear filled her as she began the ascent. How would Varn react when he learned what she had discovered? Would he be able to help them or be willing to do so? Would he turn against them altogether? His old love and loyalty were unshaken despite what had been done to him, and she recalled how even the destruction of those derelicts on Mirelle had troubled him. If he did choose to try to block her, would she detect his treachery in time and then be able to act against him?

Her spirit writhed in shame and disgust at her lack of faith in the man. The War was over, and Varn Tarl Sogan was sworn to the Federation's cause. He would uphold it, whatever the cost to himself.

The deepening shadows and the low, erratic course the two scouts maintained kept them nearly invisible against the steep slope, but still neither of them breathed freely until they gained the shelter of the cabin.

Once inside, Islaen Connor reported what she had seen and

repeated Barak's warning about the possibility of a patrol entering this area within the next few days.

Jake seemed not to hear that last. "An Arcturian battleship," he whispered.

There was a faint tremor in his voice, but he would not have disowned his fear had he been aware of it. It was all too well founded.

The crew could not know the War had ended. To them, this was a hostile Sector, and they would act accordingly. If that vessel lifted now, and the Colonel reported her to be spaceworthy at least externally, she would annihilate half Quandon Sector before she was finally halted.

Sogan had gone pale. He withdrew from the others, moved away from them entirely, as if he could not bear to meet their eyes or endure the touch of their gaze at all. "This illness struck after the man refused further service?" he demanded suddenly.

"Aye. There was a kind of triumph on him even as he died."

The former Admiral stared into the fire, seemingly oblivious to his comrades.

The Noreenan woman went to him. "I don't think it's a plague, Varn, just some kind of reaction to the drugs. In that sense, we needn't fear . . ."

"No chemicals have been used. Those slaves are mind-controlled."

A deathly silence fell over the room.

"That's not possible!" the Commando-Colonel hissed after a moment. Her voice was thick with horror at the thing he suggested, this monstrous corruption of the power she herself possessed.

"Is it not?"

He looked at her briefly, then faced away again, his head bowed in a shame so thick that no mind talent was required to read it. "Could you see the Arcturians' shoulder insignia?" Bandit had already given him the information he requested, but he did not want to betray that fact before Barak of Omrai. Everything else must come out now, but her secret, at least, he could still try to shield.

"Aye."

"The ship is the *Empire's Glory*?"

She nodded. "Aye, she is."

"Then her master is close kin of mine, the son of my father's only brother. If the weakness in our line stems from our grandsire and not from my father or myself as I had believed, then Aleke could be altered even as I."

"But you never enslaved anyone!" Bethe Danlo exclaimed half in anger at the accusation he seemed to be laying against himself. "Except for Islaen, you can't deal with human minds at all."

"No," he agreed "I can only touch with certain levels of animalkind and maybe, if Islaen is right, sense trouble in an upcoming assignment. She, in turn, can intercept emotion, not read minds, and she can search a body for injury." He frowned. "On Visnu, she also transmitted in such a manner as to cover our entry into the spaceport . . ."

"I had forgotten that," the Colonel murmured.

"As had I until now.—Who knows what other forms such ability can take? In Aleke Tarl Sogan, it would be very likely to turn toward some dark road. He is a hard man and a cruel one in the sense that he is indifferent to the hardship and death he must inflict in order to gain his own will, be it upon our enemies, the menials serving him, or on our soldiers. For that reason, he has been held to the rank of Captain despite his birth and other abilities. My people do not encourage the like and have never tolerated anyone so marred in a major office. It is too often an indication of other weaknesses besides."

His voice was low. His comrades had to know all this, yet he felt soiled. No Arcturian betrayed the weaknesses of another of his race, much less blood of his own, before representatives of another people. "He would be quite capable of doing all that seems to have occurred here if, under the pressure of exile, the power to work it suddenly woke in him, even as mine did in me."

Jake took a step toward him. "Sogan, you have nothing to do with any of this."

Islaen silenced him with a sharp shake of her head. She could feel the war prince cringe, but she forced herself to remain quiet. Varn would accept nothing from any of them, but she knew he would fight his way out of this himself. They needed him, and the habit of responsibility was too deeply ingrained in him for him to refuse its demands now.

Barak of Omrai stared openly at the dark-eyed man. He had never suspected that the off-worlder was not of one kind with his companions. All of them differed so greatly from his own race that he had seen only those basic collective differences from

Omrai's norm rather than the more subtle ones which marked each as an individual.

How should he have guessed those accursed shipmen were this Sogan's people? His guest sported no close-cropped beard. He wore no scarlet uniform. He did no killing with the weapons he carried as if they were extensions of his body.

None of that mattered now. Nothing mattered. "Omrai is dead," he said dully. "No one can fight such a power."

The Arcturian forced his own concerns aside. They faced a monstrous challenge on Omrai of Umbar, and his would have to be a crucial role in meeting it. "No. Your people are strong, Barak, if they can break free so quickly, well before any of the off-world captives."

"Break free to die," the boy replied bitterly.

"They die human.—That battleship has been on-world for ten years. I know your enemies, lad. If they have not utterly subjected Omrai to their will in that time, it is because they cannot do so. They represent a far greater threat to the rest of the Sector than to your people."

"What can we do?" the Omrain asked in a low voice. The sudden change, the determination, in Sogan's manner both awed him and rekindled hope in his heart.

"Make certain that the *Empire's Glory* is no longer a danger either here or in the starlanes beyond."

Barak of Omrai studied him closely for a moment, then he straightened. "I will keep watch outside. This you will want to discuss amongst yourselves."

Islaen Connor looked at him with new respect. She knew the boy would have preferred to be a party to their deliberations and, indeed, had some right to be as his people's leader. His offer was a sign of his maturity and his ability to read a situation and the people involved in it.

"What if a patrol shows up?"

"There are places in plenty for one person to hide."

No sooner had he left them than the Colonel turned to Sogan. "Can this be done, Varn?"

"You Commandos are trained to take out Arcturian battle-craft, not me," he replied testily.

"We've never had to go up against anything like this, and you know it!"

He took a deep breath. "Aye. I am sorry, Islaen." He turned away from them to face the fire once more. "All we have is speculation. Give me a moment to try to put my thoughts together."

"Take whatever time you need. We're all feeling our way."

Bandit can help?

The question was very different from the gurry's usual declaration of her ability and right, and it sounded directly in Islaen's closed mind so that only she and not the war prince heard it.

Maybe, love, she responded in kind. *This is different from our usual troubles.*

Islaen?

Aye? What's bothering you, Little Bandit?

Varn didn't hurt the captives?

No, of course not!

Why is he . . .

The woman sighed in her heart. *That would be too difficult to explain now. Just bear with him, and don't question him about it.*

Bandit won't!

Sogan left the fire and began pacing, as if the stone floor were the bridge of a battleship. "We should be able to go after the ship, or Islaen and I should. Our shields are strong, and we are well accustomed to wielding them by now."

He eyed his consort speculatively. "Our minds are nearly always shielded to some extent, instinctively so, beyond the defenses we sometimes consciously raise around ourselves. I suppose neither of us could live easily knowing our innermost thoughts were open for the other's reading. Whatever the reason, we are well accustomed to our guards. That should serve our cause now."

The Commando-Colonel realized with a start that he was right. She had not even been aware of the barriers she did in fact keep over her mind until now. "You think that will be enough to defend us?"

He nodded. "Aye," he said slowly. "It should unless we are forced into an actual confrontation and maybe even then. Aleke will never have encountered any sort of shields blocking his approach, much less guards consciously raised and controlled. We shall have to be careful about giving him an opening, but we should be able to hold against him, or to hide from his searching at the least."

His eyes looked out beyond her, through her, for a moment.

"We have no idea of the exact nature of his abilities or the extent of his power, but rest assured that they are finite. If luck is with us, we should be able to get in and attack before he becomes aware of us, though it will be best if we two take the bulk of the work on ourselves. Karmikel, Bethe, you will do well to stay back entirely or to withdraw quickly once the fighting begins. He can probably overcome only one person at a time, and we do not know how long it takes for him to gain control, but it could be deadly to all of us if any of our number were broken."

Neither protested. The very transmissions of their minds, which they were powerless to control, could betray the party, as those of potential assailants had often betrayed an ambush or planned assault to Islaen Connor.

"Barak might serve better," Jake ventured. "You say he's shielded in part."

Sogan glanced at his consort. "Islaen?"

"I'd been thinking about that," the Colonel agreed. "As long as he keeps a hold on his emotions, he's almost impossible to pick up. At least for me."

"Maybe I am wrong altogether," the former Admiral said wearily. "Most of this is guesswork based on a very singular premise. If I am playing the fool . . ."

"If you are, you are," the demolitions expert told him. "We'll praise the Spirit of Space for it should things turn out that way, but I don't think you're off. It all fits too well, even with that strange transmission from the *Minotaur*. They wouldn't have wanted any trace of an Arcturian accent—no ship'd ever surrender to them then—so they'd have to use one of their captives and make a tape, since they couldn't chance having him with them during battle. Words forced from the throat of a mind slave rather than spoken naturally would logically sound a little off, jerky and uneven like those did."

"We must assume you're right," Islaen said. "Our mission doesn't hang upon that, fortunately. It will add a new caution to our efforts but not really alter our basic plan of action."

She stopped herself. "Sorry, Varn. I didn't mean to take over on you like that."

He gave her the ghost of a smile. "Go on, Colonel. I was just supplying you with information, such as it is. As I said before, this is your work."

"We'll all have to be involved to some extent," she said, to herself as well as to her companions. "Barak, too, though I hate risking him again. We'll want a guide to take us back there. I could find the clearing, but not without some delay, and I want to strike as quickly as possible once we do start out." Her mouth hardened. "It's not going to be easy, not with the matériel we've got on hand . . ."

"Bethe, can that atomic cannon be fired?" Sogan asked suddenly, then stopped himself and quickly described their discovery of the hidden passage and cave and his retrieval of the flier.

The demolitions expert waited until he finished and then shook her head in answer to his question.

"Not yet. I haven't been able to work on it."

The Colonel caught Varn's idea, and her excitement mounted. "We have a little time yet. Can it be done?"

"The controls are crumbling, the screens are rotten, and the materials in the firing core have degenerated into space only knows what mongrel compounds, but, aye, it can be made to fire—once—if I cannibalize the rocket's fuel supply to power it."

"What about our own extra disks?"

"Not in that gun. It'll be unstable even with the low-strength power it was designed to take."

"Do what you must."

Islaen's mind raced ahead. They had two objectives: to render the Arcturian battleship harmless and to warn the *Free Comet* about the storms that all too frequently rent Omrai's near-space before she came near enough to be caught up in one of them. According to Barak, the early signs of their gathering were minor and were likely to be overlooked or ignored unless a ship were alerted to their significance.

No, that was not all. A third burden rested on them as well. They had to get word to the Navy of the danger waiting on-world and nearly ready to lift again to the grief of the whole Sector if her party failed to neutralize it.

They should succeed against the *Empire's Glory,* she judged, or they should if they could avoid falling victim to this Aleke Tarl Sogan's essentially unknown mind-weapon. She had no doubt of her team's basic ability to take out the starship if they planned well and fortune flew with and not against them, even if they might not survive to appreciate their success themselves.

The second phase of their mission was the more difficult and must depend entirely upon the skill of one man. Jake Karmikel would have to take the flier and try to reach the Patrol cruiser with the dark intelligence they had gained.

The former Admiral would have been the better choice for that task, but the power he possessed made it essential that he accompany the attack party. That should present no difficulty. Jake might not be Sogan's equal in space, but he was good, very good, and Islaen Connor knew that her trust and Quandon Sector's were well placed in him.

TWENTY-THREE

THE FEDERATION PARTY set to work at once, Karmikel and Bethe Danlo on the cannon, the Colonel and Sogan preparing their gear and what plans they could form for their encounter with the Arcturian warship. Barak held the guard for them.

There was no confusion, and soon most of their preparations had been made.

Nothing remained after that but the wait, a fairly long one, since the power cells of the cannon required a complete recharging, a process the demolitions expert estimated would not be completed before morning.

Varn Tarl Sogan kept as much apart as possible from his comrades. This quiet time was hard for him, worse than for any of the others, although he knew it rode them as well. With no pressing detail or duty on which to focus his attention, other thoughts and memories rose to fill and cruelly lash his mind.

The explanation he had proffered for the captives' quiescent behavior was a bizarre one, and had it not been for his own strange gift and the close blood tie between him and the master of that ship, he would never have dared suggest it, nor would any of these others have considered the idea.

He still could be wrong. Drugs or torture or constant, brutal labor could reduce the spirit until little or none of it remained alive. As for the slave's death, sickness could be responsible, something the off-worlders had brought to Omrai with them. It was not Quandon Fever despite that virus' ability to jump the immunization shots occasionally, particularly in its more virulent forms. That did not slay so quickly or in the manner Islaen had described, but some other disease could have done it, a new one requiring physical contact with the invaders for its spread. Such an illness could also have accounted for the crew's heavy losses as readily as the crash.

The war prince did not believe that, but still the possibility kept looming up in his mind, accusing him. He had never felt any warmth toward Aleke and had intensely disliked his treatment both of his menials and of the men serving beneath him. Was that disapproval so coloring his reading of the present situation that he was falsely laying this abomination against his kinsman?

Even if it was entirely true, what about the crew of the *Empire's Glory*? They were but soldiers acting as they believed circumstances warranted. They would not realize the War was over. It had been fought for decades before they crashed, and although the Arcturian Empire was hard-pressed at that time, conditions had not so far deteriorated as to indicate that defeat might be imminent. That had still seemed inconceivable then.

They no longer had the right to fight, but neither did they deserve death, to become the last victims of that awesome bloodletting, and he knew full well that many would die when the Commando-Colonel attacked. When he attacked.

His eyes closed. He was sworn to the Federation, but other, older oaths held him as well, oaths he had never recanted despite his condemnation and exile. Was he to play false to them now, betray his own . . . ?

The walls of the cabin seemed to close in about him. Varn swung the entrance to the passageway open with unnecessary force and fled the room, pausing only long enough to say that he wished to check out the flier himself.

He hurried down the passageway to the cave, which was mercifully empty. The cold had driven Bethe up a short while before. Her actual work was finished, and she had elected to delay the final systems check until morning when she would be able to see how the ancient system ran with full power cells. She would have had to redo the test then anyway.

Whatever the reason for it, the Arcturian was glad to find the place vacant. He could not have borne the inevitable questions now.

He slipped outside and stood in the sheltered area formed by the mouth of the hollow, breathing deeply of the clean air. Omrai was very still, very unlike his own tormented soul.

He felt Islaen's call and angrily closed off his receptors. This he could not let her know! She would see him as a traitor then, even as he saw himself.

Sogan swore, raged, at himself. He had been a fool, a stark madman, to imagine one like him could build a life among his race's direst enemies, to actually think that he would never be faced with such a challenge to his loyalties, a challenge he must fail, no matter the course he chose to follow.

He ground his fist into the rough stone. The pain sobered him, and he drew himself under control.

The former Admiral moved away from the shadows and strode out into the glen until he stood very near the edge of the ocean.

Was it treason to prevent that battleship from dishonoring, albeit unwittingly, the Emperor's treaty? Men would die in that preventing, but if they were not stopped from lifting, others would perish, innocent colonists whose lives were his charge. He had no choice even under his own hard code but to defend them.

He remained there a few minutes longer, looking out on the sea until he felt that his composure was restored, at least to the point that he could act as a man and an officer before the others.

Only then did he realize that the communicator on his left wrist was clamoring for his attention. His shields dropped, and his consort's mind burst into his.

Varn, a patrol! Get to cover!

He started back for the cave at a run.

Too late! Even as he turned, he caught a flash of movement, and a red-uniformed figure rounded the sharp bend formed by the mountain's arm.

The two men stood motionless a long instant, then the Yeoman's hand tightened on his blaster.

Sogan threw himself aside as the weapon discharged. His own blaster was in his hand, but he knew he would be defeated in the very firing of it. The other shipmen would know full well that no native Omrain possessed any such arms. The hunt would soon be up and their hope of a surprise assault on the *Empire's Glory* ended.

Die, you bastard! he thought savagely. *You have killed us all!*

The hatred surged out from him, and in the next instant, Varn Tarl Sogan found himself in the Yeoman's mind.

That clear contact lasted only for a moment, then the will to slay plunged into that part of the other which sustained his life.

The newcomer clutched tightly to Varn's mind, holding on to him in a nightmare grasp of pure despair. Even as death claimed him, his grip did not loosen but rather was wrenched away in his dissolution with well-nigh inconceivable violence.

Sogan's head all but exploded with pain that held and expanded until all the universe seemed comprised of it, pain and the horror of what he had done. He did not hear the shipman groan or see him drop lifeless to the ground.

Karmikel flung open the outer door of the cave. "Quick, you fool!" he hissed. "Drag him inside before any of the others come snooping around!"

The dark-haired man turned slowly, as if in a trance. He made no move either to obey or to return to their hiding place himself.

Jake saw his stricken expression and the dull, lifeless eyes, and his own eyes closed. Battle shock? Varn Tarl Sogan?

A soldier's strength was little defense against that. It could hit anyone when his resilience was badly enough down. Being forced to destroy his own like this must simply have proven too much on top of everything else he had suffered, pushed even the war prince too far . . .

He reached Sogan in a few quick strides and put a steadying arm around his shoulder. "Come on, friend," he said gently. "Let's get back inside."

The Arcturian offered no resistance and came readily although seemingly with little realization of what he did. Scarcely had they gained the cave than he swayed and would have fallen had it not been for the other's support.

Jake eased him onto the rear seat of the flier and went back outside.

It was several minutes before he returned. When he did, he carefully sealed the door behind him.

To his surprise, Varn was sitting up. His hands were pressed to his temples, but the intelligence was back in his eyes when he looked up.

"What did you do with him?" he asked, speaking with difficulty, to judge by the tightness of his voice.

"Snapped his neck and made it seem that he'd fallen from the spur. It was tricky making the blaster scar that was left by his bolt look natural, but I think I managed it, well enough to fool his comrades anyway. Luckily, you didn't mark him . . . —Here they come!"

The redhead remained still for some time, then relaxed. "It worked," he said. "They've gone and taken him off with them."

"I killed him," Varn said dully.

"You had no choice . . ."

Karmikel stopped abruptly, suddenly realizing what Sogan meant, why there had been no visible wounds on the dead man's body. "With your mind?" he whispered.

"Aye. —Space!" The Arcturian gasped that last as his face contorted in a spasm of agony.

The Commando was beside him in a moment. "He got you, too?"

"I think so . . . Aye!"

Karmikel activated his communicator. "Islaen, Varn's been hit. I don't know how, but it looks bad."

"I know. His mind's sealed, but I can still feel the pain.—The patrol's gone now. Bring him up. That cave's too cold for a wounded man."

Sogan rallied enough to come to his feet. He tried to shrug off the Noreenan's arm, but Jake's hold only tightened. "Forget it, Admiral. You're pretty rocky, and those stairs are treacherous. You won't be able to tell us anything if you break your neck, and if you do, our good Colonel'll probably break mine for letting it happen."

Karmikel half carried the Arcturian up the passage and settled him into the flight chair.

Islaen sat on its edge as she bent over him. "What happened?" she asked, forcing herself to speak quietly, although her heart was beating wildly. Varn looked terrible. His face was starkly white, his lips blue, and even as she watched, his breathing became more labored. His eyes were closed, and she was not certain he was any longer aware of them. Only his mind shields remained firm. She could not pierce them to reach or question him at all.

Jake told her the little he knew. "I thought it was battle shock at first," he concluded. "It was only later that I realized it was even more serious."

The woman nodded grimly. She had felt that first awful rush of pain and knew her consort had taken an actual if most strange wound, but with the Arcturian patrol upon the mountain itself, she had not been able to leave her post here to go to him. Now it might be too late.

She sent her mind out and was not long in confirming that his body was sound enough.

The stroke had not been a physical one. She had to delve deeper, into the man himself, but shields he had cast up were of a strength she had never before encountered in him. Even semiconscious as he was, she could not breach them.

"Varn, open your mind," she commanded desperately with both voice and thought. "Please let me try to help you."

At first, she feared he could not respond, or would not, but then the barriers came down.

Islaen Connor gasped in horror. There was a wound, a deep, ragged tear in his mind itself. She could find no tissue damage, but that gash was bleeding the life out of him as surely as would a punctured, wildly spurting artery.

She gripped the grief and panic that threatened to overpower her. If she gave way to that now, the war prince was lost.

She had found the damage. Repairing it was another matter. No physical form of aid would help him, but it was just barely possible that her mind, this sometimes eerie gift of hers, might be able to do so.

She had to try it! She could not just give Varn up, let him die without putting up all the fight in her power for his life.

Her hands grasped his, although she realized the contact could not influence the outcome. Her eyes closed as she centered all her attention on the enormous task before her.

They had fully melded once, after lifting from Hades of Persephone. Now she strove to achieve such a union again, not to share being and experience but to become literally one with him, to use her strength and will to close that wound and to drive his own desire to live to complete the healing process. That must still be active, or he could not have held on so long. If it were not, if it had faded into oblivion in these last few minutes, she had little hope of success.

An hour's quarter went by. Total silence gripped those within the Omrain cabin while the Commando-Colonel did battle for Varn Tarl Sogan's life. At the end of that time, her head lifted. Her face was pale and drawn with exhaustion and glistened with sweat, but she smiled up at her comrades. "He should make it now." She ran her hands over her face. "Prepare a sedative, Bethe, enough to keep him out until dawn. Half the normal strength should be sufficient."

The war prince's eyes opened. They slitted against the light and the intensified pain the sight of it sent through him. "Not yet." His voice was low but reasonably steady.

Islaen gently brushed his cheek with the tips of her fingers. "Sleep's the body's and mind's best healer. You need a lot of it, friend, more than we'll be able to let you have."

"Not yet," he repeated. "If my wound sours, we could lose what I have learned."

Islaen took the needle the Sergeant had readied but put it on her lap. "All right, Varn. Tell us what happened. Take your time. We have the whole night to kill."

"It will not take long."

He described the incident and then lay still for a few seconds, gathering both his thoughts and his strength. "It was as if I fired a bolt into him . . ." Sogan paused. "No. It was more like the spears some barbarians use. In hurling it, I penetrated his mind myself, joined with it. He, or some inner part of him, realized he was slain and clutched at my life in an effort to make it his own. As death wrenched him away, he tore me."

The Arcturian shuddered but went on. "That resistance on the part of one side or the other is what kills the captives when they break their chain, I think. They rip themselves open when they wrench free. If the mind slaver withdrew voluntarily, without that violence, they should suffer no harm. Indeed, he almost certainly must do so occasionally to rest himself, probably while they sleep."

"You could have withdrawn without hurt if he hadn't seized you?" Islaen asked.

"That I cannot say. Maybe, or I would have suffered less severely at any rate. The wielding of that spear may be a damaging process in itself."

"Not for your cousin, apparently, or he couldn't keep up with it," Karmikel observed.

"No, but that is part of his talent, not mine. My gift is for communication and limited interaction with a number of nonhuman species, not waging war or casting others into bondage."

The redhead frowned. "You were never able to read anyone before except for Islaen. How could you do so much now?"

Varn's eyes darkened. "I do not know. We were of one race and one caste within it. Perhaps that was enough to create a natural bond or link between us."

"Could you actually read him?" the Colonel asked.

He nodded, then winced as his head seemed to explode in

response. "Aye, as clearly as I do you, though in a different manner." His mouth hardened. "He felt little surprise at finding me there, and he knew what was about to occur. That was the worst of it all. This was a process he had witnessed before. He feared it and accepted it as inevitable, whatever his hopeless struggle to live a little longer."

Sogan's voice grew harsh with purpose. "That renegade must die, Islaen Connor."

The woman felt the hate and anger swell in him. "Easy!" she warned, afraid of what he might do to his scarcely closed wound.

She lifted the needle and checked the dosage. "You've had about enough, Admiral."

"Aye," he agreed wearily. "I can think of no more right now that would help us."

He felt a sharp prick and, within seconds, nothing more.

TWENTY-FOUR

VARN TARL SOGAN tried to resist the voice calling him in his mind but at last woke and opened his eyes. His head still throbbed, but less severely now, more an aftershock than a signal of danger.

The Commando-Colonel was kneeling on the pallet beside him. *I'm sorry, Varn, but it's time to shift.*

You should have been less generous with that dose last night, then, he grumbled, but sat up, quickly reaching for the tunic she held out for him. Omrai of Umbar was too damn cold for his liking.

An ear-splitting whistle lashed into him like a small, deadly dart, but he held out his hand to give the gurry a landing place.

Varn! Varn's cured now?

"In the greater part, small one. Just be a little quiet for a while until the process is complete."

Yes, Varn! Sorry!

The Arcturian laughed softly. She was purring so rapidly and so hard that she seemed to be in dire danger of vibrating right off his palm. *One of the company seems glad to have me back at any rate.*

Give the rest of us a chance! Islaen said, laughing herself as she slipped into his arms, putting the hen to flight.

As their lips met, she let him feel the full of her joy and a little, a very little, of the fear she had known for him.

What did you do? he asked after a few moments. *I was not much aware of anything at that stage.*

The woman described the new use to which she had put her mind.

I'm only glad it worked, she finished. *For the first few minutes, I was afraid I couldn't manage it.*

You have a fine gift, my Islaen, to give life back to one nearly dead. I . . .

She felt the change in him. He strove to sever his contact with her but moved too slowly, and she blocked his exit. *No more of that! You're no monster because of what happened. You didn't even realize it was possible, so how can you think of fixing guilt on yourself? Besides, that Yeoman had to be eliminated after he saw you, and this left no mark on him to betray us. Whether your subconscious recognized your strength and moved you to use it or not, you did act in our defense.*

Sogan's head lowered but then raised again. *I know that, but it was bad, Islaen. No one not actually experiencing it can know how bad.*

He sighed and drew her to him again, this time just holding her.

Islaen rested against him, her eyes closed, thinking how very close she had come to losing him and glorying in the miracle of his love for her.

At last, she gently freed herself. *We'll have to be moving soon,* she told him. *We let you sleep as long as possible. Finish dressing as quickly as you can and get something to eat. Once we see Jake off, we'll be starting out ourselves.* She got to her feet. *I want to have a final look at that cannon. You should be just about ready by the time I return.*

The former Admiral entered the central room a few minutes later. As usual, he went first to the fire, seeking warmth from it, but the glare of it bothered him, and he swiftly turned away again.

There was no mistaking the pleasure of his comrades at seeing him. All three greeted him warmly, then Bethe studied him critically. "That's more like it," she told him. "You look spaceworthy again. How do you feel?"

"Nearly myself."

"Liar," Jake declared calmly. "Your head's about ready to come off. You can't even stand to look at the fire."

Sogan shrugged. "It is nothing like yesterday. Compared with that, anything feels good."

The Noreenan handed him a couple of capsules he had already taken from their medical kit. "These should take the edge off it. They're a sovereign remedy for an opaline hangover."

"I wish I had so happy an excuse for this," Varn said as he accepted and swallowed them dry.

He sat down at the table. Although he felt little interest in the food the Sergeant was removing from the fire, it might be a long time before there would be another chance for a meal.

As he ate, he watched Barak. The Omrain boy had welcomed him along with the others but had quickly fallen silent and was now sitting at the farther end of the room, his eyes hurt, his expression sullen.

Sogan realized with a twinge of guilt that he had some right to be. He had wholeheartedly cooperated with the off-worlders, had taken part in a mission he greatly feared for their sake, and they had not even trusted him with the knowledge that they possessed transport. More, they had directly lied to him regarding it and, by extension, about their purpose on Omrai.

Once his meal was finished, the Arcturian walked down to him. Drawing one of the chairs away from its place by the wall, he sat beside him. "We could have done nothing else."

Barak nodded, but the pain did not leave him.

Varn sighed. "Islaen had no choice. None of us did. It is not always wise or possible to trust those outside our own unit in our work. By the time we had come to know you well enough for such confidence, we had learned what we faced as well, and everything started moving too rapidly to allow time for explanations."

The Omrain's eyes lowered. He himself had been raised to command, and if secrecy had never been part of his people's lives, he knew that other races were not as fortunate. The off-worlders had done no more than their reading of the circumstances demanded. Rightly so. Because of their caution, had he been captured near the Big Ship and his mind broken, he could have said no more than that his guests were survivors from a blasted starship. He could not have betrayed the secret of their weapons and their actual purpose.

"Do not explain. A leader amongst you must obviously hold many things close. I do understand that need, even though I do not envy you it."

The demolitions expert had worked on the atomic cannon through most of the night, and just prior to Varn's waking, she had been able to report that the ancient weapon would fire.

It was to inspect this that Islaen Connor had gone, and when she returned to the cabin, there was a strong air of satisfaction on her.

Bethe accepted her praise, but she again warned that an attempt to use it could result in the death of the gunner. The screens were rotten, and nothing could be done to repair them. They could rupture under the sudden forces of firing.

The Colonel nodded a trifle grimly, but she did not waver in her purpose. She must accept that danger if her plan was to succeed.

Bethe Danlo was very definite in her assertion that there would be only one shot. That was disappointing, but it would have to suffice—would suffice if the fire could be accurately directed—and the Sergeant assured her there would be no difficulty with that.

"Is it still possible to use the rocket?" asked Islaen in an afterthought.

Bethe looked at her in surprise. The Commando knew she had cannibalized the fuel core for the cannon. "Not unless we discover an atom cache."

"Our own disks?"

She shook her head doubtfully. "I can make the hookup easily enough, but it wasn't designed to handle that much power. It'd be torn apart before it had gone a hundred miles."

"It need go only a hundred yards. I'd prefer to use robot guidance on it, and it must be able to carry a substantial payload."

"No problem. The nose is fitted out for cargo already. We can preset the controls before launch."

"Excellent. Separate the cannon from it to give us two weapons, and we'll be set."

It was a matter of minutes before the work was completed. The demolitions expert gave the few necessary instructions to her comrades so that they would all be able to operate both the rocket and the cannon for maximum effect, then she turned her attention to helping Jake with his final preparations. In a very short while, he would be spaceborne, alone in the vast void and screened from its eternal cold only by the tiny, fragile Commando flier.

Once the others had returned to the cabin above, she and Karmikel started work. Neither had much heart for speech, and they labored together in silence until both were at last satisfied that nothing more remained to be done. After that, they stood looking at the flier, each conscious of what any failure on its part would mean—death for the one and planet-bound exile for the other.

Jake's head turned to the woman beside him. Her slender body was straight, ready to meet what fate would send. Her face was pale and tired after her long night's labors, but she was unweakened by her weariness. She seemed fragile all the same, despite her strength. Everything within him wanted to take her into his arms, to shield and defend her, and once more, the fear welled up in him that he might never now be able to do so.

The woman's thoughts were equally bleak, equally uncertain, but she felt his eyes on her and forced a smile. "See that you don't take any wrong turns out there and get yourself lost."

"No fear of it!"

His fists clenched by his sides. If he did, he would never see her again. He found he could not endure that thought. "Bethe," he said suddenly, hurriedly lest his courage dissolve, "did you mean it when you said you'd have no more part of me?"

She looked up at him. "No, you big space tramp! Of course I didn't!"

His eyes closed in his relief, but a new fear twisted his heart. Whatever he faced in the starlanes, the Sergeant's risk was infinitely greater. The screens on that cannon were so rotten as to scarcely exist at all. "Remember this, Bethe Danlo," he said fiercely, "no matter what happens. It's you that I love. Not Islaen or anyone else. Only you."

She came into his arms and buried her face against his chest. "Come back to me," she whispered. "Don't leave me here without you."

"I won't fail you. I vow that on my very soul."

All too soon, it was time for him to go.

Karmikel settled himself at the controls and maneuvered the little vessel outside.

Varn Tarl Sogan came with him to check that his space seals were firmly in place.

"The Spirit of Space speed you," he said as the canopy was about to close.

"And you as well, friend. We all have our work before us on this one."

The Arcturian signaled that the seals were sound and moved back into the shelter of the cave. The lifting exhaust would not be such as would scar the glen, but neither would it be the gentle air jet that carried the flier over Omrai's surface.

Sogan watched until the vessel had disappeared from sight but did not remain outside after that. There was a bitter bite in the air, and he would have to endure enough of it once their own mission began.

The remainder of the team and Barak were already in the cabin when he returned there. They had been watching the flier as well.

Islaen gave him a tight smile and then went to get her pack, saying they would do well to leave as soon as possible.

To their surprise, the Omrain shook his head emphatically. "We cannot go now. The sea-cold is upon us."

The Commando-Colonel looked at him in horror and swore bitterly. A day's delay might or might not affect their work, but Jake . . .

The same thought was in all their minds, the same blame. They had felt this cold before. Why had they not remembered? Barak could not be faulted. It had come on very suddenly, and he was not trained to think in relation to space as they were.

"The full force of the storm hasn't struck yet," she said in the end. "Perhaps it's the same in space. The flier may get through without being too badly hit."

She had voiced the one hope remaining to them. If Jake Karmikel were lost, then the *Free Comet* was almost certain to follow, well-nigh ensuring that none of them would ever leave Omrai again.

The ice formed very rapidly. It was later in the season now, and the temperature plummeted far below what it had been during the first storm in a fraction of the time.

Looking out at the glacier which covered Omrai's surface, the off-worlders were glad Bethe had taken the time she had to repair the cannon. Had they started out as planned or earlier, they would all now be dead.

TWENTY-FIVE

THE ICE STOPPED forming late that afternoon, and the temperature rose.

Sogan sighed as he watched what little of it he could see through the nearly covered window. They would be held here at least another couple of days and probably more. It was too late now for any perceptible amount of the ice to melt before nightfall again brought in the cold.

If the Arcturian could accept such a delay, his commander could not. Islaen Connor would wait not longer. A thought had just struck her as she gazed helplessly out at the imprisoning glacier. If she could implement it, they could leave very shortly, or before the first light at the very latest, even if they ran into difficulties with some of the details.

She started impatiently down the passageway, calling for the others to follow. There was purpose in the Colonel, and both her own comrades and Barak of Omrai were quick to obey. They found her already kneeling beside the rocket examining the castors on the transportation sling. Without a word of explanation, the woman went over to where the curragh lay against the wall. She smiled. The wood was already shaped and was iron hard. She began to break it apart with the aid of a pencil-thin diamond saw from her gear.

Her companions watched the Commando-Colonel curiously until she paused to explain her intention at last. Varn Tarl Sogan raised a quizzical eyebrow at the plan Islaen outlined, but he and the others readily joined in. He had some doubts about the idea, but he had yet to see that guerrilla fail, and so he kept them to himself. She had enough to do without having to deal with his less daring thoughtways.

Soon the wheels of the rocket sling had been immobilized. Islaen and Varn fastened the wooden strips that remained of the curragh to the base, forming a sledge.

The Commando studied the results with satisfaction. She had made the skis considerably broader than the wheels for stability. They would be traveling over rough country, and the rocket had not been balanced for movement of this sort. She did not want to risk a crash once they set out.

After a final check of their equipment, they covered the glittering metal with their blankets so that Umbar's light would not reflect from it to betray them, then Islaen told them, Barak of Omrai along with the rest, to push the sled outside while she gathered up their already prepared packs for them.

They positioned the vehicle and then waited impatiently for her to join them. All were as warmly dressed as possible, but the night was bitterly cold, and they moved about, trying to keep their circulation going.

Islaen Connor left the cabin. She, too, shivered, but the chill did not concern her. The exertion of the journey would soon warm them.

She had more immediate matters to worry her. Sleds like this were heavily used for both pleasure and commercial travel during Noreen's long, sharp winters, and she knew the handling of them, but her homeworld and Omrai of Umbar were very different planets. What would have been a relatively simple task on flat plains or gently rolling hills would have to be otherwise on these wooded mountainsides, especially with a totally inexperienced crew to aid her.

There was no help for that. She instructed her comrades in how to guide the sled over the ice. They listened intently. The mission and their lives depended on their mastering these skills quickly.

The rocket was heavy, and their combined weight when they rode it would add considerably to its mass. They would reach high speeds over any part of the trail having even a moderate downward slope. If they could not handle the vehicle, there could be a crippling accident, fatal both to them and to their hopes of destroying the Arcturian warship.

Islaen positioned her team as best she could, Barak on the left side, alone since he was slightly heavier than Varn despite his

youth and small stature, Sogan and Bethe Danlo on the right.
She herself claimed the very rear. It would be her part to act as
a living rudder.

They would ride, walk, or push depending upon conditions on
whatever part of their route they happened to be crossing.

For now, they would have to push, and all of them took their
places.

The war prince bent close to Bethe, and his gloved hand
closed over hers. "The flier is small and very maneuverable," he
whispered. "It could ride out turbulence that would be the death
of a bigger, less agile craft, and Karmikel is one of the best pilots
I have seen. He will bring it through."

"Thanks, Varn," she said softly. "If you're not just saying
that, it means a lot just now."

"I say what I believe. Instilling false hope is no kindness."

There was no time for more as they began manhandling the
sleigh around the bend from which the Arcturian Yeoman had
appeared. They rounded it, and the steep slope leading up to the
trail they must follow rose before them.

There was no easier way. The company braced themselves
against the sled.

It was difficult working against the weight of the rocket and
the slippery surface of the ice. They needed most of their
strength merely to keep it from sliding back down, and all four
were glad to rest against the sledge, their breath coming in
gasping sobs, by the time they had it balanced at the top.

The Colonel allowed them only a moment before giving the
order to mount. She pushed hard against the sled to start it and
stepped quickly onto the left rear runner as it swept past her.

The brakeman's task was never an easy one, and Islaen soon
found herself wishing for Jake's bulk and strong muscles.

She could expect no relief. She was the only one of the team
familiar with this method of transportation, and this was not a
responsibility she could relinquish to anyone who was less than
skilled.

They were going faster than she had anticipated at this stage.
The ice was hard and very smooth, and the slope proved more
pronounced than it had appeared.

The woman had been worried about guiding their less than
ideally balanced vehicle over the unknown, rugged trail, but this
fear, at least, proved almost needless. The glacier was so thick
that it completely covered most of the brush and smaller

boulders and almost everything else that might have constituted a threat to their progress.

Gradually, the party accustomed themselves to the sleigh. Their commander's load was eased as the others learned to anticipate the needs of their craft more exactly and acquired the skill to meet them as they arose.

Barak's heart beat wildly. He had watched carefully while the off-worlders fashioned the skis, and he now set himself to learn every possible detail he could about the handling of the sled, both his own task and Islaen's, whom he kept under as close observation as he could. The Omrain boy was filled with a marvelous excitement, for he saw in this sledge the birth of commerce on his homeworld.

In a bare two months Omrai's long winter would have laid hold of the planet, and his people would have buried themselves in their cabins to wait it out as they had since the *Space Queen* crashed so many generations before.

All that could change. It must and would change. With vehicles like this one, craft constructed to carry cargo, it could become the most active season of the year. Crops grown in the south could be sent north, preserved from spoilage by the cold, and traded there for the sea catches and fuel wood of that region, or the northern goods could be brought south. The direction of the trade flow was of no importance. It was the idea itself that mattered.

He could hardly bear the wonder of it. This night could well mark the beginnings of the climb back to the stars for the offspring of Omrai, a climb they would now be able to at least partly make themselves and not depend entirely on the charity of others, and he who had so recently thought to witness her final destruction would be the moving force behind that beginning. It was a mission of unthinkable, inconceivable worth, and it made his life and the knowledge he bore seem both priceless and incredibly fragile.

It was very dark. Omrai's single satellite was in its new phase, and only the distant stars sent their faint glow to the planet's frozen surface.

The company was well into the woodlands now. The heavy growth gave them cover, but it brought a new danger as well.

Islaen strained to catch the shadowy images of the trees along their course, trying to sight them in time to avoid striking any of them.

At this speed, with the uncertainly balanced sled, considerable forewarning was necessary, and she could expect little help from her comrades in this. Even Barak, whose eyes were used to his homeworld's night, was not equal to the task. The work was too unfamiliar for any of them to calculate the alterations in course with the necessary degree of accuracy, much less transmit the information to her or move in time to aid her.

The night was cold as well as dark. There was a high wind, its bite further sharpened by the speed of the sleigh, making the chill seem even deeper.

Islaen Connor could have laughed aloud. Despite the demands being made on her, she would not have changed this part of their journey. She had all but forgotten the thrill of skimming over the surface of a planet on a night such as this, where all was silent but the roar of the wind and the hiss of the skis against the smooth ice. It had been long, very long, since she had last known its like, not since her leave the winter before she was assigned to penetration duty on Thorne of Brandine, and not even the deadly nature of their mission could lessen the pleasure of the run for her.

Her companions were enjoying it as well if the touches she was receiving from their minds spoke true, Varn enormously so despite his dislike of the ever-gnawing cold.

Only Bandit was not happy, although she took pleasure in her humans' delight. She was huddled beneath Islaen's clothes, right between her breasts, her claws fixed in the cloth above her to hold herself in place. She was shivering fairly constantly, violently whenever the wind drove through to her in an exceptionally sharp gust, and she frequently informed those who could receive her thoughts of her opinion of Omrai of Umbar and her weather.

No sound escaped the gurry. The unit's discipline was part of her, and she knew enough not to make unnecessary noise when they were thus engaged in an active portion of a mission.

The night passed. Dawn came suddenly and brilliantly. The off-worlders dropped their goggles over their eyes to shield them from the glare, as Barak did with the wooden slats which were their on-world equivalents.

Islaen weighed breaking their journey. They were all tired enough to warrant that, but she decided against it. They would not halt, not yet. They would not be able to keep up this speed much longer. Soon the ice would begin to decay under Umbar's rays. There would be time for rest then.

It was a somewhat eerie journey. The glacier was like crystal. She could look into its depths and see the lush plants beneath it, the leaves still and fresh. She knew that a considerable amount of activity was taking place beneath the ice. The life processes of the vegetation continued, although the animals had gone into brief hibernation. The bristles she had noticed on the leaves the day they planeted were piercing the ice, breaking it down and combining its chemicals with those stored in the leaves, generating heat as they did so. They more than Umbar herself were responsible for its rapid disappearance once the sea-cold ended.

Much of the tension she had felt throughout the night left her with the coming of the light. Guiding the sled was no problem now that the trees were clearly visible long before they became a threat.

Umbar burned down on them. The glacier was disappearing rapidly, most of it evaporating directly into the atmosphere whence it had come. There was comparatively little water left after it.

That was still too much. The amount of ice was enormous, and by midmorning, its surface had become rough and wet enough to mire the skis.

The Colonel watched for a sheltered place in which to take their rest. Such sites were no rarity in rugged country like Omrai's forested mountains, and she did not have to search long before discovering a dry rise on the leeward of a steep hill from which the ice had already melted.

She and Barak secured the sled while their comrades set up and camouflaged the camp. In a few minutes, Bethe Danlo had prepared a meal from their rations. After eating, the three not on guard lay down to rest and immediately fell into a deep sleep.

The Commando-Colonel claimed the first watch. Even now, she eyed the ice impatiently. She knew they needed this break, but she disliked any delay that went beyond what was actually necessary to satisfy their absolute requirements. They must move as soon as the way was passable once more.

To her relief, the glacier continued to melt rapidly, nearly as rapidly as it had formed. Not a quarter of it remained by the time she surrendered her post to Sogan.

* * *

It was well into the night before the Colonel felt it was feasible to start again.

In truth, she was pleased with this timing. They had covered most of the journey on the sleigh. Less than half a night's travel would bring them to the Arcturian base. That would place them at target by dawn.

They would have to wait for the light. The *Empire's Glory* must be clearly visible for her plan to have the maximum chance of succeeding, but neither did she want a long watch on the perimeter of the clearing. By the same token, the Commando-Colonel would not have wished to make their approach in the light, when the possibility of premature discovery was at its greatest.

Sogan removed the skis and fastened them to the sling while his comrades dismantled the camp and erased the few signs they had left. He tested the transport device. The wheels moved easily, as though they had not stood unused for all the long generations since the *Space Queen* crashed on Omrai.

As soon as Islaen judged the ground to be hard enough to support the rocket's weight without miring the wheels, she ordered her small force to start out.

Their pace was slower now as they had to move the heavy sling with nothing but the strength of their own muscles.

The off-worlders no longer wondered why Barak's people had fallen to such a primitive state. Even with these wheels, their task was monstrously difficult. On a planet where no metals existed to make even the crudest tools and no tamable animals large enough to bear a man's weight, any form of vehicular advancement was all but inconceivable.

Their labor would have been lightened by activating the engine for a few seconds to give some momentum to the sling.

The Noreenan smiled at the thought of it—the burst of flame, the roar shattering the silence of the woodlands. The Arcturians would be upon them before the engine could be disconnected again.

At least, the land still did not betray them. Although it was now fairly flat, it did not slope against them.

The guerrilla wondered how far they actually were from the base. She had not yet received any contact from the shipmen, but that could be no criterion in this case. As she did not know the actual extent of this Aleke Tarl Sogan's power, she would have to assume that it was at least as great as her own and conduct herself accordingly. She did not dare make an active attempt to contact the invaders for fear that it might be read.

Varn was keeping an equally close guard on himself. There was no need to warn him of the possible dangers involved here.

Despite his fear of searching actively, the war prince kept some of his receptors open, enough to give them some guidance. They were unquestionably nearing the ship. There were few animals in this area, and those were extraordinarily quiet, living in the permanent state of terror that was born of long-term contact with the worst spirit of his species, the spirit that conquered the weak and slew the proud. By analyzing the touches he received, he was able to place their position in relation to the base with a high degree of accuracy.

Sogan could feel the beat of his heart increase until he imagined that it must betray all he felt, his fear and other, lesser thoughts.

He concealed his discomfort. His comrades had a right to believe they could fully depend upon him. They trusted him, and he would do nothing to lessen that now, with the confrontation so near to hand.

The Arcturian's eyes closed. He did not fear the battleship or her crew any more than a healthy respect for his people's combat abilities demanded. He knew those beside whom he would fight, and he knew what they had been able to accomplish during the War. They would do as much now barring a direct betrayal by fortune, and that, too, both he and they had faced in the past and overcome.

What of his kinsman? That thought ever ran through his mind. If the gods showed any kindness at all, Aleke would be slain in the initial attack, but if he were not, how could they face him?

They would have no choice. They must face him, or he must. Aleke Tarl Sogan must die. For the Empire's sake as much as the Federation's, for the sake of their house's already smeared honor, he must be slain, but even the contemplation of such an encounter filled the former Admiral with stark terror. How could he hope to stand against the force that his kinsman possessed and had unleashed? How could he bear the corruption of it? Reason itself rose up to oppose any such contest. The power to slay or destroy was not his that he should presume to wield it against a man to whom it came as readily as his own contacts with Islaen Connor did to him.

He hastily calmed himself as he felt the Colonel's thought brush against his shields. His barriers lowered a little, and their minds linked. He felt it then, the unmistakable touch of human minds, many of them. Varn shivered. One pervasive, tremendously powerful pattern hung over all the others, arrogant, harsh, and utterly ruthless.

His feelings settled. With the target almost upon them, there was no place in his mind for any wasting emotion.

TWENTY-SIX

JAKE KARMIKEL WAS glad when the space seals slid into place. There was a cold wind coming in from the sea. He raised his hand in farewell to Sogan and set the controls for lift-off. His hand closed over them.

The glen soon disappeared into the larger landscape of the coast. There was no sensation of motion, no pressure in the small craft, but the instruments spun as it gained altitude and speed. Already Omrai was shrinking into a ball. The sky turned purple, darkened still further until the black void of space stretched before him.

Scarcely had he penetrated it than the flier shuddered, then ripped free of his command. The instruments spun erratically. Jake's heart stopped at the sight of the readings they showed, but he calmly increased antimagnetization to maximum and fought the controls until he regained mastery over the vehicle.

He would not be able to hold it long. Waves of pure, angry energy swirled and eddied about it, battering, pulling, twisting in a rampage of fury.

Each wave tore into the flier, striking it with physical force. A vessel with a greater surface area could not have held together. She would quickly have been wrenched apart by the savage, contradictory forces pummeling her, or, at best, if her master were very skilled, she would crash on the planet below even as the *Space Queen* had crashed centuries before.

Jake Karmikel was skilled, and he drew on all the knowledge and all the art he had acquired over the long years to help him win free of this interstellar nightmare.

There was some pattern in the turmoil. A vessel this tiny could ride some of the waves, sparing itself from at least part of the storm's incredible fury.

At last, he found a place that was momentarily neutral. He hit the drive hard, and the flier shot outward, away from the turbulent area, in the brief moment given him.

The Commando-Captain halted when he was well out of the danger zone and ran a check on his systems.

They seemed to function in spite of the buffeting they had taken. He would have to hope they would continue to do so during the long voyage before him.

He looked back once more on the blue-green planet and shook his head in silent wonder. What he had experienced was only the gathering of the storm, its preliminary rumblings. What must these lashings be at their height?

Jake looked out on the infinite universe. He suddenly felt very insignificant, and very alone.

His task was a hopeless one. The stars themselves looked to be mere points of light that were in reality marvelously huge. What was a Commando flier or even the *Free Comet* by comparison? How could he presume to imagine that these two minute specks of space dust could somehow contrive to meet in all this vast blackness?

They would meet! His will and his mind decreed that they would. The Noreenan closed his eyes, concentrating on all he had learned in an obscure course on astral navigation he had taken in his youth and on all he had learned since then in the starlanes.

He looked out into the void, this time carefully studying the brilliants all about him. These were strange stars, far off the commonly traveled lanes.

His confidence held, and he calculated rapidly, checking his findings against the instruments.

Karmikel frowned. They differed very slightly, but that difference could mean the failure of his mission.

Again, he went through the process and again reached the same figures. The Commando hesitated a moment, then moved out on the course he had plotted, ignoring the readings on the instrument panel.

This done, he checked the transceiver. It functioned, praise the Spirit of Space. He set it on the *Free Comet*'s frequency and opened the channel.

Little more was left for him to do but to keep the flier on course. If the cruiser approached as he figured, and if he had calculated correctly, then his mission would succeed. If not, he would die and perhaps the Patrol ship as well, and his comrades must very probably remain forever on Omrai if they survived their attack on the Arcturian camp.

For a long time, a couple of Omrain days, he received no response to his broadcasts. The guerrilla feared he had chosen wrong, that it had been his calculations that were at fault rather than the badly jostled instruments. He despaired of success, but there was nothing for it but to continue on his present course. It was too late to turn back. He did not have the fuel left to retrace his path now.

Then he heard it, a faint echo coming over the transceiver. His hand was shaking as he gave it maximum amplification. The *Free Comet* was acknowledging his call.

Jake Karmikel slipped the last of his fuel disks into place and moved the flier into its highest space speed.

A speck soon appeared that grew until the cruiser was clearly visible to him. The two vessels closed rapidly, and he hurriedly readied his vehicle for pickup.

The flier drew alongside the *Free Comet*. The air lock opened, and the little machine slipped inside the Patrol starship.

TWENTY-SEVEN

ISLAEN CONNOR LAY in the last cover before the cleared space that was the Arcturian base.

All was very much as she had noted earlier. Her experienced eyes searched out the camp's weaknesses. There were many. The unwilling invaders expected no trouble here.

She turned her attention to the battleship herself. Despite her previous visit, the size of the *Empire's Glory* stunned her. She had seen vessels this large only twice before, both times in deep space.

In truth, she had never seen one of these, although she was familiar with the design. The Empire's scientists had developed the plans for circular vessels like this in the last decade of the War. They were devastatingly effective in large-scale battles between the fleets of the two ultrasystems and might have turned the course of the War had they come even a few years earlier. As it was, only a few prototypes had actually been built before the final collapse of the Arcturian war machine.

The Commando was satisfied. They would be able to do enough damage to the warship that she would no longer represent a threat to the colonies in Quandon Sector. Whether they would be able to remove the danger from Omrai herself was less certain, although the Colonel planned to take whatever steps were possible to secure this planet as well and to free the prisoners and bring them and her company to safety, perhaps the most hopeless phase of the mission.

The latter was almost irrelevant. The lives of a few guerrillas against the fate of star systems was a very small matter, but she was resolved to bring them all out of this if it was humanly

possible to do so. Islaen Connor had spent too many years with
the Commandos to consider her own life as anything but of
secondary importance on such a mission, but neither would she
sacrifice it needlessly. The guerrillas had developed a keen sense
of survival to balance their willingness to die if need demanded.
They could not have functioned without it.

The attack should begin soon. Barak lay close beside her.
Sogan and Bethe Danlo had broken away from them before they
reached the perimeter of the camp, taking their weapons to the
places from which they could best sight their targets. The first
moves must come from them. Bandit had unwillingly obeyed the
Colonel's command to withdraw into the trees before they had
come into actual sight of the base. She would have no part in the
battle to come.

The minutes passed slowly. Varn should be in place. The first
strike would come from him. His target was the engine, the
stellar drive, his task to see that the warship remained forever on
Omrai.

Islaen studied the ship. It was imperative that the war
prince succeed. From what she could judge, the repairs were
almost completed on the hull, and she knew the internal damage
would have been taken care of first. Perhaps all that the
Arcturians needed was an adequate fuel supply before they could
lift.

Ordinarily, they could not have hoped to pierce the hull from
this distance with any weapon they possessed, but the quantity of
titanone needed to restore the *Empire's Glory* would not have
been easy for a nongovernment vessel to get even on a highly
civilized planet, and the Arcturians had been forced to make
their repairs with solar steel, most of that not top quality. If Varn
Tarl Sogan could send his rocket into that part of the ship where
the stellar drive systems were located, the starship would not
leave Omrai.

Bethe's target was the command spike. Once that was blasted,
the shipmen would have no mechanical guard systems, no ability
to direct or fire the huge pletzar banks. Without those, Omrai's
fight was all but equalized. The invaders would be forced to
depend on their own suddenly inadequate powers. Patrols could
be isolated and destroyed, the attackers disappearing into the
shadows to strike again once the Arcturians' ability to summon
quick and deadly assistance was gone.

Only the lasers would remain to threaten the colony, and if all went as planned in the first, most urgent stages of their mission, the Commando hoped to take those out as well.

Her attention fixed on the spike. There was no sign of cannibalized metal there. It seemed to have suffered little damage in the crash, but Islaen felt that the atomic cannon would be enough to destroy it if the demolitions expert could send her single bolt where she intended.

As it was retracted during combat, only the crown had been sheathed in titanone. Most of the casing was of the lighter solar steel, albeit of the highest rating.

This retractability was their greatest danger. Bethe must fire quickly after the former Admiral's attack, or they would lose the opportunity entirely.

That failure would be deadly to the team and to Omrai. The Arcturians would almost certainly turn the full power of their pletzar banks against the planet, reducing all this part of her to lifeless rubble.

Such a course would be fatal to the crew as well, but suicide was an acceptable alternative to defeat to the men who fought under the inflexible code of the Arcturian warrior caste. Only the news of the War's end, and with it their right to act aggressively against Federation peoples, would be likely to stay them, but they would most assuredly act before that could be announced to them in such a way that they would believe and accept it. It was essential that the power to do so be taken from them at once.

The Commando was growing restless. This waiting was hard. One never became so accustomed to it that it could merely be endured, as physical discomfort can be borne and, at last, almost forgotten.

She had no choice in the matter. Nothing could be done to ease it either for herself or for her comrades. The Omrain, too, was growing more anxious for the fight to begin. Islaen frowned. The fool! He was allowing his excitement to take him, letting it completely overwhelm his shields. She was receiving his every emotion without even having to open her receptors to probe for them.

She struck the boy hard, a savage blow right into his side.

Barak's body convulsed. He would have cried out, but the woman had covered his mouth, preventing even a gasp . "The

mind slaver wouldn't have been so merciful had he found you!"
she hissed.

The Omrain nodded. He was ashamed rather than angry and
vowed to himself that he would not so weaken a second time.

Islaen turned back to the ship, silently marking the seconds
until the attack.

The charges had been laid in the rocket and set to detonate
fifteen seconds after impact. The automatic pilot had to be
adjusted on the actual launch site, however, and it was this
which was holding up the fire.

The Commando-Colonel licked her lips nervously. An error in
this or a failure of the rocket, and their mission was over.

She had placed her trust well, she told herself savagely.
None knew better than the former Arcturian Admiral the place
on the great hull that covered the stellar drive. He most assuredly
could hit it in theory. If only he could do as well in
practice . . .

He must be ready by now! Islaen unconsciously pressed
herself harder against the ground. There was a sharp roar,
tremendous for so tiny a vessel. The rocket shot forward with a
speed that left a silver rainbow tracing its course. Sogan would
already be diving through the brush, trying to get as far as
possible from his now-marked hiding place.

The missile smashed into the Arcturian warship. Its sharp,
hard nose easily pierced the worn metal covering the engine.

The explosion came a moment later. It had a peculiarly hollow
sound, and Islaen Connor smiled. Whatever else happened this
day, the Arcturians were planet-bound.

The Colonel raised herself a little to better observe the ship.
The command spike had begun its retreat with the first warning
flash from the rocket. It was sluggish from long disuse and a
slightly faulty mechanism or it would already be beyond their
reach. What was holding Bethe?

A ball of fire broke from the brush opposite the place where
the Noreenan lay.

A moment later, the whole area, to a radius of perhaps one
hundred yards, was enveloped by a searing white flame that was
so intense as to be almost pure light.

Islaen flattened, burying her face in the cool ground. Only the
fact that she had been watching the fireball's effect on the ship
had saved her from at least temporary blindness, and even with

that, her eyes throbbed and teared, as if trying to rid themselves of the terrible excess of light they had taken.

She did not see or care to see the command spike shatter and fall in a spray of molten steel. She felt drained, artificially emptied, and an overwhelming sense of loss filled her soul. It had always been bad to have a comrade fall, but this was many times worse. The War was over, and this assault in which Bethe Danlo had given her life should never have had to take place but for fortune's grim humor.

Her grief was sharpened by the fact that she could not even send her mind out to confirm the spacer's death. Shielded as she was, she could still feel another mind searching the perimeter of the base, one that moved openly and carried with it the promise of death and worse than death for those responsible for this assault.

Their contact had been brief, a mere brushing of patterns, but it had been enough for her to feel the force behind the Arcturian Captain's probe. The raw strength of it stunned her.

Islaen shook her head as though to clear it of the memory. What chance would she have if ever a confrontation came? Her shields might be supple and strong, but how long could any defense stand against what that man possessed? His gift was not a tool or faculty for gaining knowledge but a weapon, one in whose use he was all too well schooled.

She did not despair despite her appreciation of her handicap. In one respect, at least, they were favored. Whether because of his rage, which now threatened to fill the whole of the camp, or because of some innate weakness, all that great force had swept unheeding over the Commando. Islaen Connor had been very aware of the Arcturian and remained aware of him beneath her shields, but he had not perceived her.

She was certain of that. There had not been even the faintest of responses, no reaction whatsoever, and she knew within herself that she would not have failed to detect the slightest tremor of recognition in him. She had spent too great a part of her life refining her talent for reading the emotions of those around her for her to err in that now.

The intensity of the Arcturian's anger spurred her, and once his probe had passed over her to seek elsewhere, the Commando carefully reached out to the prisoners. They were free, dazed and frightened, but free.

Releasing them was Barak's job. She had other work to do.

While the Omrain broke down the slave pens and led the prisoners to safety, she would have to penetrate the *Empire's Glory* and neutralize her lasers before a large part of this section of the blue-green planet could be reduced to ashes in the fury of punitive activity that would otherwise follow fast upon this attack.

TWENTY-EIGHT

AFTER PRESSING HER blaster into Barak's hand in case he should encounter and have to battle any of the crewmen in the course of his efforts, the Commando-Colonel dashed forward. She hoped he would not be called upon to use the weapon, but she had schooled him in its management before they left the cabin and knew he could at least aim and fire it should the need arise.

She ran hard across the open place. A second, two, and she was beneath the great ship, secure for the moment in her shadow.

She paused to see whether she had been observed. The camp was alive with soldiers. They still darted in every direction, each with his own assigned purpose.

It was an incredibly short time since the raid began, and this base had not experienced or expected danger in ten infinitely long years, yet the crewmen were responding as if this were a front-line installation. With discipline like this, she thought, it was scant wonder that their kind had made such awesome opponents.

She was satisfied they had not detected her, however, and their commander was no more perceptive. Islaen was relieved to note that his powerful mind no longer swept the camp. At least, Barak would have the chance to get the prisoners out of his range before he realized the truth if, as the Colonel thought, he now believed that the attackers had perished in the explosion of the atomic cannon.

Her eyes automatically went to the seared place. Only a faint glow remained, and that would soon be gone. At least, the cannon had not been so primitive as to leave the area contaminated after its own destruction.

Her mind returned to her own task. Her refuge would not remain secure for long.

Islaen Connor snaked along the cold ground beneath the battleship until she came to the now-useless weapons banks. She smiled without humor. Useless to all but her.

In another few seconds, she located the air lock covering one of the projectile tubes. The Commando had formed this part of her plan early, and the tools she needed to force it were near to hand.

The task was delicate and took more time than she liked to give. It was not difficult in itself, but the Empire had acquired a powerful respect for Federation guerrillas over the long years of the War, and they had put intricate alarms on every possible entry place to their vessels.

The woman swore softly as precious seconds were lost. In this matter, too, the crewmen had retained their discipline and thoroughness.

At last, the hatch slid back. The tube inside was empty, as she had known it would be. It would be a waste of matériel to keep weapons banks armed that were now located facing downward, for all purposes permanently, a few feet from the planet's surface.

The Colonel returned her tools to their places in an outer compartment of her slender, body-hugging pack and took from it two packets. One she slipped into a pocket sewn inside her tunic specifically to receive it. From the other, she removed heavy-looking magnetic gloves.

With their aid, she hoisted herself into the tube. The Noreenan paused only long enough to slide the air lock closed behind her. Then she began to climb.

Her pace was rapid. She had spent a lot of time opening the lock, and she was determined to win it back now.

It was darker than the void inside the ship, but the raditorch she strapped to her arm before the raid provided sufficient illumination for her purposes.

It was hard work, painful work, since her hands and wrists were forced to bear the whole of her weight. Soon her breathing became labored, and her muscles began to lose their strength.

A sharp projection showed above her. Islaen made for it with a surge of renewed strength, reached it. She clung there until her heart returned to something approximating its normal beat.

The Commando felt encouraged. This was the trigger, the device that armed the projectiles as they sped from the ship. About fifty feet above that was her turnoff point—if the weapons systems of this ship were truly of similar design to those on the older, more conventionally built vessels.

Islaen Connor began to climb again. She went more slowly this time. It would be a mistake to try to reclaim lost seconds on this part of the ascent. She had tried that at the start and had only succeeded in nearly exhausting herself. She could have paid for her impatience with her life had her arms or her will been less strong.

Islaen found the narrow opening where she expected it to be and turned into it without hesitation, confident of her course. The way would be horizontal until she reached her goal, and the guerrilla paused a moment to remove the heavy gloves. They would be more a hindrance than an aid in the narrow tunnel.

This was a ventilating duct, one of the many that crossed the weapons systems of any large ship to assure a constant flow of cool air and to better distribute the warmth generated in their operation, especially when the stress of battle caused overheating, a frequent problem that the scientists of neither ultrasystem had been entirely able to solve.

The Colonel did not fear that she would become confused in the giant maze. Federation guerrillas knew the twisting inner ways of the Empire's starships better than most of the crewmen who served on them, although only a few, scarcely a dozen, had ever actually penetrated one like this. Fewer still had survived to speak of it.

Unlike those of Federation vessels, these ducts had not been designed to serve as passageways, and Islaen was glad of her slight, slender body. Anyone larger could have negotiated the tunnel only with the greatest difficulty, if at all. As it was, she was forced to wriggle along in the manner of a worm burrowing through Noreen's rich soil.

No, not a worm. She must place herself lower on the biological scale than that. Hers was more the part of a microorganism invading the heartwells of some great creature.

It was an eerie thought, and the woman hurriedly put it from her. Such an analogy normally would not have troubled her, but she was conscious of a deep sensation of loneliness now, and she did not wish to encourage any thoughts that might aggravate it further. There was no friend here, no one to take up her task if she should fail . . .

She had never felt that so intensely before, although it had been true many times in the past, on planets crawling with crack Arcturian troops. But this was not like being on a planet at all. Aye, that was the crux. On-world, she felt some degree of advantage. Though she recognized it as illogical, that feeling helped. Here, in the center of the vast machine, only the enemy who had built it could truly be at ease.

It was hard work pushing her way through the duct, although nothing in comparison with the climb up the tube, and it was dangerous. If the Arcturians fired their lasers now, sending shock waves and superheated air through the vent system . . .

Her hand went to the hidden pocket above her breast. Soon her clothes were dark with her sweat.

Islaen Connor moved, crawled, through the duct for what seemed a much longer time than it actually was. The canker fear that she had somehow missed her exit began to gnaw at her spirit.

A glimmer of light showed ahead. She switched her torch off. There would be no further need of it until her return.

The vent ended abruptly, opening into a large room all but filled with machinery. Many breaks showed in the walls. The Commando frowned. This hive effect was not seen in the older ships.

She soon reconciled herself to the design. It stood to reason that a circular vessel would have her systems centrally located. That explained the unnaturally long time she had remained in the duct before coming upon the chamber.

The Colonel dropped lightly to the deck after carefully marking the location of the vent. She must be able to find the correct one, and do it quickly, if she was to escape at all.

Islaen glanced around the chamber to orient herself. All was as it should be. The secret of the new ships lay in their greatly increased efficiency rather than in radically new equipment.

There was so much of it. Here in the protected heart of the ship lay the key to the entire vessel.

The guerrilla ignored the large, strange machines crowding the room. Her interest lay with the terminals that all but covered the walls. There were many, so very many, each packed with multicolored chips set in bewilderingly complex patterns. Even a master technician would have had difficulty in assigning to every one of these its proper duty, and this she certainly was not. Varn Tarl Sogan could not have done so, and he knew his ultrasystem's war craft as well as anyone.

That knowledge was not necessary to her work. The Arcturians color-coded their many systems. In a situation like this, where so much was located in so small an area, some kind of easily read, accurate method of identification was essential for their own technical people, particularly in times of crisis.

Islaen knew what to seek. Her eyes rested uneasily on the rarely used service entrance from the body of the vessel, then passed on. Soon she located what she wanted.

She spotted a complex coded with the scarlet color of the Empire, the controls for the now-useless pletzar banks. To the right of them was a series of rust-red microcircuits. These would be the key to the lasers.

The Colonel removed the packet of explosive from her inner pocket. The warmth of her body had rendered it soft and pliable. A distinctive, not unpleasant odor rose from the substance when she kneaded it. The Commando broke off several small pieces and set them into place almost automatically, joining the whole with a hair-thin fuse.

Her fingers worked almost without direction. It was a familiar task for her. How many of the Empire's installations had she actually blown? A hundred? More? Islaen shook her head. There were too many over too long a period of time. She could no longer remember.

Leaving the pletzar and laser banks, she turned her attention to the projectile controls in the center of the room. These, like the pletzars, had been negated by the destruction of the command spike, but the Noreenan feared that an exceptionally resourceful technician might be able to work from this cabin to achieve one final blast of revenge. It might not do the damage of the lasers, but if it could be detonated quickly enough, it would take not only the battleship and her unit but probably even Barak and the escaping captives unless they could move a lot faster than she believed possible.

The arsenal itself would be in some other highly shielded storeroom. There was no point in trying to locate it. Even with her training, it would take more time than she had to discover the route through the single duct out of all those leading from this room. There would be only one, and that way very indirect. Of that she was positive. The Arcturians would no more risk exposing their explosives to extremes of heat and shock through the ventilating system than did Federation designers.

There was another way to destroy the missiles and the other things stored with them, at least in theory. If she could send the detonation command back along the circuits in reverse of their usual direction, she might be able to blow the entire arsenal.

Morris Martin, the former CO of her unit, had worked out a method of doing just that and had discussed it in detail as an interesting possibility, but even he had treated it entirely as a theoretical problem without even the slightest thought of ever implementing it.

Morris was dead now, slain soon after they planeted on Thorne, and that discussion took place a very long time ago. Did she remember enough to actually make the attempt?

But even as she wondered, the Colonel fixed a charge to the terminal. She used a minute amount of the explosive, enough to send an impulse back through the circuit without blowing the controls. Fortunately, the Arcturian firing frequency was well known, and she could set for it without hesitation.

Islaen Connor worked carefully, very carefully. She must turn the full power of the explosion in upon the weapons themselves. If the force of such a combined blast blew outward, those in the camp and its immediate environs would suffer almost as heavily as if the shipmen themselves succeeded in setting off their weapons.

At last, Islaen slipped the detonator into place. The fuse was a long one, and she concealed it well. For further security, she attached disrupt caps at key places in the intricate system. It was unlikely that anyone would come here, but if the worst happened and the fuses were found and pulled, the whole would automatically be triggered. When all was at last ready, she activated the spark timer.

Islaen Connor ran for the vent and clambered into the duct. The way was easier this time. She was working with gravity, and she now knew her route. The light from her torch was almost unnecessary.

The Colonel made good speed on her retreat. The major part of her mission had been accomplished as far as she was able to move it. She need not fear capture so greatly now and could lessen a little of her caution for haste.

She reached the projectile tube. Islaen paused to slip on the magnetic gloves and fasten them in place.

Her descent was rapid, almost too rapid. She braked herself with her legs. In a matter of seconds, she had reached the trigger. She held on there and placed what little was left of her explosive.

Islaen slid the remainder of the way, slowly enough so that she struck the air lock lightly. The Commando opened it a fraction, averting her face as she did so. When she felt her eyes could bear the light, she scanned the surrounding area. Safe. She dropped to the ground and began running. Very little time remained on the fuse now. The Colonel gained the woods. She kept going without breaking stride. Hers was a woodsman's flight, rapid but at the same time noiseless and hidden from unfriendly eyes. She gave the control of it over to her instinct, reserving her conscious mind to watch for the enemy.

Islaen opened her receptors slightly, taking care to broadcast nothing of her own pattern. There were hostile contacts but none near. She was moving away from them. Her heart leaped as she touched with Varn, and she altered her course to join him.

A sharp explosion. She automatically threw herself to the ground. That would be the tube. Soon the major blasts . . . Another explosion, stronger and louder, and then a third, this time merely a dull rumble. The ground beneath her heaved once and was still.

The Commando-Colonel relaxed. She had succeeded almost completely in turning the force of the explosion back upon itself. Only a very little part of its power, a few waves, had sped outward, not enough to threaten even those in the Arcturian camp.

TWENTY-NINE

ISLAEN SOON FOUND Sogan. He was crouched at the edge of the area blasted by the atomic cannon's destruction and was bending over a badly seared body. To judge by the reddened look of his hands, he had not waited for complete cooling before retrieving it.

Her eyes widened as her mind instinctively reached out to what had been Bethe Danlo. This was no corpse! Life remained, threatened and scarcely detectable by conventional means but still reasonably strong.

The Arcturian looked up and nodded. *She lives. I think most of the blast went over her, causing heavy surface damage but little internally. Let me have the renewer quickly.*

The Colonel had already ripped her pack open and pulled out a device resembling a large, clumsy-looking antique blaster.

Varn almost snatched it out of her hand and turned the invisible healing ray on the felled Sergeant. Speed was essential now. If they were to make good their escape, they must be well out of this area before the shipmen could begin an organized search.

A twig cracked. Both wheeled, Islaen's spring-sheathed knife snapping into her palm as she turned.

Barak faced them. The Colonel's blaster was in his hand, set at broad beam to kill. His eyes were blank, his face lax in a way that explained his seeming treason. The woman dropped her knife and Sogan the renewer. They obeyed his mechanical command to move. A feeling of hopelessness closed around Islaen's heart. There was little doubt of their destination.

She had been completely unaware of the boy's approach, but

204

that was hardly surprising. She had not been able to pick up anything from those other mind slaves earlier. It was impossible to make contact with something that, for all practical purposes, no longer existed.

Scarcely had the three passed out of sight than a tiny feathered form swooped to the ground beside the Sergeant.

The gurry was whimpering softly. She had obeyed her orders and had neither interfered with the battle nor attempted to contact anyone, friend or foe, but she had witnessed most of it and had seen the disasters which had befallen the members of her party. Soon now, their destruction would be complete, when the evil man in the huge ship turned his hate on Varn and Islaen.

She wanted desperately to help them, but she could not. She had felt that other's power and the dark, violent emotions behind it and knew the goodwill she projected would have no effect upon him. He was not mad, but he was as much a renegade as any deranged Jadite creature afflicted with the lust to slay . . .

Bethe was hurt, and her she might aid. Islaen had been burned once, worse than this, and Bandit had helped Varn keep the renewer on her. She might be able to do that again now.

The trigger was slender, and its touch was light, easily managed by her supple toes, but the device itself was heavy. Varn had tied it in place for her the other time. Could she maneuver it well enough alone?

She had to do it! Bethe was dying, and it was a gurry's life to help and protect those with whom she allied herself, Jadite goldbeast or human.

Luckily, the barrel was pointing in nearly the right direction. By tugging and pulling at it, the little hen finally aimed it at the place where she thought the spacer's injuries were gravest.

Still whimpering in her distress and fear and weariness, she activated the ray. Maybe if Bethe recovered enough, she would be able to do the rest herself . . .

The prisoners had gone a little more than thirty yards when two scarlet-clad Yeomen approached them. Ignoring Barak entirely, they glared at the pair.

"Your names, vermin," one demanded in excellent if heavily accented Basic.

The former Admiral glared at him coldly. "Varn Tarl Sogan," he responded haughtily in his own language.

Both Arcturians straightened into an approximation of their race's stiff salute, although they were too much warriors to lessen their guard on their captives. They recognized him now, right enough, even beardless and clad in this alien costume. The war prince was famed throughout all the Empire's fleets, and they had seen tapes in plenty dealing with his exploits. Even had that not been true, they should have known him, resembling as he did their own commander.

"Sorry for the arms, sir . . ."

"Proper security measures, Yeoman. I should report anything less.—Your Captain survived the crash?"

"Aye, sir. He will want to see you."

"And I need to see him. Take us to him now. You will be fulfilling what I am certain are your orders as well as my wishes."

He was about to direct them to Bethe Danlo but restrained himself in time. The demolitions expert was near to death and in no pain. She would do better to go this way than to fall into Aleke's power. At least, she would be human in her ending and not some sort of animated corpse.

He made himself glance indifferently at Barak, whose blaster had never wavered in its fixed threat. He did not know how much his kinsman had learned from him, but he must assume that everything the boy had known was now the slaver's knowledge as well. Whatever he was to accomplish, he would have to work as closely as possible through the truth.

"Since this is your—creature now, see that you control it."

"Aye, sir. He will not fire unless you try to escape."

Sogan did not look at Islaen. Her mind touched his once, very briefly, assuring him of his complete trust, then she withdrew again. A coldness filled his heart as he realized that it was probably for the last time.

THIRTY

THEY SOON REACHED the base itself and Varn Tarl Sogan had his first real look at the *Empire's Glory* since the attack.

It was apparent at once that, whatever their fate now, they had succeeded, utterly and absolutely. The starship was pitted with still-smoldering holes. Her weapons banks were demolished, and even the slaves who might have cleaned away the wreckage had been freed. Barak had accomplished that much before being discovered and overcome. At least, none of them were to be seen in the encampment.

That knowledge was likely to be their only comfort. The war prince had felt little hope from the time they were taken, and what confidence remained to him was soon gone.

He knew his people, and he did not need Islaen's help to recognize the crew's feelings of anger and hatred, their desire for revenge, as well as their amazement as some of them recognized or half-recognized him. Another emotion merged with these others, and it was that which made him fear.

Arcturians were soldiers of the highest quality. They respected courage and daring even when they suffered as a result of them. It was obvious from the looks they cast that they pitied the captives, and this they would not have done if death or even torture were to be their fate. The prisoners faced something worse.

They entered the ship herself, still under their guards' and Barak's blasters, and moved down huge halls that were the battlecraft's main highways. In many places, the walls or ceiling or floor were bent and twisted from the force of the explosions which had killed the vessel. Men hurried along them, most hastening in response to the orders being broadcast to them over the intercom. The calm voice issuing them was one Sogan remembered all too well.

At last, they came to a large cabin, the bridge of the battleship, located at the base of the shattered command spike. The two Yeomen ordered them inside, then left them to the Omrain's steady guarding.

A lone man waited for them there. He was typically Arcturian, tall and slender of body with the olive skin and dark hair of the Empire's race. The inevitable short beard just covered his chin and skirted the jawline. His eyes were chillingly cold, and a bitter anger lay behind them.

Barak set Islaen's blaster on the table in response to the Arcturian's wordless order and withdrew to a place against the wall.

Aleke Tarl Sogan toyed with the weapon for a moment before putting it aside and turning his attention to the prisoners, motioning with his own blaster for them to stand a little farther apart from one another.

He glanced once at the Commando, then turned from her as if she were something of no consequence. Only the fact that he kept her carefully covered showed that he continued to be aware of her existence at all. His eyes linked with Varn's. "You come under very strange circumstances, kinsman. And in very strange guise."

The war prince shrugged. "I have work to do. A beard and uniform would hinder it."

He walked slowly around the bridge, as if he were again an Admiral of the Arcturian Empire touring one of the ships under his command. The controls were laid out in the conventional manner, and for a moment, his heart twisted with longing and regret. Had he managed things differently, this might still be a living vessel and his the command of her . . .

Several times, his fingers touched the controls or ran across the various instrument panels. No mark was left behind to betray dust or a buildup of grease.

The other man watched him, stiffening at his presumption but saying nothing until he completed his inspection.

Varn faced him at last. "She appears to be in fine order."

"Did you think that my command would not be?" he asked haughtily.

"No, but less could be expected and condoned under these

circumstances. I am glad to find such tolerance is not needed here." The war prince sighed. "I am sorry to the depth of my soul, Aleke."

He meant that. He hated this man for the evil he had wrought, an evil he now knew went beyond the creation of mind slaves, which might be excused if not praised by the better part of their people by reasons of the circumstances in which the Captain found himself. There could be no accepting the rest. Aleke Tarl Sogan was a renegade both among their own race and to humankind at large, but still Varn grieved with him over the death of his ship and all such a command meant to an officer of their caste. He was too familiar with that pain himself not to empathize with his kinsman now.

"Why, Varn?" the Captain asked.

"Because we had no choice." His head lowered and raised again. "The War is ended. The issue went against the Empire, and you could not have been permitted to lift to work ill against those whom we are no longer permitted to fight by the Emperor's own order and formal treaty."

"You might have come to me with that news."

"In this guise and in company with Federation Commandos?"

Aleke started and looked swiftly at his other prisoner. "Commandos? A woman?"

He nodded. That was his own reaction that day on Visnu when he had come to slay the Colonel. It was known that approximately half the Federation Navy was female, but it was difficult to imagine they held places in the elite, tough guerrilla units. "Commando-Colonel Islaen Connor."

"What is your connection with our enemies' forces?"

The former Admiral smiled bitterly. "It was necessary that I uphold the Empire's honor."

All this while, the two men had been studying, testing, one another.

The war prince kept his shields tight around his mind, leaving only a few closely guarded receptors open, but even with so little part of his senses functioning, he could feel the enormous power of the other as it slithered over the barriers he had raised, searching for a way past them.

As he had been able to read the mind of the Yeoman he slew, so could he read his kinsman's thoughts now, for Aleke had cast up no shields himself.

The Arcturian commander remained open only a short while.

A shock of surprise went through him when he learned he could not penetrate his cousin's guard, and he hurriedly brought his own defenses to bear.

The movement was slow, clumsy. He was unaccustomed to it and had to struggle to raise his own shields.

Then they were in place, and Varn lost contact with his mind. He was sorry for that but decided to make no effort to breach the other's guards, not yet. He was satisfied for the moment. He had learned one very useful piece of information. Aleke was apparently unaware of his own mutation or Islaen's. He had merely set Barak to work after breaking him without bothering to question him. That lapse, a rare one for his kinsman, might be made to work to their advantage now. At the least, it would postpone the inevitable clash between them a little longer.

That battle would, must, come. Aleke Tarl Sogan could not afford to let him leave his bridge alive.

Varn did not allow his awareness of that fact to appear in his expression. He was very careful to conceal what he had learned, to conceal that he had even been aware of any contact between them at all. He could not hide the fact that he was shielded against invasion, but he could make it seem a natural gift, something beyond his control and knowledge, and Islaen would use the same ruse, he knew, should she be tested.

The former Admiral's mind was working feverishly. They must escape, and quickly, or be either broken or burned down, and they must not leave Aleke Tarl Sogan alive when they went.

His earlier determination to slay the man had been sparked by anger and the burning desire to avenge the clouded honor of his house. The brief chance he had been given to observe the base and all he had learned from Aleke himself before his cousin raised his shields both altered that motive and firmed his resolve. The potential for still more evil rising from him was so great and the probability of its fulfillment so certain that the Arcturian commander simply could not be permitted to live.

Implementing that decision would not be as easy as reaching it. The war prince eyed Islaen's blaster hungrily without appearing to do so. Would he be able to distract his kinsman long enough to leap for it and fire?

Unlikely. Aleke was vigilant and was not so foolish as to underestimate soldiers who had accomplished what these two had against him. His own blaster would discharge if either of them tried to move. Indeed, it was almost certain that he was trying to tempt them into making the trial by leaving that weapon there.

The Captain was in truth strongly on the alert. He had never before encountered a reaction such as this in any of his victims, and he was wary of it.

Now he wished he had questioned the Omrain slave, but there had seemed no need then, and it would be impossible to probe him now. He could not turn that much of his strength from the war prince, not while he remained so much of an unknown quantity, and he did not wish to kill his cousin outright without first solving the mystery he represented. The answers could too easily mean life or death for him in the future.

Aleke grew more tense as the minutes passed without his being able to breach his prisoner's defense. He still did not wish to reveal the full extent of his strength, nor did he dare do so while the other captives were in the room. To do that would require his total concentration, leaving him at their mercy.

The Commando remained a distinct threat, yet he wanted her alive so that he could question her should he continue to be unable to break his kinsman's mind.

He would have to terminate them both eventually, of course. It would not take long to burn them, but they were standing just far enough apart that there would be a minute delay in dropping them, perhaps sufficient time for one of them to move against him.

His patience gave out at last. He need not concern himself with the woman, or the slave either, for now. His crew could guard them. The war prince was of greater import. It would be well to break him at once.

"Take her to the pens," he snapped to Barak.

The boy turned mechanically to obey.

Varn Tarl Sogan looked from him back to the Arcturian. Anger filled him, cold, clear, utterly implacable. Barak of Omrai was not fair to the eye or one whom he would ever voluntarily choose for a companion or comrade, but he had seen the fineness of spirit, the courage, of him, and he refused to see him further degraded by this thing whose blood he shared.

"He shall not go."

The Omrain froze. A shudder passed through his body as the Captain left him and wheeled his mind to face this challenge.

Varn's eyes met his. "I will that he stay if he so desires."

The other man smiled coldly. "You are very ready with your

orders, Admiral. You seem to forget the situation in which you find yourself."

"I have told you the situation. The War is ended, and you are presently in violation of the treaty we signed concluding it, criminally so if you refuse to submit to its terms."

"Who else knows that?" he replied in a low, triumphant hiss.

"Your entire crew. I activated the intercom on general ship frequency at the start of our interview. —Leave it be, Aleke! You face mutiny if you close it now!"

The captain laughed, although he quickly withdrew his hand from the switch. "Mutiny? I think you do not appreciate . . ."

"Fool! Do you imagine you command spineless menials? You can use your mind's power to break only one victim at a time, leaving the others free to act. They were forced to bear with you before, but the news I have brought and the fact that a war prince now addresses them alters that. The basest menial in all our ultrasystem would be required to uphold the Emperor's word and the Empire's honor above the will of a renegade, much less warriors of our caste."

Aleke stiffened, but Varn went on swiftly, his voice as hard and cold as justice itself. "Aye, I name you a renegade. I know full well what you have done here."

"I did what conditions demanded of me," his cousin replied with frigid dignity.

"In the harm you have caused to Omrai's citizens and the civilian craft servicing this Sector, perhaps, though you will find I shall not stand alone in my repugnance for some of your methods. A mutant such as yourself will find little tolerance and no welcome whatsoever anywhere within the Empire."

His eyes bore into the other's. "You are not ignorant of that fact. As soon as your talent woke and you chose to utilize it as you did before witnesses, you knew that all hope for a life of worth or importance among our people was ended. You never intended to return home but rather planned to seek a more passive and comfortable colony and make it your own infant kingdom. To do that, you needed fighting men, but not the officers who would condemn such deviation from your orders and oppose it. As a result, those officers had to die and most or all of the noncoms with them. —Say nothing! There are none here now, and a crash does not slay so selectively. Those murders will not be ignored. You will face and pay the full penalty for them."

Aleke slammed his hand down on the switch, silencing the intercom.

The former Admiral made no effort to reactivate it. His purpose had been accomplished, as the other well knew. Whatever happened on the bridge now, the Captain's fate was sealed. His crew would either kill him outright or withdraw from the *Empire's Glory*, sealing him within and leaving him to perish of want or by his own hand in the corpse of his dead starship. It would not even be mutiny, since a war prince had directed them to their course. Varn had been careful to use only that title, which, unlike his lost military rank, could not be stripped from him.

That victory multiplied the danger to himself and his companions a thousandfold. The Arcturian commander was now filled with blind, white-hot hatred and bitter purpose. All else might be lost to him, but vengeance he would have.

Motioning with his blaster, the Captain forced the woman and the Omrain to the farther side of the bridge. They would watch their ally broken into a groveling slave, and then they would meet their deaths at his once-trusted hand.

Varn Tarl Sogan knew his enemy well enough to guess his intention. He realized there was no hope of reaching Islaen's blaster, but he had known from the beginning that this would be settled between them with another weapon, one forged in them by some strange, unwelcome quirk of birth, a weapon that set them apart from all the rest of their race and from the remainder of humankind as well.

Varn tried to compose himself, to concentrate on what he must do. He had used the analogy of a spear to describe the force he had used to kill that poor Yeoman. So it was, a spear fashioned of the mind's invisible, potent energy. He set himself to forming another like that first.

Omrai's gods had favored him greatly in sending him that earlier encounter. Tragic and nearly fatal as it was, it had taught him not only how to summon and fashion his weapon but how to use it as well, how to direct it against that part of his enemy's brain controlling his life systems. If he could do that here and strike true with it, death would come instantly, more mercifully than this man before him deserved.

Accomplishing that would be no easy matter, and victory was by no means guaranteed. This was Aleke Tarl Sogan's talent, apparently the prime channel or one of the major channels of it, whereas it was but a secondary and newly awakened aspect of his own. He would be hard-pressed to overcome so expert a killer with it, and only the fact that the Captain had never before encountered a true shield or any sort of active opposition gave him real hope.

Victory was too uncertain for any of them to depend upon it, but perhaps it was not necessary that he actually conquer. If Aleke was deeply enough absorbed in their duel, Islaen or Barak might then jump him or go for the Commando's blaster. He would not be capable of doing either himself . . .

A sudden blast of force smote violently against his mind. It was strong, his kinsman's sending, but he had anticipated its coming. His shields held firm.

Realizing his first wild rush had failed, Aleke withdrew and began seeking for some weakness in the war prince's defense, even as Varn searched his.

The former Admiral realized his opponent was trying to elicit physical aid from the other prisoners, and he knew a moment's fear, but he relaxed again in the next. Too much of Aleke's power was tied up in the duel itself to seriously threaten either. Islaen's shields were as strong as Varn's own, and as long as he could keep the Captain occupied at least on their present level, even Barak would not be overcome a second time.

Soon the Arcturian commander recognized the futility of his efforts and ceased all attempts to go beyond the fight itself. The strain of this silent combat was too great to so squander his resources.

Barak seized the blaster, but neither he nor the Commando made any attempt to interfere with the strange warfare being waged by the two Arcturians. Not only would it be difficult to avoid burning down both if the boy fired, but they were afraid to distract their champion or to inadvertently do him injury while his mind was so closely engaged with the other's. Not unless it was obvious that his defeat was upon him would they move.

Varn had at first been concerned that Aleke's shields would be equal in strength with his power or nearly so, but he soon found this not to be the case. They had been clumsily erected and even now were deeply fissured and of uneven strength, a readily understandable weakness, since the Captain had never had any reason to develop them and had had no experience in their use. That he had attained this degree of facility gave testimony to his innate strength.

Whatever the imperfections of his defense, it did little to damage his cause. Such was the power of Aleke Tarl Sogan's mind and the ease with which he could harness it to take the offensive that the former Admiral dared not make a direct attack against his shields. He knew he could not meet the force his cousin could generate head-on.

What frontal assault could not accomplish might sometimes be gained by stealth. A very small part of his mind crept through one of the fissures scoring his enemy's defense. It was risky work, but if he could bring enough of himself inside the other's mind to form his own spear there, he should be able to strike the death blow quickly and from such short range as to finish the duel.

Aleke's spear slammed against his shields again with a hard, angry blow, growing frustration adding both keenness and determination to it. Once more, the war prince's defenses held firm, but he had been concentrating so heavily on formulating his own attack that he instinctively returned the strike.

Too late, Varn recognized his error. He had not been ready, not nearly ready, to show his hand. His opponent gasped and reeled back, but surprise more than injury had unbalanced him. He was wounded, aye, but his life centers remained intact, and Aleke whirled on the invader as would a pain-maddened wild thing.

Before he could act either to withdraw or to defend himself, Varn Tarl Sogan was struck such a blow that he was driven to his knees.

Another followed it and another, strike after strike slamming into him with ever-increasing fury and effect until Varn fled his cousin's mind to the security of his own in a near panic.

Temporary security. His shields were beginning to crumble under the constant hammering and strain.

He groaned in his soul. Once they went, the closing of the duel and the vile fate his kinsman had planned for him would be upon him.

He had been such a fool to think . . .

His shields shattered, but even as they did, a new strength surged into him, and his defense stood firm and whole once more.

Islaen's thought was with him. He rested against her an instant, then he braced himself to meet his foe once more. He had to take Aleke now. Islaen Connor's shields would hold them for a while, but if the assault continued at this level, they would eventually break, sealing the doom of both.

That he would not allow! His own mind was defiled by its contact with this renegade's, but never would he permit such corruption to soil her.

Whatever he did must be accomplished quickly. Aleke was surprised now, or should be, at finding a sound defense in the place of the crumbling barrier he thought he had shattered. If he guessed the truth and went for the woman while she herself was unguarded . . .

The former Admiral made himself think. His power to fight like this rose slowly, never achieving anything approaching the force his kinsman seemed to possess in unlimited supply. As long as that remained the case, he would not be able to match Aleke.

What was the source of their weapon? It was energy somehow generated by them or within them, probably in much the same manner in each of them save that in him it was released too slowly and in too small a volume to meet his present need. He must find the reservoir. Shallow though it likely was, if he could release the energy stored there and cast it at the moment of release, even Aleke Tarl Sogan should not be able to stand against it. The effect would be that of a mental planebuster.

Desperately, he sought for that power source, knowing he had to find it quickly, while he still had the strength to work his will. Already he could feel himself weakening from the wounds Aleke had given him, and his foreman's attacks were becoming ever heavier and more insistent. Either he claimed what he sought now, or he must resign both himself and his consort to the Arcturian Captain's will.

There! He felt and concentrated upon something far within him. It was like a well, dark and deep and sealed or blocked so that only a small trickle of the energy it held could escape from it to rise for his use.

He had to have more! His will demanded it, and he thought he felt an answering stir in his innermost mind, but the blockage held, and no increase came in the power feeding the slowly forming spear that was his last and, if unstrengthened, hopeless defense.

Will and desire were not enough. In stark desperation, he drew on the one strength he had left, that feeding and maintaining his own life in the face of his injuries. He would have to trust that Islaen would be able to sustain him long enough for him to accomplish his will.

He knew he would grow no stronger. He gathered himself. Even as he did, he ordered the Commando-Colonel to withdraw lest she be destroyed in his failure or by some backlash of force should he succeed. Once and twice more, he drove his will against his own inner mind, trying to force open a pathway to the power he sought.

Suddenly it came, so suddenly that he was ill prepared to receive it, a rush of energy that all but overwhelmed him both by its volume and by the incredible violence of it.

Anger rose with it, raw, primeval, savage, melding with the original power he had released and transforming it into something alien and terrible.

Once loosed in his upper mind, the altered force waited, swelled and coalesced into a single vast wave that tore outward in a furious surge that barely gave his shields, which had regenerated during the brief respite Islaen granted him, time in which to draw apart to allow it passage.

Varn realized in horror that he was powerless to brake this monster he had created, was utterly incapable even of commanding its course.

The nightmare wave rushed upon Aleke's mind. The Captain tried to flee but could not withdraw rapidly enough to escape it entirely, and the crest of it swept over that part of him left trapped beyond his guards.

He screamed at its touch. It was searing, like an open flame against his eye.

The war prince tried desperately to check the madness of his assault. The renegade's defeat was certain now. No barrier he could hope to raise would stand against this vengeance weapon, a weapon untempered by mercy or pity or any other softening force. He wanted the man dead, not this, not what he instinctively knew must follow, yet he was powerless to check it.

The advancing wave slowed a fraction after the first contact as it gathered again for the assault against the Arcturian commander's mind. A spear formed, awesome and terrible. A moment, less, it held, then it struck Aleke's guards.

His shields vaporized at its touch, and the whole dire force roared into his unprotected mind like magma exploding from a volcano.

The Captain screamed once again in the anguish of a soul in its mortal pain.

Varn's own cry followed fast upon it. He fought madly to dissolve the fearsome thing he had raised.

It wavered, then dispersed entirely, as if it had never existed.

Too late. Even as it faded, its strength ebbing back from where it had come, the former Admiral again knew the horrible severing of conscious life and will that left him alone and reeling in that which had been a human mind.

This was worse, infinitely worse, than his encounter with that unfortunate Yeoman. He watched, sickened to the depths of his soul, while the thing which had been Aleke Tarl Sogan fell to the deck and lay gulping like an air-drowning fish. He willed himself to return to that blasted mind, to give the shell its end, but he could not slay it. Nothing remained for him to act upon.

Slowly, wearily, he withdrew again. He could do nothing more, for Aleke or for himself. There was a price to be paid for the summoning and too abrupt dissolution of a force such as he had drawn to his aid. Gray mists rose about him. Varn saw a dim image of Barak use the forgotten blaster to put an end to the mechanical animation that maintained the shell of the destroyed man. Enough awareness remained to him that he realized the boy acted out of pity more than hatred or revenge. After that, the cloud closed in completely, and he saw nothing more.

A call reached him through the dark mists enveloping him, demanding action from him, fearful . . .

Islaen! Sogan fought his own weakness and the deadly inertia which would have kept him where he was, safe in this eternal state of partial life until he passed out of what had become an accursed existence altogether. His consort needed him. He could hear and feel that in her, and he struggled to respond.

Would he be able to do so? The war prince knew he had been gravely wounded, more than heavily enough to shatter his life. Islaen Connor was maintaining him now, pouring her strength into him, but she could not continue that for long, not without destroying herself as well.

That he must prevent! Sogan pulled away from her, determined to stand or crumble on his own, sparing her further trial.

He was immediately conscious of intense pain and was certain his death would follow fast, but he knew in another moment that it was but a shadow cast by closing wounds, worse than he had experienced that morning in the cabin, aye, but of the same nature.

He felt the Commando's touch then, carefully prompting and guiding the healing he could all but feel taking place within himself.

The Arcturian's eyes opened. "Islaen?"

She was kneeling beside him, her face tense, her blaster in her hand. "Varn! Praise the Spirit ruling all space!—It's not over yet. Do you think you can help us further?"

"I can try," he said weakly, sitting up with her help. "What has happened?"

"Nothing yet. We've sealed the door, but the crew'll be wanting in very soon, and I don't know how they'll respond to me.

"The transceiver's still working, and I was able to raise the *Free Comet*. She's coming to take us all off if I give her the signal to do so."

"Can she manage?"

"It'll be tight, but, aye, she can, provided our prisoners are quiet and ordered. Otherwise, she'll have to wait for the Navy. That'll almost certainly mean one hell of a bloody mess before it's settled."

"Help me to the intercom!"

The woman could not raise him alone, but with her aid and Barak's, he got to his feet and staggered to the instrument panel. By the time he finished his transmission, the former Admiral was bearing his own weight once more.

The crew of the *Empire's Glory* accepted the war prince's authority, and for the next three days, Varn Tarl Sogan functioned as if the past had returned once more, a nightmare past in which he healed his command's wounds and prepared it for surrender.

Grief and shame and inner despair lashed him almost as powerfully as they had years before when he turned over his fleet to Ram Sithe, but he gave no sign of that either to the Arcturian soldiers or to his own comrades as he greeted Marta Florr and repeated again the words no member of his race or caste had once ever thought to utter.

He saw the crewmen settled and assured them that they would be well received by their own people, better than the bulk of the defeated Navy had been, since they had striven so long under such seemingly impossible circumstances to win back to space and their duties again.

Last of all, with a deep misery he was hard-pressed to conceal, the former Admiral confessed how matters actually stood with him with respect to their people and withdrew from the warriors who he believed could now only despise him.

That final duty completed, his will released its hold, and he yielded to the barely closed wounds whose demands he could no longer ignore.

THIRTY-ONE

ISLAEN CONNOR SQUARED her shoulders as she came into the hangar and forced herself to meet the anxious looks of her two comrades with a tired smile.

"Taking a break at last?" Jake asked.

She nodded. "He just dozed off. He'll be waking again soon, but I thought I'd stretch my legs a bit."

"You should stretch out," he told her sternly. "You look about done."

"I will later, once things are settled."

"He's doing all right now, isn't he?" Bethe Danlo inquired. She still looked and was tired after her own ordeal, but she was healed thanks to the renewer, thanks to Bandit's work with it, and she had submerged her weariness in her concern for her comrades, Islaen as well as Varn.

"The wounds are healing nicely," she replied carefully, not meeting the other woman's eyes.

"What's the danger that he'll turn a blaster on himself?" the Sergeant asked bluntly, ignoring Karmikel's angry gasp; they had been discussing that possibility, but he had not imagined she would raise the subject with Islaen.

"Suicide's an acceptable course for one of his race," the Commando-Colonel replied evenly. "We're not even permitted to interfere when one of them makes that decision. Seven of the prisoners have gone that route already, and Varn has the same right of choice."

"You'd let him die?" she demanded incredulously.

"Not before, not while he was so ill, but now his mind's clear. The decision's his, and if he chooses to go . . ."

For one of the few times in her life, her control shattered. She turned from them, burying her face in her hands.

Jake reached her in the next moment and took her in his arms. "Easy, lass," he murmured. "Don't give up on our Admiral yet. He's not one to run, and I don't think he'll ever walk out on you."

She regained her grip on herself and pulled away from him. "Sorry," she muttered.

Bethe watched her for a moment, and her eyes hardened with a determination she was careful not to let either of her companions see. "Get her out of here, Jake," she ordered. "Make her eat something."

"I'm all right now," Islaen said hastily. "Varn shouldn't be . . ."

"If you don't take a break soon, we'll have you on the flat of your back, too.—Go on," she added more gently. "I'll stay with our patient."

The Colonel nodded, yielding to her will. "Very well, but call me back if . . ."

"Your consort'll survive your absence for half an hour," she told her dryly. "Get going now, while you have the chance. —Leave Bandit," she said quickly, fumbling in her belt pouch and producing a red-striped pellet. "Peppermint. Since the *Comet*'s crew learned she likes sweets, I've been inundated with donations. Don't worry, though. I'm careful not to give her too much. At the rate you two are going, she might too easily end up fatter than either of you."

That elicited the smile she had been trying to win. While Islaen was still thus distracted, Karmikel deftly slipped his arm through hers and maneuvered her out of the hangar, then hurried her through the corridor beyond until they left the exploration wing altogether.

The demolitions expert waited, stroking the gurry and talking to her. When she was certain her comrades would not return for any reason, she straightened. "Come on, pet. We have a job to do."

She, too, left the hangar and hastened to the war prince's cabin. She paused outside the door. "Whistle if Varn's awake or when he wakes. I don't want to break his sleep."

Bethe quietly slipped inside. Sogan's eyes were closed, and Bandit remained quiet.

The woman sighed. Even in sleep, his expression was tense,

set, showing no sign of peace or rest. No wonder Islaen was afraid for him, knowing all she did about him.

The spacer studied him closely. He was very thin, she thought, but apart from that and his pallor, he did not look too bad now. If only he would will for life and not death . . .

Her eyes closed as despair rose up in her. Jake was right. She did love this man, although not in the way she did the Commando-Captain. She did not want to see him die, of his wounds or by his own hand.

Her head raised. She was a lot less tolerant than Islaen Connor of some of his people's ways, and she was prepared to fight with whatever weapons she must use to prevent him from putting that blaster set so near his hand to his head.

She resisted the impulse to remove it. The custom of a unit such as theirs demanded that it be there. Hiding it would only delay the inevitable anyway if he did resolve to use it. The choice would have to be his. Islaen was right about that.

Bandit gave a sharp whistle as his head tossed restlessly on the pillow.

"Varn?" she whispered softly.

His eyes opened and brightened in the same moment. He was pleased to see her. More than pleased. He had not realized until he believed her dead how much the blond spacer had come to mean to him, and her survival was the one fair spark in those last, dark hours on Omrai.

His expression shadowed. It was small thanks to him that she was still alive. "I have not yet asked your pardon . . ." he began.

The woman frowned. "For what?" she demanded. "I was better off slipping quietly into death than winding up that mind slaver's creature, which was the only fate you could've envisioned for me at the time had I been brought back to the battleship. Even Jake agreed with your choice and, more, gave thanks for it, and he's anything but an impartial judge."

His eyes closed, and Bethe hastily shut the door to block out the bright hall light. She knew that his headache was still severe and that glare intensified it.

Bandit gave an impatient whistle, and Sogan roused himself again. He raised his hand to receive and caress her. "Gently, small one," he said softly. "We have all been a worry to you on this one, have we not?"

Yes!

He translated that for the woman, who laughed and reached over to scratch the feathered head. "She came through it all like a proper heroine as usual," she said.

Bethe Danlo's eyes were soft when they flickered to the former Admiral. Varn's open affection for the gurry was one of the things which had first drawn her to him. He had never disclaimed Bandit or refused her his affection, although association with so comical-looking a little creature must occasionally sting an Arcturian officer's sometimes exaggerated sense of dignity. Even now, he did not turn away from her or ignore her.

That strengthened her resolve. She knew without having to read the gurry that Bandit was using her power on him, but that would not alter his mind or stay his hand indefinitely if he decided as they feared he would.

The Sergeant stepped a little back from him. "I didn't come here to talk about what happened to me," she said rather sharply. "I want to know how long you're going to keep this up. Islaen's been strong for you ever since you two ran into each other on Visnu, and if you don't start returning that service real soon, she's going to crash as badly as you have."

He sat up, ignoring what the sudden movement did to his sense of balance. "What! Where is she?"

"With Jake, getting something to eat, I sincerely hope. She's scarcely left you at all these last four days, certainly for nothing so trivial as that."

"I must see her."

Bethe smiled. The fight was back in him again, and she could be certain now that he would do nothing against himself, at least until he assured himself of his consort's well-being. "Soon, my friend. Very soon."

She left him, taking the gurry with her. "You can tell Islaen she's wanted, pet," she told Bandit when they were in the corridor once more, "as soon as she's through with her meal. Don't disturb her before that. —Stay with Jake yourself, mind you. This must be settled between them."

She nodded at the little hen's hopeful chirp.

"Aye, we've won a battle. It's still the Colonel's job to win the war, but I think we've just given her a good fighting chance."

The Commando-Colonel came into Varn's small cabin, timidly because she did not know what she would find.

To her surprise, he was sitting on the edge of his bunk. "Where do you think you're going?" she demanded in alarm.

"Nowhere for a while, I fear," he replied ruefully. "I just tried."

He studied her. The dim light was more than sufficient to confirm Bethe Danlo's report. "Space, woman! Have you had no rest at all?"

"Some," she lied.

Islaen's eyes went of their own accord to his blaster, and she steeled herself. She knew from his manner that he had made his decision, and she trembled in her very soul because she feared he had been attempting to reach the weapon before she came in. He could be trying to conceal that fact now . . .

"Are you going to use that?" she asked bluntly.

He shook his head. "No. You deserve more from me than that."

"You deserve more!"

"Maybe," he replied indifferently. "Sit beside me, my Islaen."

The woman complied. She let him draw her close, although she took care to keep most of her weight on herself.

Suddenly, all the fear she had known for him swept through her, and she turned her face from him, raising her shields as she did so.

Instantly, his hold tightened. "The Spirit of Space curse me!" he muttered savagely. "There is no excusing the grief I have brought you."

He had tried to go to her in mind but had been forced to revert to verbal speech in the same moment. His wounds were still too raw to permit even so light a use of his talent.

She looked up at him in concern. "Easy, friend! Not too fast. —There's nothing to excuse, and even if there were, one makes all sorts of allowances for the wounded."

"How are they?" he asked after a brief pause. "Your prisoners?"

"As comfortable as possible. They're pretty crowded, but they realize that can't be helped."

"Suicides?"

"Seven."

He looked surprised. "I had imagined there would be more by now."

"There will be two, maybe three, others," the Commando

said with regret, "but you handled the surrender well, and Marta Florr is carrying her part. Telling them they would be received with honor at home made a lot of difference, I think. —They're concerned about you," she added. "No one's ever survived an encounter with their former Captain, and they want better for you, although none of them have much hope of your pulling through. They'll be glad to learn they're wrong about that."

Sogan's open disbelief angered her. "It was never your fighters, the officers and men of your fleet, who condemned you! Even you have to admit that. Most of them agreed with your sparing of Thorne, and these soldiers are no different. —They know the full story now, too, the part you left out plus a description of your present work. I made sure of that. Your record here would bring glory to any war prince, and they're proud to own you as one of their kind."

His head lowered. Little else that she might have said could have meant more to him. He had not wanted the hatred of those men.

His consort knew she had done well in telling him that, and she began to hope that he might now be willing to take still more from her.

She eyed him speculatively. "They'll keep quiet about what actually happened on Omrai. Their commander's murders disgrace only him, but according to their brand of logic, long-term association with a mutant just about qualifies them as class-one pariahs themselves. An officer might feel compelled to report it all, but none of them are left, and the Empire's rankless soldiers are not bound so powerfully to your code. They won't spread the tale. I didn't tell them that you used the same means to overcome him, of course."

He just shook his head. "Your people cannot be kept in ignorance now that this stain has arisen more than once in my house," he said dully, "especially since it took so deadly a turn in Aleke."

"No. I've informed Ram Sithe already and have given him all the information we have, but I presented it in such a way as to conceal our own roles."

Varn looked at her sharply. "Are you sure about that? Sithe's not readily fooled."

"He wasn't," she told him, "but he can pretend to be. He's assured me point-blank that we'll be completely protected."

Her brows lifted, and she shrugged. "He said two live troubleshooters are a lot more useful to him and to the Federation than a couple of dead guinea pigs."

The war prince's head snapped up. "Islaen . . ."

"Under those circumstances, I'd go your route, friend, and he knows it."

Sogan nodded after a moment's silence. "There are others who know."

"Barak and the captives?"

"Aye."

"I had a long talk with our Omrain comrade. There's a good chance that mental power of one sort or another may be latent in his people or be developing in them, and in many of his planet's other creatures as well. He'll not betray what could be a major strength of theirs, not until they're very sure what they're about. It'll take the close study of several generations to get any of the answers they need. As for the prisoners, they remember their capture and the never-ending labor but don't realize what actually happened to them."

She frowned slightly. "There may be some risk of memory returning later, but I doubt it. They didn't know what was going on when Sogan took them over, and after that, the faculty to appreciate their situation was submerged along with everything else that made them human."

"What will happen to them? Some must be pirates, since their ships were taken as well as legitimate craft."

"All will be treated, naturally. Those who're wanted by the Navy or Patrol will then be held and the rest released with victim's compensation."

"Captain Florr?" he asked.

"She knows nothing, not even that you've been ill. You were on your feet and functioning when you came on board and for some time afterward. She's pretty certain of your race and that you're not lowly born within it after the part you played in the surrender, whatever her official acceptance of my explanation that you speak Arcturian better than I do and so naturally took over that part of it. She believes you're merely very wisely keeping a low profile. None of us and none of your own people are inclined to disillusion her."

He gave a sigh of relief. Everything seemed to be working out, after all, despite the potential for disaster which had hung over them through this whole mission and in its wake.

All sense of ease left him suddenly. Before his will could block it, his memory returned to that dire encounter on the bridge of the *Empire's Glory*. He recalled, relived, the pain and the terror he had know then, and he shuddered openly in his horror of the abomination he had wrought.

How could he have done it? How had he dared? Both he and Islaen Connor had considered the possibility, if not of precisely this nightmare, then of other violence. They had rejected it utterly, morally and in the field.

Islaen had once thought to try her talent against the wills of opponents, the vile developers who had lured the Amonite settlers to Visnu of Brahmin almost to their deaths. Those men were vermin, filth fit only for extermination, yet he had recoiled from such a deed and had called to her to stop, which she had quickly done when the realization of what she contemplated was brought to her attention. Now he himself had done as much, worse, to his own blood.

His eyes closed. He had sought only to slay, not to break his kinsman's will or turn him into a living tool. Certainly, he had not wanted what did happen. He had not even considered . . .

What did his intentions matter? He had done what he had done, and he had not even been able to give clean death to the sorry thing he left in place of a man. Barak of Omrai performed that kindness for him.

The Commando's mind brushed his, but he recoiled from her touch as if he feared he would defile her. "I cannot forget it, Islaen," he whispered in near despair.

"No," she said somberly. "You're too fine a man to be able to just set it all aside. You're too fine to have had this put on you in the first place."

She caught hold of his hands, forcing at least that much direct contact between them, as her eyes locked with his.

"Varn, you have to accept that there is no guilt on you and no reason for shame. There's none in our eyes, and there must be none in yours. You fought with the only weapon left to you to defend yourself and to defend us against a man who merited death a dozen times over, by your own law as well as by the Federation's, a man who would have gone on creating an ever-widening circle of evil had he escaped death then."

He wrenched his hands free and pressed them to his face. "I did not slay him. I . . ."

"You were forced to use a weapon almost totally unfamiliar to you. It exploded on you just like that atomic cannon blew up on Bethe."

"You might have been trapped," he said slowly as his eyes seemed to focus on some grim vista invisible to her. "Had your withdrawal been slower . . ."

"That didn't happen," she said sharply. "It won't now, unless you're planning to use that weapon again."

Even through his shields, she could feel his loathing and fear. "No!—Nor is it a weapon. That term cannot be put on a force one is totally incapable of controlling." His brows drew together. "It was my hate that destroyed him. I must own that, I suppose, since it rose out of me."

"You never expected such a response?"

"No, though after my performance on Hades . . ."

"Forget Hades, damn it! —Look, what happened was not by your willing, and now you know enough not to summon it again. That's all that matters or should matter."

Her voice softened once more. "I know it's worse on you because he was your kinsman, but in truth, Aleke Tarl Sogan wasn't an Arcturian or a Terran or anything else. He was a renegade, worse than any other we've ever encountered. Even Thurston Sandstone was but a madman, someone to be pitied once we made sure he couldn't work any more harm. Sogan violated his oaths and code. He betrayed the Empire's trust by his planned conquest of a private kingdom . . ."

"Aye, Islaen Connor. I know all that. I knew it well enough to determine his death before we ever joined battle, but I can pity him, aye, and understand him in part. I share enough of his guilt to permit that."

He shook his head quickly when she stiffened. "No, not our mutation. There is no evil in that in itself."

He stopped but then shrugged and continued. Now that he had begun, it was his to finish it. "There are times, all too many of them, when I think I should willingly cast away everything I have won merely to be on the bridge of such a ship as the *Empire's Glory* again, even if I had to conquer a planet or star system to maintain her."

"You would not do so if actually given the chance, would you?" she asked him quietly.

"No, of course not." He spread his hands in a helpless gesture. "What difference when I wish it?"

"All the difference in the universe!"

Islaen Connor was furious with herself. This must have been riding him for some time, certainly since they encountered that derelict squad on Mirelle. She should have recognized it and done what she could to counter at least the guilt that came with it, even if there was nothing else she could do to resolve it.

"You have a right to want," she told him, "especially a real command. That's what you were trained to do, after all."

The Commando-Colonel's eyes fell. He would never have one again. Not even Ram Sithe could swing that, and she felt wretched in her inability to secure it for him. Varn Tarl Sogan allowed himself to desire so little, and he asked for almost nothing . . .

He read her unhappiness and its cause readily enough. "I should refuse such a post if it were offered to me," he said softly. "It would mean the end of our work together, and that I would never permit."

The Arcturian's fingers brushed her too-pale cheek gently. "Our unit holds a singular position in all the Federation. I am proud to be part of it. I should not accomplish a fraction as much at the helm of a peacetime battleship, and you know it is real purpose that I want, not empty status. Perhaps I cannot bury all my longing for the old ways, but I know there can be no peace or contentment for me anywhere but at your side. Unless you will it, I shall never quit you."

She gave him a tremulous smile. "Then we shall be together forever, Varn Tarl Sogan."

They remained quiet for a while. Islaen saw that he was tired and started to rise, but his hand stopped her.

"Stay a moment. —I know I mentioned Noreen to you, but I would like to return to Thorne for now. I cannot face any further challenge for a while. You could go on to your kin yourself, but I want, need, to have you with me."

That last was a question, one of a kind rarely heard from him.

"We travel together or not at all, Admiral," she said rather severely.

The Commando took a deep breath. She made herself speak casually. "We're bound for Brandine's space already, just as soon as we pick up the *Fairest Maid*. We're to base out of

Thorne, according to Ram Sithe's orders, and she is home, after all."

His eyes closed wearily. "Aye, my Islaen. She is that."

The man realized what he had said. His eyes opened again, and he smiled at her, accepting the admission and the decision he had made. "She is home in truth, Islaen Connor."

CLASSIC SCIENCE FICTION
AND FANTASY

__DUNE Frank Herbert 0-441-17266-0/$4.95
The bestselling novel of an awesome world where gods and adventurers clash, mile-long sandworms rule the desert, and the ancient dream of immortality comes true.

__STRANGER IN A STRANGE LAND Robert A. Heinlein
0-441-79034-8/$4.95
From the *New York Times* bestselling author—the science fiction masterpiece of a man from Mars who teaches humankind the art of grokking, watersharing and love.

__THE ONCE AND FUTURE KING T.H. White
0-441-62740-4/$5.50
The world's greatest fantasy classic! A magical epic of King Arthur in Camelot, romance, wizardry and war. By the author of *The Book of Merlyn*.

__THE LEFT HAND OF DARKNESS Ursula K. LeGuin
0-441-47812-3/$3.95
Winner of the Hugo and Nebula awards for best science fiction novel of the year. "SF masterpiece!"—*Newsweek* "A Jewel of a story."—Frank Herbert

__MAN IN A HIGH CASTLE Philip K. Dick 0-441-51809-5/$3.95
"Philip K. Dick's best novel, a masterfully detailed alternate world peopled by superbly realized characters."
—Harry Harrison

For Visa and MasterCard orders call: 1-800-631-8571

FOR MAIL ORDERS: CHECK BOOK(S). FILL OUT COUPON. SEND TO:

BERKLEY PUBLISHING GROUP
390 Murray Hill Pkwy., Dept. B
East Rutherford, NJ 07073

NAME_____

ADDRESS_____

CITY_____

STATE_____ ZIP_____

PLEASE ALLOW 6 WEEKS FOR DELIVERY.
PRICES ARE SUBJECT TO CHANGE WITHOUT NOTICE.

POSTAGE AND HANDLING:
$1.00 for one book, 25¢ for each additional. Do not exceed $3.50.

BOOK TOTAL	$ _____
POSTAGE & HANDLING	$ _____
APPLICABLE SALES TAX (CA, NJ, NY, PA)	$ _____
TOTAL AMOUNT DUE	$ _____

PAYABLE IN US FUNDS.
(No cash orders accepted.) 279